DEMON KING

CLAIMED BY LUCIFER BOOK ONE

ELIZABETH BRIGGS

DEMON KING (CLAIMED BY LUCIFER #1)

Copyright © 2020 by Elizabeth Briggs

Cover designed by Sylvia Frost, thebookbrander.com

ISBN (paperback) 978-1-948456-06-7

ISBN (ebook) 9781948456661

www.elizabethbriggs.net

1

HANNAH

Only a desperate woman made a deal with the devil—
and I was on my way to ask him for a favor.

I couldn't help but wring my hands while we went up,
up, up in the elevator. Generic club music played softly in
the background as I stared at the sleek mirrored walls and
dark silver buttons, trying to avoid looking at the two
imposing men either side of me. There was no escaping
them. They filled the entirety of the space with their broad
shoulders, thick necks, and well-pressed black suits, barely
leaving me room to suck in a breath. They were hot as hell,
just like everyone I'd seen in The Celestial Resort & Casino,
but scary enough to make me wonder if coming here was a
huge mistake.

Who was I kidding? Of course it was a mistake. But it
might be the only way to find my best friend.

The elevator dinged, signaling we'd reached the penthouse, and when the door opened, I let out the breath I'd been holding. More models-turned-security guards stood outside a big, black, shiny door. As I stepped out of the elevator, that black door was thrown open and a man in a disheveled gray suit rushed out. His wide eyes were full of something like panic or fear, and he jostled hard against my shoulder as he tried to escape.

"If you're smart, you'll turn around and run," the guy yelled before one of the muscular guards grabbed him by the arm and dragged him toward the elevator. He didn't even struggle, and soon the elevator door shut him in, barely droning out his last word. "Run!"

I swallowed hard but steeled myself as I headed for the open door. Each footfall felt like one step closer to my doom. I glanced between the guards perched on either side of the door, but they barely acknowledged me as I walked through. I'd already gotten approval to speak with Mr. Ifer from a man in a suit downstairs, so I supposed they were expecting me.

Just inside the door was a small foyer with a huge painting of stylized black wings spread wide on a pure white canvas. I knew little about art, but found myself staring up at it, drawn to the way the brush strokes looked like angry slashes.

I shook myself and continued down the hall, along black marble floors with a touch of silver veining in them, and entered a large living room. The sight of expensive, black leather couches and a grand piano made me freeze. I'd expected to meet Lucas Ifer, CEO of Abaddon Inc and the rumored mob boss of Las Vegas, in his office, not his own home. Momentarily stunned by the sight of it all, I took in the backlit mirrored bar along one wall, the large, sleek fireplace across from it, and the floor-to-ceiling windows on the end with an impressive view of the Las Vegas Strip, not to mention the infinity pool on the balcony.

The man I'd come to see leaned with his hand on one of those large windows, staring out at his domain like a brooding king. Or a kingpin, maybe. I could only see his profile, but it was striking enough to make my heart miss a beat. I cataloged him while I waited for his attention to land on me, as I didn't dare disturb such dark, dangerous perfection. An impeccable black suit framed broad shoulders and tapered down to narrow hips, before hugging a perfectly rounded ass. Sunlight kissed short, thick hair that looked almost black except for highlights of rich, chocolate brown. Below that, perfectly trimmed dark stubble accentuated a chiseled jaw, leading up to the cheekbones of a god.

Whatever I'd expected from the man they called "the devil" in hushed whispers, it had not been this.

"Come to ask for a favor?" His voice washed over me with a delicious British accent that somehow made his words sound both smart and sensual. "As you saw, it didn't go so well for the last fellow. Then again, he tried to renege on our bargain. I trust you won't do the same."

His words rolled off his tongue like sex and sin, but also reminded me why I was here. I shook my head a little to clear my thoughts and to snap out of the daze he'd put me in. "Yes, I am. Here for a favor, that is."

He turned from the window to face me, and the light and dark played over his face in the most beguiling way I'd ever seen. The full force of his presence hit me in the gut like a fire bursting into life from the strike of a match. Forget the men outside—they were nothing compared to him. I actually forgot how to breathe under the weight of those eyes, an emerald color I hadn't realized was humanly possible until today. And that mouth...dear lord, was that a mouth made for sinning. I could already imagine it whispering naughty things in my ears before his lips left a trail of lust down my skin.

Something about him was familiar too. I searched my limited memory for a time I could have met him, but surely I would've remembered someone this remarkably gorgeous. No. There was no way we'd met.

Yet... I knew him somehow. Instinctively, primally, deep in the core of my being, he felt like something I... It was right on the tip of my tongue. The thought I couldn't grasp before it slid away. I refocused, but it was no use. I couldn't put my finger on it. Maybe I knew him from before the accident? Seemed unlikely, and surely if he knew me, he'd say something.

I realized I was staring and jerked my gaze away, out over the view. Las Vegas in the daytime wasn't nearly as impressive as at night, when the city was lit up as if some preschoolers had sprinkled giant tubs of glitter over an expanse of desert. Even so, the bustling city against the back-drop of the mountains in the distance momentarily took all of my focus, giving me a second to gain my bearings again.

"Tell me your name," Lucas said.

His voice, that accent, *my god.*

"Hannah." I finally met his eyes again. "Hannah Thorn."

"Hannah." My name rolled off his tongue like a sip of expensive Scotch. I shook my head and blinked away the thought. I didn't drink. Why would I think about the smooth burn of a drink I'd never had?

He tore his eyes from me like it was difficult for him to do so. Almost as if he was drawn to me as much as I was to him. A fanciful notion, and one I immediately dismissed as he walked behind the bar.

"Drink?" Lucas held up a decanter and a crystal tumbler that sent a rainbow of light shards bouncing around the room.

"No thanks. I don't drink."

He hummed low in his throat, a sound of dissent. "Pity. We could have a lot of fun if we got drunk together."

He reached for different glasses and shoveled ice into them. Three perfect cubes hit the sides of the glasses with a chinking sound. Then he grabbed a jug of clear liquid from under his counter, and I held up my hand in the universal gesture for *stop.*

"I meant it. I don't drink."

"And I don't give alcohol to anyone who isn't a willing recipient." He picked up his glass and took a big swallow of the contents. "Sadly, just water."

He held the second glass out to me. As I wrapped my fingers around it, our hands brushed against each other, and the fire in my gut erupted again, sending heat all over my body and down to my core. The feeling that I knew Lucas redoubled, like a memory just outside my grasp, or a word on the tip of my tongue. And with it came a rush of desire so strong it took my breath away.

His gaze intensified. Did he feel it too?

"Sit." Lucas gestured toward the black leather couches.

I perched on the edge of one and held my glass in both hands, my grip tightening as my nerves stretched thin. Anxiety wound in my chest and mixed with the desire pooling between my thighs, making me feel light-headed. I glanced at the nearby piano, trying to bring my emotions back under control. This was all too big. Much too big. What the hell was I even doing here?

Lucas sat on the couch across from me and spread one arm along the back. He rested an ankle on his knee in the perfect picture of poise and calm control. "Now, how can I be of assistance?"

I took a deep breath, trying to channel some of that calm control for myself, even if I only pretended. I was perfectly happy to fake it, even if I would never make it. Not around someone so disarming.

"My best friend is missing," I blurted out. *Way to fake poise.* "Her name is Brandy Higgins. She was staying here, in this hotel, for a conference, but she never came home. I tried to find her myself, but I haven't had any success, and when I went to the police they were dismissive. Especially when I told them she'd been staying here."

"You must be a very loyal friend. Very few are brave

enough to ask me for a favor." He looked at his drink and shook the ice around in the glass, the sound it made almost musical. "The rest are extremely desperate. I wonder, which one are you?"

I glanced down at my hands, but then forced myself to meet his eyes, trying to channel bravery along with my desperation. "Both. Brandy is more than a friend. She's like a sister to me, and she has a little kid and a sick mom at home counting on me to find her. I've been living with them ever since her divorce to help out, but if she doesn't return..." The thought was too terrible for me to consider. I straightened my spine and stiffened my shoulders, shoving my anxiety into a tight ball in my chest as I faced Lucas with determination. "I heard you're called the King of Las Vegas, and that nothing happens here without you knowing about it. I figure if anyone can find Brandy, it's you."

I didn't mention the other rumors I'd heard about him, like the fact that he was basically a mob boss who ran the city, and how people referred to him as the devil in nervous whispers and behind locked doors. Even the police seemed afraid of him.

"You both sound like a proper pair of saints," Lucas noted, his lips quirking at the corners. "You said she went missing here, in The Celestial?"

"Yes, a few days ago."

He nodded slowly, like a man in no kind of a hurry, a man with nothing to lose and with the luxury of time on his side. Time I sure as hell didn't have. "You understand there is always a price for my help?"

Panic wrapped an iron band around my chest, and I sucked in a shaky breath. I'd known this was coming, and I had no idea what he'd want in return for his help. "I don't have any money."

"Oh, I don't trade in money." He laughed, but his face flashed with something villainous. "My currency is dark deeds and dirty secrets."

I swallowed hard and glanced at the hallway, wondering if it was too late to escape. I had no secrets, none that I remembered anyway, which meant he would want a dark deed of some kind. Would he ask for something illegal? Something dangerous? Something I would regret for the rest of my life? I nearly ran out the door, but then I pictured Brandy's son looking up at me with barely contained tears as he asked when his mom was coming home, and my resolve hardened. I looked Lucas in the eye and nodded.

He leaned forward, no longer casual. "Are you willing to do whatever it takes?"

"Yes," I said breathlessly. "What do you want?"

"You."

My jaw dropped, and my stomach dropped lower. Possibly through the floor. All the floors. "Me?"

He chuckled, the sound a dark melody full of wicked promises. "Six nights with you. Here in my penthouse. Mine to do with as I please."

I gasped at the sensual pause between each of his last three words. Then I shook my head, certain I'd misheard. Misunderstood perhaps. Yes, that last one. "Excuse me? You

expect me to give you carte blanche to do anything to me?
For six nights?"

"Would you prefer seven?" A sinful grin crossed his lips
as he leaned back against the soft leather of the couch. "I
will warn you, I don't rest on the seventh day."

"*Seven?*" My thoughts scrambled, and all I could do was
stare at him. Was he serious?

He nodded. "Yes, let's make it seven nights. One for
each deadly sin. Even better."

Shit. I really shouldn't have questioned that six nights
thing. I ran the scenarios through my head, my face warming
as I saw many of them in glorious detail. Yes, the man was
insanely attractive, but he was proposing something six
degrees of indecent. Not to mention, he was a total stranger.
A very gorgeous, very *dangerous* stranger. What he was
asking of me...it was too much. Maybe there was some other
way I could find Brandy. Someone else I could go to
for help.

Lucas watched me, waiting for my decision. "Tick-tock.
Time is slipping away. The longer you wait, the less likely
we'll find your friend alive."

Fear pulsed through me at the thought, but he was right.
She'd already been missing for days. I needed to make a
decision quickly, but I had to be sure about what I was
getting myself into. I cleared my throat. "Let me get this
straight. You want me to stay here with you for seven nights
while you...do whatever you want to me. Sexually."

His gaze darkened to a glower, and I nearly trembled at

the intensity of it. "I have never forced myself on a woman, and I never will, if that's what you're worried about."

A breath of relief left my lips. "I had to be sure. I've never done anything like this before."

"I promise no harm will come to you by my hand. But as for sex..." He rose to his feet and walked the few steps toward me, making me look up at him. Then he bent forward and rested his hands on the back of the couch on either side of my head, caging me in. "Don't you know who I am? They call me the devil for a reason. Temptation, lust, sin, all wrapped up in a neat little package. Oh, who am I kidding? A *huge* package. Trust me, before the week ends you'll be begging for every single thing I do to you."

He was entirely too close, his face inches from my own, his green eyes burning like a fire had been lit from within. Desire rushed through me like I'd never felt before, but it was mixed with a heavy dash of fear. My gaze dropped down to his mouth, only a breath apart from mine, and I ached for him to close the space between us, even as I wanted to run from him.

I forced my eyes back up to meet his intense gaze. I couldn't think of another way to find Brandy. I'd tried everything I could, but nothing had worked. If I didn't do this, I'd fail completely.

This was my last chance.

"I agree," I said, with as much courage as I could muster.

"Excellent." He straightened up and walked to the other side of the room casually while my heart raced in my chest. He picked up a pad of paper and a pen, then handed them to me. "Write down everything you know about your friend's disappearance. Names, dates, and so forth."

As I scribbled down all the details, apprehension making my handwriting look like someone else's, he watched me closely. I kept glancing up as the pen scratched along the paper, unable to keep my eyes off him. Why did I feel like I was signing away my soul with our deal?

When I'd written down everything I could think of, I gave him back his notepad and pen. He closed his hands around mine to take them, and heat shot down to pool between my thighs again. Unexpected longing rose in my chest, and I swallowed as I tried to bring order and coherence back to my thoughts.

"Where are you staying?" he asked.

"This cheap place off The Strip." I looked away, embarrassed to say the name of it. I'd scrambled up every penny I had to come here, but it was nothing compared to this penthouse. "Double Down Motel."

His face twisted with disgust. "Give me your room key. I'll have all your things brought here."

"What about my car?" I asked.

"My people will handle that as well."

I raised an eyebrow at that, but pulled out my keys and handed them to him. He had *people*? I thought people who had people were just a myth. Who actually had *people* to do shit for them?

"Good." He pocketed them and held out a hand. "Now follow me."

Every time I touched him I felt...things. I kept my hands to myself. "Where?"

"To your new room." His voice dripped with promise. "Though I suspect you'll soon prefer mine."

We walked down a corridor and he threw open a door at the end. Unlike the rest of the penthouse I'd seen so far, which was all decorated in black and silver, this room was done in neutral tones. The queen-sized bed had one of those padded headboards behind it and was covered in lush blankets, a thick duvet, and soft-looking pillows. On the other side of the room was a cute sitting area and a desk in front of windows looking out at The Strip. A door led to a walk-in closet as large as my old apartment, and another opened to a massive bathroom all done in Carrera marble.

"This is your guest room?" I asked, as I took it all in, spinning in a slow circle. If this was for guests, what did his bedroom look like?

His lips quirked up in amusement. "It's yours now. Make yourself comfortable. Order anything you like from room service. My people will bring your things along shortly, while I begin my investigation into your friend's whereabouts."

I shook my head, part in denial, part in wonder. This situation made no sense, and I was starting to wonder what the catch was. Maybe this was a case of mistaken identity of some sort. After all, why would he want me—*me*, of all people—for seven nights? I was just a basic bookworm with a nice set of boobs and a cute smile, who worked in a flower shop and wore flip-flops and jeans. Nothing special. Not compared to the women he probably surrounded himself with all the time.

Nerves churned in my gut as I considered the full force of what I'd just agreed to. Me. Here. In this penthouse. For seven nights.

And *him*. Doing whatever he wanted to me.

For the next week, he owned me. Completely. But it would all be worth it if he kept his side of the bargain.

I turned toward him. "Do you promise to find Brandy?"

"I will. Dead or alive, I will find her."

He looked me in the eye, and I didn't doubt his conviction. Lucas Ifer was a man who got things done, and if anyone could find my friend in the dark underground of Las Vegas, it was him.

He offered me his hand, and I took it to shake. The moment his skin touched mine, an electric tingle rushed through me, with that same fleeting sensation of familiarity and long-lost desire.

His fingers tightened around mine almost possessively. "It's a deal."

2

LUCIFER

The door to the guest quarters closed behind me with a barely perceptible click as I stepped into the wide hallway. There I paused to draw in a deep breath as the enormity of what had just transpired hit me fully.

She was *back*.

My heart raced with anticipation. I could hardly believe it when she walked into my penthouse without warning, but the second we touched all doubts had vanished. She'd returned to me. Finally.

Hannah Thorn. A new name. A new look. But still undeniably *mine*.

I pictured her on the other side of the door, probably examining her new bedroom. Long golden hair framed a heart-shaped face with blushing cheeks and bright blue eyes, not to mention her very kissable lips. Lips I would soon be claiming, along with the rest of her small, curvy body. I only had to convince her over the next seven nights that she belonged to me.

While I found her friend, of course. Couldn't forget that part. She'd led Hannah to me, after all. Yes, I needed to find this Brandy woman, if only to thank her.

Besides, I didn't take lightly the disappearance of a human female in my hotel. Though demons fed on the energy of humans, I had strict rules about not harming them, especially within my domain. Of course, now that we'd made Earth our permanent home, the entire world was technically my domain. Still, even the youngest demons knew not to break the rules in the king's own castle.

The Celestial Resort & Casino was my flagship hotel, a shining gem on the Las Vegas Strip, designed to entice humans to sin in any number of ways, all so my demons could feed safely while still remaining hidden from the world. In fact, I'd covertly built the entire city over the last forty years to be the perfect haven for demons. Sin City, they called it, and I was its King.

I stepped outside my penthouse and adjusted my suit as I eyed my guards. "No one goes in or out, except by my command."

They bowed their heads as I entered the elevator. If Hannah really wanted to leave, I wouldn't stop her, but I couldn't have her running around the city alone either. Now that she'd been returned to me, she needed to be protected at all times.

For years my heart had been cold and black, a hard piece of coal waiting for her to return and ignite it. I'd searched for her for so long to no avail, only to have her walk into my life out of the blue. Looking for *me* this time. Oh, the irony.

I took the elevator down one floor to my war room. As I stepped inside the large space, I could almost inhale the power of my rule—a heady scent indeed. I paused as I took in the room, dark lord of all I surveyed. Live feeds and surveillance footage filled huge TV screens, and my industrious staff operated computers on too many desks to count as they followed every thread and whisper of sin this city had to offer. Greed, envy, lust...all mine, mine, mine. A huge switchboard took up an entire wall as they made connection after connection, following people, emotions, and things. Flashing lights moved around on a large world map on the wall, showing various demon, angel, and fae activities.

Samael was in his office, as I expected him to be, from where he oversaw everything in the command center. He acted as my right-hand man in most matters, and he'd been by my side ever since I left Heaven to rule Hell. Gadreel was in there too, looking at an open file atop the black desk. He was one of the younger Fallen, only about two centuries old, but he'd proved his loyalty many times and had risen in the ranks to become Samael's assistant.

I poked my head into the office. "Meeting. Now. Get Azazel too."

They both snapped their heads up, one dark and one light. Samael furrowed his brow. "What's this about?"

"She's returned." I didn't need to elaborate. They knew who I meant.

Gadreel's blond eyebrows darted up. "Are you sure?"

I thought of the sparks I'd felt when I touched Hannah's hand. "Yes, I'm certain of it. Funny enough, she found me this time."

Without waiting for a response, I turned and headed for our meeting room. The windows facing out to the rest of the command center turned opaque as soon as I flipped a switch, giving us complete privacy. The room was sound-proof too, even from supernaturals with enhanced hearing. I took my seat at the end of the conference table, sinking into the plush leather executive chair. Seconds later, Samael walked inside, followed by Gadreel and Azazel. They shut the door behind them, and took seats around the table.

"I hear she's back," Azazel said, as she kicked her legs up on the table, showing off studded black leather boots. She was my top security official and my fiercest blade, able to wield any weapon with ease. Tight black leather was her armor of choice and anger her fuel to fight.

"Yes, and I need you to guard our new guest," I said. "She's in my penthouse, and I can't allow her to leave it unless you're by her side. I want you protecting her at all times."

Her face twisted with annoyance, but she nodded. She would never disobey a direct order from me, even if she didn't want to follow it.

I leaned forward and caught her eye. "I realize being a bodyguard may seem beneath you, but in truth I've given you the most important task of them all. Hannah's life will soon be in danger, and you're the only one I trust to keep her safe."

Her annoyance faded and she bowed her head. "I won't fail you, my lord."

"What is her name now?" Samael asked, his hands folded calmly on the table.

"Hannah Thorn."

"Ah. The woman asking about her friend."

I should have known Samael would already have some information on her. Little happened within these walls that he didn't know about. "Yes, and we need to find this friend with all haste. She went missing in The Celestial a few days ago." I pulled out the pad of paper and handed it to him. He scanned it quickly, while I continued. "I also want everything you can dig up on Hannah's life. Family, boyfriends, work, what she eats for breakfast—I want every single detail."

"It will be done," Samael said, with his usual smooth confidence.

I pulled out Hannah's car keys and room key next, then tossed them to Gadreel. The blond man caught them with quick reflexes. "Gadreel, I need you to go to the Double Down Motel" —I shuddered simply saying the name— "And retrieve her things, along with her car. I trust you can figure out which one it is."

"Won't be a problem, my lord," Gadreel said, as he examined the room key with distaste. Hannah had referred to the Double Down Motel as *this cheap place off The Strip.* That description oversold it.

"You have your orders. For the time being, let's keep Hannah's presence here between the three of us." I rose to my feet and glanced between my loyal Fallen, while determination burned in my chest. "I lost her before, but I'm not letting her go this time. Not again."

3

HANNAH

As soon as Lucas closed the door behind him, I glanced around the guest room in wonder, still struggling to believe this was all real. Two days ago I'd been packing my bags to head to Vegas to find my friend, and now I would be living here for the next seven nights, at the whim of a man they called the devil. Sure, I'd agreed to the deal, but that didn't make it any less terrifying. Especially now that Lucas was gone and I was alone with my thoughts.

He'd better find Brandy. And alive, too.

Please let her be alive.

I moved to the large window overlooking The Strip and wondered for the hundredth time where she was and what had happened to her. Sunlight glinted off the various hotels and casinos, and I remembered how excited Brandy had been to come here. She'd been invited to a librarian conference over a three-day weekend, winning some award that paid for the entire trip. She'd asked me to come too, to have a girls' weekend with her in Vegas, but I'd turned her down. My florist shop was small, but it demanded almost all of my attention just to keep it afloat. Plus, I enjoyed working there in the place once owned by my parents, finding exactly the right flowers to brighten people's homes or convey the things they couldn't always bring themselves to say. No matter how much I'd wanted to go to Vegas with Brandy, I'd said no. Now it was one of my biggest regrets.

She'd gone to Vegas alone, and then she never came home.

The last time I heard from Brandy was after she checked in to this very hotel, when she'd called to say goodnight to her son. That was six days ago.

When she didn't answer her phone or come home at the end of the weekend, I knew something was wrong. I felt it right in my gut, and I never ignored my instincts. With a sick mom and a little kid, no way would Brandy run off. Someone must have taken her.

Over the next day I made dozens of phone calls, trying to find her, but it was useless. It soon became obvious I'd have to go to Vegas myself and figure out what happened on my own. I begged my part-time helper Maggie to watch the flower shop for a few days, and then I scraped together every penny I had and hit the road in my beat-up car, driving the five hours through the desert until I reached Sin City.

Before I left, Brandy's mom Donna had taken me aside and begged me to find her daughter, while she'd sobbed into a tissue streaked with blood. Donna had terminal lung cancer and could barely find the energy to make herself a sandwich these days, but she promised she'd manage looking after Brandy's son Jack while I was gone. Then, on my way out of the house, Jack grabbed me around the waist and asked me to bring his mom home soon. Both times I'd blinked back tears, and swore to them that I would find Brandy.

What else could I have done? Brandy had treated me like family from the moment we'd met in the library where she worked, and she'd given me a place to live when I needed it most. I should have gone with her to Vegas, and guilt was eating me alive for that decision. I'd chosen my responsibilities over my friend, and I wished more than anything that I could go back in time and redo everything. If I could get Maggie to step in and help at the shop now, why couldn't I have done that before? Brandy would have done it for me in a heartbeat. Why, why, why did I let her go alone?

I had to find her, and it was all on me. Brandy had nobody else in the world to go looking for her, and I couldn't let her drop off the face of the Earth. Vegas would eat her alive and forget her, allowing her to become another statistic. The police here were proof of that. When I went to report her disappearance they blew me off, especially once they found out Brandy went missing in Lucas's hotel. They'd closed ranks immediately, speaking in low voices to one another with pointed glances, suddenly all deferential about Mr. Ifer. He probably had each and every one of them on his payroll. They eventually took my report, but I had a bad feeling it was in a pile somewhere never to be seen again.

My only option had been to start doing some detective work myself, but I kept hitting dead ends. First, the staff at The Celestial Resort & Casino couldn't find any information about a librarian conference. When I looked it up myself online I only found one sparse website for it, and no other mentions anywhere. It was almost like it never existed at all. Or like someone had set up the whole thing just to lure Brandy to Las Vegas. But why? Had she gotten herself involved in something bad? Some sort of business with the mob? I found that hard to believe.

I started poking around the hotel, asking questions and playing detective, but I was no Nancy Drew. I had no idea what I was doing, yet I asked people as many questions as I could think of, and slowly but surely my intuition tugged at me, telling me something wasn't right. I wore my cheap flip-flops up and down The Strip, visiting all the places Brandy might have visited. No one gave me any information, almost like Brandy hadn't existed at all. I hit brick wall after brick wall. I needed access to video cameras, phone records, and credit cards, but I didn't have a badge or any connections. And I was running out of time and money.

Then I heard about Lucas Ifer, the owner of The Celestial, along with a lot of other places in Vegas too, according to rumor. They called him the devil in hushed tones and made him sound like a dangerous mob boss, but it soon became apparent that not much happened in Vegas he didn't know about. Plus he was known for making deals, and he was able to get you anything you wanted. For a price, of course.

By all accounts, Lucas Ifer was the King of Las Vegas. If the police couldn't help me, and the people on the street couldn't help me, I had to come to the castle. I just hadn't expected the castle to be in the sky. Now I was trapped in this tower like Rapunzel, except my hair was definitely not long enough to get me down.

I sat on the edge of the bed, my heart pounding. I was basically being held captive as a sex slave for a mob boss, and there was no telling if he was going to find Brandy. Or if she was even alive.

No, I had to stop thinking that way. I believed Lucas would honor our deal as long as I did. I felt it in my gut, and my gut was never wrong. Even if my gut also told me that he was the most dangerous man I'd ever met.

I leaned back and ran my hands along the smooth, soft duvet cover and blankets. This guest room was huge and luxurious, but it was sparse too, and I got the feeling it wasn't used very often. I debated ordering room service, but my stomach was too twisted up in knots to eat anything. Still, if I had to stay somewhere for seven nights, I would be hard-pressed to find a hotel room nicer than this one.

Damn it. Seven nights away from home and from my shop. I sincerely hoped Maggie was able to keep an eye on the place that long. She was in her late sixties, and I worried running the whole thing might be a hardship for her. I'd had to agree that she could say cash or check only, which was going to suck. Most people preferred credit, but Maggie was hopeless with the card machine. I grimaced at the thought of returning to a business that had collapsed under the weight of going old-school. The place wasn't doing all that well before I'd left, and I owed it to my parents to keep it afloat.

Taking out my phone, I dialed her quickly. No answer. It was almost five, and she was probably closing up the shop. I sent a text instead. At least she was pretty good with texting.

I'm delayed in Vegas. Please do your best at the shop. Will be gone 7 more days.

I'd deal with the fallout when she replied. As I waited, I considered texting my sister too, but Jo was an enormous worrywart. She tended to be overbearing, and I didn't need that on top of everything else. If it had been up to Jo, I never would've left Vista. If I told her about what I'd agreed to now, she'd completely fly off the handle.

Maggie's reply reassured me. **I'm fine. Take your time. Win lots of money.**

She ended it with a bunch of money bag emojis. I shook my head, wondering if she was unclear on why I was here, or just perpetually optimistic. I took a few moments to call Donna, but she didn't answer either. Probably making Jack something to eat. I sighed and left her a message telling her I was doing everything I could to find Brandy, but I would be here for another week. I apologized profusely for being away so long, and my throat tightened with emotion as I hung up.

With all my bases covered, there was nothing else to do but wait, which I wasn't very good at. If nothing else, I could explore my new surroundings. Surely that was allowed.

I got up and opened all the drawers in the room but they were empty. I stepped inside the giant walk-in closet and twirled around, but it was bare except for a few hangers. I moved into the massive bathroom next, my eyes going wide at the sight of all that marble and the huge shower and even bigger soaker tub. I'd never been in a bathroom this fancy before. Or this big. I was tempted to take a bath and try to wash away my worries, but I was curious about the rest of this place. If this was to be my home for the next week, I should get familiar with it, shouldn't I?

I opened the bedroom door wide enough to peer out into the hallway, but didn't hear a thing. Lucas was gone, off to investigate Brandy's disappearance, or so I hoped. I walked back out across the marble floors into the living room, gazing across the black and silver space that exuded power, danger, and luxury. The place could really use a few flowers or ferns to give it some life and color. Maybe some succulents even. Something to make the space feel less cold and dead.

Then I realized I wasn't alone after all.

A gorgeous Black woman stood in front of the entrance to the penthouse. Leather crisscrossed her body like some sort of armor, and her dark hair was scraped back so tight it drew her skin taut over the most wicked cheekbones I'd ever seen. The hilt of a blade peeked above her left shoulder. Something about her tickled my instincts, but not like the familiarity I felt around Lucas.

"I'm Zel," she said, like she didn't care if I remembered or not.

"Is that short for something?" I asked.

"Azazel."

I could see why she went with Zel. "I'm Hannah."

"I know. Lucas ordered me to protect you."

"Protect me or prevent me from leaving?" I asked, raising an eyebrow. I had no doubt she could snap me in half with a lazy bend of her pinky finger, and she didn't sound pleased about her new job as my bodyguard.

Her dark eyes surveyed me with something like disdain. "If you leave the penthouse you need an escort at all times."

"Why?" I tilted my head with a frown. "Is Lucas worried I'll run away?"

"Lucas protects what is his."

And that included me now, I realized with a shiver. "What if I leave the city?"

She pinned me with a threatening gaze. "You won't."

I truly was a captive. I had the illusion of freedom, but Lucas had made sure if I went anywhere, his bodyguard-slash-spy would keep tabs on me at all times and make sure I didn't run away.

Zel didn't seem inclined to chat, so I continued through the living room and around a corner, discovering a small, well-appointed kitchen on the other side of the bar, along with a dark dining table that seated six. I couldn't imagine Lucas doing much cooking, although this kitchen seemed like a chef's dream come true. I didn't recognize the brand names of any of the appliances, which made me think they were ridiculously high-end. I opened up the stainless steel fridge out of curiosity, and was surprised to find some food inside, including an impressive selection of fancy-looking cheese. I spotted foods with labels in foreign languages, and I examined tins and jars containing things I'd never even heard of. To my relief, I spotted a container of Heinz ketchup in the door. Something I recognized. Something that proved Lucas wasn't all pomp and circumstance.

I shut the fridge door and headed down another hallway, with the distinct sense I was going down the rabbit hole and through the mirror. Nothing in this penthouse felt at all real. Everything was spotless, like dust didn't even dare to exist within these walls, and I'd never witnessed such luxury or wealth so prominently and unashamedly on display. I was hesitant to touch anything, for fear of breaking something. I didn't need to add to my tab with Lucas.

At the end of this hall, I found a big set of double doors like the ones that led out of the penthouse to the elevator. I tried the handle, but each one was locked. Certainty flowed through me that these doors led to Lucas's private chambers. I rested my hand on the smooth wood and felt an intense craving to know what was on the other side, along with a whisper of something that felt a lot like desire. I shook off the feeling and turned around.

I wondered what Lucas would think of me looking around his space, and then I realized he almost certainly had cameras everywhere. He likely already knew that I'd been poking around like a mouse when the cat was gone. Well, what did he expect? I couldn't sit around the guest room all day staring at my nails, waiting for him to return. I snorted at the thought.

I walked out onto the huge balcony that wrapped

around the entire penthouse, and marveled over the pool that seemed to flow right over the edge and into the sky. The sun was starting to set, and Las Vegas was waking up with all its noise and lights. Soon my first sinful night with Lucas would begin. With a tremor of fear running down my spine, plus a heavy dose of curiosity, I wondered what he had planned for me.

Back inside, I found another set of double doors and assumed they would be locked too, but to my surprise, they clicked open—and then I walked into a librarian's own personal heaven. A vast room filled with hundreds of books stretched before me like something out of a movie. The bookshelves around me seemed impossibly high, and Belle would've been at home tucked into a corner here, waiting on her Beast. Old leather editions were housed with glossy modern volumes, and I longed to flip the pages just to inhale all the scents the paper released. Brandy would've chained herself to the ladder that provided access to the upper shelves.

In one corner of the room was a seating area with plush, dark chairs and large paintings on the wall behind them. On the other corner stood a massive desk with nothing on top of it, and a silver sword hanging on the wall behind it that seemed to glow with an inner light. The legs on the desk were exquisite carved wood, wrapped in tiny wraith-like figures that turned out to be horned demons and gothic angels on closer inspection. Every time I blinked, the carvings seemed to move, and I stepped back and shook my head. I'd never been a good sleeper, and it had only gotten worse since arriving in Vegas. The long nights must finally be catching up to me.

I turned in a circle, taking in the library with awe. I wasn't sure what the next seven days and nights would hold, but this library might make it all worth it. Like Brandy, I was a total book nerd, which was how we'd met, after all. I'd strolled into the Vista Library looking for something to read during the boring shifts at work, and we'd been best friends ever since.

Dark wooden pedestals stood around the room, displaying ancient-looking vases and other pieces of art under spotlights, like in a museum. I had no doubt each one was priceless. An old Greek vase caught my eye, and I moved closer to inspect it. Intricate black figures depicted a scene on an orange background of a large man in a crown sitting on a throne, offering a plate of berries or seeds to a woman standing before him. A small placard on the pedestal read, *Hades Tempts Persephone, c. 350 B.C.* My mouth fell open as I studied it with reverence. I was a huge history and mythology buff, and this vase hit both of those notes.

I'd expected a lot of things from Lucas Ifer, but I hadn't imagined him as a connoisseur of ancient art and old books somehow. I stared at the vase for far too long, and then turned to the bookshelves to get lost in them. Row after row, both fiction and nonfiction, covering so many genres and topics it made my heart sing. I soon got overwhelmed and grabbed a notepad and pen to make notes on which books I had to read during my time here. There was no way Lucas would be around twenty-four-seven, even within the bounds of our deal, not if he had a city to run. This was the perfect way to distract myself from worrying about Brandy all day.

"I see you found my library." Lucas's smooth voice interrupted me, and I turned toward him. He stood in the doorway in his impeccable suit, all brooding darkness and beguiling shadows.

"It's incredible. I could stay here forever getting lost in these shelves." I was halfway through the room and my list had already gotten longer than I could manage.

A wicked smile danced across his lips. "I can arrange that, you know."

I stiffened, remembering why I was here and how he controlled everything in my life for the next few days. "On second thought, seven nights is plenty."

He let out a low, dark chuckle, the sound so sexy it made my toes curl. "What do you like to read?"

"History and mythology mostly, but I also love romance. Historical, paranormal, fantasy romance... It's my guilty pleasure, I guess you could say." I clamped my mouth shut the second the words came out. I wasn't sure why I'd confessed that to him, especially when men were often so derisive about romance novels.

"No reason to feel guilty when it comes to pleasure...or romance." He sounded amused, but at least he wasn't mocking me or putting down the genre. "Those are my favorite genres as well."

I gestured at the Greek vase. "I guessed that from the art. Very impressive."

He followed my gaze with a mysterious smile. "I find history so...fascinating, don't you? Especially how it can be depicted so differently from what truly happened."

"But how would you know what truly happened?"

His smile grew wider and became downright devilish. "That is the question, isn't it?"

"Excuse me." A voice interrupted us just as I was about to lose myself in Lucas's dark gaze. I shook myself and turned toward the door, where another far-too-attractive man stood. He wore a suit like Lucas, but didn't pull it off quite as well, even with his broad shoulders. The tips of his sandy blond hair touched eyelashes of the same color, and big blue eyes looked out at me from a face that could have belonged to any boy next door. Only this place didn't have a next door, so where was this guy from? Where were any of these people from?

"Yes, Gadreel?" Lucas asked.

"I've brought her things from the motel, as you asked." Gadreel's eyes landed on me and lingered, like he was intrigued by my presence. I wondered if Lucas made these sorts of deals with women regularly, or if I was the first one to become the devil's plaything for seven nights.

Lucas idly waved a hand. "Put them in the guest room."

"Of course, my lord." Gadreel gave a quick bow before exiting the room. Did Lucas really demand such old-fashioned obedience from his people?

Lucas's intense gaze turned back to me. "If you're wondering about our deal, I assure you my best people are looking into your friend's disappearance and should have some leads soon. I expect we'll know a lot more tomorrow."

I swallowed, feeling a tiny trickle of hope and relief. "Thank you."

"I always fulfill my end of the bargain." His emerald eyes drew me in, and I was powerless to look away. "Now, it's time for you to fulfill yours."

4

HANNAH

A long black limo drew up at the curb outside the front of The Celestial. I was pretty sure we got in at the back while the front was arriving at our destination. The spectacle was even more eye-opening than my low-cut black silk dress, which Lucas had delivered after he'd discovered I'd brought nothing formal to wear to Las Vegas. Or more accurately, that I didn't own anything formal. Nothing that would live up to his standards anyway.

I'd never been in a limo, as far as I could remember. It was leather-everything with windows tinted so dark they seemed to be part of the interior walls rather than actual windows. My gaze kept drifting to the sunroof and the Vegas lights that played through the glass like some kind of neon kaleidoscope. I pictured myself hanging out of it and waving at passing cars like in a movie, but I refrained. This wasn't a joyride, or a date even—this was part of a deal with a dangerous man to find my missing friend. I couldn't forget that, no matter how glamorous it all was.

Or how gorgeous my captor was.

Lucas was the epitome of cool, calm, and collected as he sat back in his seat and straightened his tuxedo cuffs. Yes, he wore an actual tuxedo. Even in my new dress, which probably cost more than my monthly salary, I felt completely out of place at his side.

"I've decided each of our seven nights will represent one of the Deadly Sins," he said, with a roguish smile that made my knees weak.

My breath caught as I imagined what those sins were. Wrath, envy, *lust*. "And tonight is...?"

His mischievous green eyes danced with amusement, as though he knew exactly which sin I was thinking about. "Tonight is gluttony. I hope you're hungry."

A silent sigh of relief left me. Gluttony I could handle. "Starving, actually. I haven't eaten since this morning."

Lucas tutted. "I did tell you to order room service."

My hands twisted in my lap. "I've been too worried about my friend to eat much. Do you have any leads on what happened to her?"

"Not yet, but my people are combing the hotel's security footage now." He looked me right in the eye with complete confidence and seriousness. "I promised you I would find her, and I will. Do not doubt that."

I nodded slowly and looked away before I lost myself in his dark, burning gaze. Worry for Brandy still stifled me, but I tried to push it aside. There was nothing more I could do at this point, except have faith that Lucas could find her.

The limo stopped outside the Bellagio, a massive hotel that looked like some kind of fairytale castle framing the huge lake of water and gorgeous fountains. The window slid smoothly down in front of me and music floated on the night air, while the fountains moved in time to it and lights splashed across the water.

"Look at the fountains," I said with a gasp. When I turned to Lucas, he watched me with an unreadable expression on his all-too-handsome face, and I turned quickly back to the fountains.

The car drew to a smooth stop right in front of the hotel. Other cars raced by, but I lost myself for a few moments in the spectacle and the music. I'd never seen water sway like that before. Like it was alive.

Lucas stepped out of the limo when the driver opened the door, then he turned and held his hand out for me. I scooted over as best I could in the snug dress, trying not to snag it on my gorgeous heels. They'd arrived with my dress, and I'd nearly died when I saw the red bottom of the heels— the signature style of Christian Louboutin. I didn't know much about fashion, but Brandy did, and she'd always coveted his shoes. Maybe I could sneak these back to Vista when this was all over and give them to her.

I took Lucas's hand as I stepped out of the limo, and his eyes raked over me with something like hunger in them. Then he slowly lifted my hand to his lips, pressing a lingering kiss inside my wrist. I released a breath and met his gaze in surprise. The heat from his lips traveled right through me, straight to my core, and probably scorching my panties right off. How did he know that was my spot, the one that drove me wild and stoked my desire like nowhere else?

"You look exquisite," he said in a low voice.

"Thank you." I smoothed the dress, my cheeks flushing. "Anyone would look nice in such an amazing dress."

"I wasn't talking about the dress."

He took my arm like a true gentleman, even if the look he gave me was anything but gentlemanly. Being this close to him made my heart race, and it wasn't only with fear. He was far too good-looking, and the power and danger he radiated both intrigued me and made me want to run away all at once.

We entered the hotel and I tried not to have wide tourist eyes as we walked down the gorgeous entryway. Everyone scrambled to make sure our path was clear, parting like waves in front of us, and more than one person gave Lucas a deferential nod. He strolled by as if he owned the place, even though this wasn't his hotel. That swagger was something billionaires always had, I guessed. People whispered as we walked by, my ears picking up the hiss of the sound but none of the words. Their eyes followed us, and more than one woman lost interest in her date as Lucas passed in front of her. Others shot me curious or even dirty looks. I was on the arm of Vegas's most handsome, richest bachelor, and people definitely noticed.

At Lucas's side, I felt like the queen to his dark king.

Most surprising of all—I found myself secretly enjoying the thrill of it.

We stopped in front of a restaurant called Picasso. I knew nothing about the place, except that it was one of those restaurants that listed the chef's name under the sign, so you knew it was going to be expensive and have dishes you couldn't pronounce. Lucas led me across the shiny floors to the hostess, who waited at the entrance like she was expecting us.

"Mr. Ifer?" She was polite, but her deferential body language said she knew exactly who he was. "It's a pleasure to welcome you to Picasso. We have the terrace all ready for you. Right this way."

We followed her inside the restaurant, which was completely empty other than the three of us. A bit creepy, but it allowed me to marvel at how beautiful everything was. We walked along colorful carpet under mosaic ceilings and between tables covered in white cloths, past walls decorated with unusual geometric art.

As the name of the restaurant clicked in my head, my jaw dropped open. "These paintings. Are they *real* Picassos?"

"They are," Lucas said casually, as though we weren't basically walking through an art museum.

I didn't think anything could top seeing real Picasso paintings up close, but then we walked outside and I gasped at the view. We were directly behind the gorgeous fountains, which towered over us against the backdrop of the

Vegas lights, and close enough that I could feel the spray of water in the air.

He tightened his arm around me as I watched the fountains, mesmerized by how they danced and twined to the music with the kind of grace I'd never master. The droplets were like sprites or fairies and a lump formed in my throat as I imagined what Brandy's reaction would have been to this magical sight.

"Your box for the fountains is on your table." The hostess indicated the white-covered table with two red chairs on either side of it. The rest of the large terrace, which likely seated many guests on a normal night, had been completely cleared out, giving us a lot of space and privacy —plus this amazing view.

Lucas held out my chair for me, and I sat as gracefully as I could, praying I could keep it together in such an exquisite place. It would be just my luck to drop my dinner or spill my drink all over this dress. The whole thing was completely overwhelming, and it was hard not to gawk as the server came over and launched into a spiel about how the restaurant featured both authentic Picasso masterpieces along with decadent food inspired by the regional cuisine of Spain and France. Oh and over 1,500 selections from the finest European vineyards—not that I drank wine, but it still sounded impressive.

The server then handed me a tiny menu, just one sheet of embossed paper with six different things on it. I scanned it and picked the item that looked the least strange, because most of it was gibberish to me. "I'll have the lobster salad please."

The server gave me a pitying smile and spoke with a French accent. "Oh no, you don't need to choose anything. These are the six courses you'll be receiving throughout the evening, personally selected by our master chef. I guarantee it's the finest food you'll eat in Las Vegas."

My eyes dropped to the menu again. *Six* courses? Yes, I was hungry, but could anyone eat that much? And what were half of the things on this menu anyway? Suddenly I just wanted a hamburger and fries. And to be back in Brandy's house sitting on the couch in my yoga pants, with her by my side while we watched Netflix.

The server handed Lucas the wine list, and he perused it while I stared at the table, feeling completely out of place and over my head. When I told the server I would only be drinking water, he gave me a look that made me shrink down into my chair. Luckily Lucas ordered a bottle of wine for himself, and the server seemed pleased with his selection and disappeared.

A second later, another man in a uniform brought out some toasted bread with fancy little tomatoes drizzled in sauce—our first course. I grabbed a piece of bread and nibbled it, ultra-aware of where to put my hands. Anywhere but on the dress. Don't want to ruin this thing before giving it back to Lucas.

I glanced up and noticed him watching me again with those inscrutable eyes, looking impossibly handsome in his tuxedo against the backdrop of the fountains. Like something from a dream or a fairy tale.

"You seem nervous," he said, in his sexy, lilting voice.

I let out a sharp laugh. "Is it that obvious? Expensive dresses, Picasso paintings, and fancy meals are really not the norm for me. Not to mention..."

"Not to mention, what?" he asked.

I swallowed hard. I'd been about to say that I'd never been the woman on a billionaire's arm before, but that didn't seem polite. "I just don't understand. Why? Why are we doing this?"

"It will all make sense in time, I promise." He studied me for a moment longer and then picked up the small box in the middle of the table. "I love this restaurant, and not only for the food and the art, but because of this feature reserved for its most...exclusive guests."

"What is it?"

He opened the box and showed me the list of songs inside, which had buttons next to them. "You pick a song, then push the button beside it and it'll start the fountains to that song. It's spectacular."

Straight away, my gaze focused on *Con Te Partiro*. It made me cry every time I heard it, but I pointed at it anyway. "This one," I whispered.

Lucas's gaze dropped to my finger and his jaw tensed, just the smallest shift in his muscles. "Time to Say Goodbye," he said, with a degree of emotion I didn't expect in his voice. "A fitting choice."

I pressed the button next to the song title and the music

started slowly, the illuminated fountains arching and winding together sinuously like lovers about to be parted. A rush of emotion suffused me straight away, like I knew it would, and I lifted my napkin as stealthily as I could to dab at the corner of my eye, careful not to smudge my mascara. I should have chosen a different song, but this one had called to me.

We sat in silence as the fountains danced in time to the music, while the opera singers' voices surrounded us. We were so close to the fountains it felt like we were inside them, and the mist made goosebumps on my skin in the cool night air. Lucas watched with a stony expression, but his jaw clenched when the song got to the big climax and the fountains shot high into the sky.

When the fountains' dance ended and the water stilled, Lucas returned his attention to me again. It was at that moment our second course, the lobster salad, was brought out to us. I'd already eaten most of the bread with tomatoes—it had been delicious—and I was ready to dig into this too. I just wasn't sure how I'd eat four more courses after that.

"Tell me about your life," Lucas said, as he picked up his fork.

I shifted in my seat, uncomfortable with this line of conversation. "There's not much to tell. I live in Vista, a small city near San Diego. I run a florist shop there."

"A florist shop?" He let out an amused chuckle. "How appropriate."

I wasn't sure what he meant by that. Was it an insult or a

compliment? I decided to ignore it and instead took a bite of salad. Flavor exploded across my tongue. Wow.

He barely touched his food, but instead continued his interrogation of me. "And you said you live with this friend, Brandy?"

"Yes, after she got divorced she needed some help with her son, and I was struggling to pay the rent on my apartment. It worked out for both of us. But now her mom's sick too..." My chest ached as I thought of my second family and how they were all counting on me to find Brandy—before it was too late. "I'm just really worried about her."

He tilted his head as he studied me. "I can tell you truly care for these people."

"They're all I have. Well, them and my sister, but she lives in San Francisco and I don't see her very often. She runs a company and she's pretty busy with that."

Our plates were swept away by quick-fingered servers, and another course laid in front of us. This one was some fancy scallops dish with potatoes, and it was also delicious.

"So you're not in a relationship then," Lucas continued.

I let out a nervous laugh. "What's with all these questions?"

He pinned me with an intense gaze. "Answer me."

His directness and abrupt focus on my relationship status startled me, and I considered lying to protect myself, but I couldn't do it. Honesty was important to me and I prided myself on never lying. Not even to someone who probably had no trouble bending the truth...or worse. "No, I'm not in a relationship right now."

He leaned forward. "But you've been in relationships in the past. How many? Were any of them serious?"

His tone sounded so possessive it made my spine stiffen. I shook my head, setting down my fork. "That is really none of your business."

He sat back, languid and casual again. "I'm simply trying to understand you. Are you the type of woman who has long-term relationships, or are you more into casual flings?"

I snorted. "More like the type who sits at home and reads books instead of going out on dates."

That got a laugh from him, low and husky and sexy as sin. "Lucky for me then that I have such an extensive library. Still, I find it hard to believe you've been single all this time. You're a gorgeous woman, Hannah. Surely some men or women have taken an interest in you in the past. Did none of them strike your fancy?"

"I've dated a few guys before, but it never got serious," I admitted, my cheeks flushing at his compliment. "It never felt right with any of them, and besides, all my time is spent managing the shop."

Satisfaction gleamed in his eyes at my answer. I expected him to continue this line of questioning, but instead he sipped his red wine and asked, "You're the manager? Or the owner?"

"Both." I paused, debating how much to reveal. What could it hurt? This would only last seven days and then I'd never see him again. "It was my parents' shop, but they died five years ago. My sister and I inherited it in their will.

Jo is too busy with her own business, so I run the place myself."

"I'm sorry to hear about your parents," he said.

My throat grew tight with that familiar sadness and the loss I felt every time I thought of the accident five years ago. Not because I missed my parents, but because I didn't remember them at all. Not only were they taken from me, but I'd lost all my memories of them too, in an especially cruel twist. Was it any wonder I would fight tooth and nail to hold onto my loved ones now?

Before he could fire off any more questions about my parents, I asked, "What about you? Why does the King of Las Vegas need to bribe a woman into spending a week with him? I thought you were a billionaire playboy. That's what the internet says about you, anyway."

"Don't believe everything you read on the internet." His expression became distant as he looked out at the water as the fountains splashed a playful rhythm. "I had a great love once. The kind they write books about."

"What happened?" I asked in a hushed voice.

He turned his hypnotic eyes back on me. "I lost her."

"I'm sorry," I found myself saying, echoing his words to me a minute ago. The tone of his voice made me think that his great love had passed away, and my heart squeezed in sympathy. I couldn't imagine having something like that and then losing it.

He gazed at me with unblinking intensity. "Perhaps it will be different this time."

I wasn't sure what he meant by that, so I took a long sip

of water just as our next course was brought out, some tiny pieces of steak with figs and honey. I'd already forgotten what course number we were on. All I knew was that the food kept coming, and it was all amazing.

I pushed another button in the little box and the fountains started up again, this time dancing to that Celine Dion song from Titanic. Soon another course came, some lamb with kale and asparagus, but I was already so full I could only take a few bites.

"Tell me about your life," I finally said, once I gave up on trying to eat anymore. "It's probably a lot more interesting than mine."

A perfect eyebrow arched up. "What would you like to know?"

"How did you do all this?" I asked, gesturing around us. "This restaurant is obviously very expensive, and we've got the place all to ourselves, plus control of the fountains at Bellagio. How?"

"Easy—I own it all."

My brow furrowed. "I thought you owned The Celestial."

"That's what I want most people to believe, but for you, the truth." He gestured toward The Strip, where I could see the glowing signs of the other casinos through the mist of the fountains. "I own nearly every luxury hotel and casino in Las Vegas. Some through shell companies, so it doesn't seem as though I dominate The Strip quite as much as I do, but for all intents and purposes, Las Vegas is my city."

I sat back in my chair, stunned. I knew he was a

powerful billionaire and that he controlled Las Vegas, but to own all of that—damn. "Is that why they call you the King of Las Vegas?"

"One of the reasons." He paused before sipping his wine. "But that's not what you really want to know, is it? You want to know why they call me the devil."

My face grew warm, embarrassed that my thoughts were so obvious, or that he could read me so easily. Of course that was what I wanted to know. I'd heard those whispers—the ones people muttered when they thought I'd turned away and was no longer listening. There were also the rumors about what happened to people who crossed him. "Why do they?"

His eyes flashed with dark humor for a second before he answered. "Because I *am* the devil. My true name is Lucifer."

I couldn't help but laugh. "Seriously? That's your birth name? No wonder you go by Lucas. Your parents must have hated you."

"My father certainly does, but that's beside the point. I am *the* Lucifer, formerly known as the Lightbringer, also called Satan, the Prince of Darkness, Father of Lies, King of Hell, and a number of other titles that people have bestowed upon me over the years."

My laughter faded as I realized he was completely serious. "I'm sorry...what?"

Our server brought our final course, a fruit tart for dessert, while I stared at Lucas. As soon as we were alone again, Lucas picked up his fork, as though we were having a normal conversation. "I realize it's difficult to believe, but I only speak the truth to you."

While he took a bite, I could only watch him, my stomach twisting. "You're trying to tell me you're *actually* the devil. Fallen angel. Evil incarnate."

"You absolutely must try this tart, it's truly divine. I should know." He met my eyes again, and this time the look in them made me tremble. "Evil? Probably. Fallen? Definitely."

Shit, what had I gotten myself into? My thoughts swirled chaotically, and I poked at my tart with my fork as I tried to gain control over them. I was being held captive by a crazy billionaire who believed he was the devil. I should run away right this instant and never look back. But I couldn't. He was probably the only man in Vegas who could find Brandy, and I'd sacrifice myself any number of times for the safe return of my friend.

"Is that why you make deals?" A nervous laugh bubbled out of me. "Are you going to steal my soul? Should I be afraid?"

"Oh, Hannah. Your soul already belongs to me." His eyes smoldered and a villainous smile spread across his lips. "And you should be *very* afraid."

5

LUCIFER

My spoon guided my coffee into a slow swirl in my mug—an exercise in controlled chaos—as I skimmed the newspaper front page. A relic of an older time, but one I refused to give up, even if I managed most of my business online these days. Hell, I still remembered when newspapers were invented. To see new technologies change the world and then become obsolete years later—such was the curse of an immortal.

Besides, the headlines about Earth's latest problems were a good distraction from thoughts of Hannah. Just knowing she was in my penthouse brought me a sense of calm that had been missing for years, but I was certain she didn't feel the same. Ever since I'd told her the truth about who I was she'd become closed off and nervous, and had retreated to the guest room as soon as we'd returned from dinner. She didn't believe me. Not yet. But she would.

As I sipped my coffee I gazed out at the midday sun. Normally I spent my nights awake and slept during the day, as fit my role as Lord of Darkness, though I didn't need much sleep after all this time. However, with Hannah here, I'd adjusted my schedule to accommodate her mortal needs. Besides, I had plans for us today.

The elevator opened outside the penthouse door with a familiar ping, capturing my attention. Samael walked inside a moment later, his dark brow furrowed as he approached. Like many former angels, he had an ethnically ambiguous look with dark bronze skin and rich brown eyes. Many humans guessed he was Middle Eastern, or perhaps Latino, but the truth was often too much for their fragile mortal brains. Like me, Samael had been born in Heaven, though we'd lived in Hell for much longer. Not that either Heaven or Hell was home anymore.

"Good morning," he said, in his usual serious tone. "I have an update for you on the missing woman, along with a complete report on Ms. Hannah Thorn."

I nodded and sipped my coffee as he slid a thick beige folder toward me with Hannah's name on it. "What have you found?"

"Our surveillance footage of Styx Bar showed Ms. Brandy Higgins sitting with Asmodeus on the night she disappeared."

My attention piqued, I stopped in the act of opening the folder. Asmodeus was an incubus who ran most of my strip clubs in the city—and Samael's son, with the Archdemon Lilith. "Is that so?"

"They spoke for a short time, and then they left the bar together."

"Have you questioned Asmodeus about this?"

"I tried." A muscle in his jaw ticked. "My son is missing as well."

My hand tightened around the folder. Asmodeus was old and powerful, not to mention extremely loyal to me. If he was missing too, that pointed to a much larger problem than a lost human woman. Who could kidnap him? And why would they do such a thing? Was Asmodeus the target, and Hannah's friend simply in the wrong place at the wrong time? It felt too much like a coincidence, and I'd learned those were rare among immortals.

I opened my mouth to issue Samael further instructions, but before I could speak, Hannah's bedroom door opened with a quiet click. She shuffled sleepily into the kitchen and her eyes widened when she saw we were already in there. Her startled gaze flowed over Samael, curiosity obvious in her body language, then landed squarely on my naked chest. Interest flickered in her eyes, but she quickly dragged her gaze away from my body as her cheeks flushed. Her obvious desire for me stirred heat at the base of my cock, but I needed to take this slow, to bring her to me willingly. Still, it seemed she wasn't above a bit of temptation, judging by the way she'd eyed me. And I did love to tempt.

I stood quickly and pulled out a chair, gesturing for her to take a seat beside me. "Hannah, this is one of my closest advisors, Sam."

"Nice to meet you." She clutched her robe—which

looked as ancient as I was—tight at her throat, a hopeful look lighting her eyes. "Are you helping to find my friend?"

"Yes, I am." Samael held himself stiffly, though his words were polite. His dark eyes scanned her, no doubt taking in every detail and filing it away in his vast mind.

"Find Asmodeus and find the girl," I told him.

His gaze snapped to me and irritation crossed his face. "Of course I will."

He sounded almost offended, and I wasn't sure if he thought I was questioning his capabilities, or his devotion to his son. In truth, I simply wanted both of them found immediately. "I have no doubt you will."

He bowed his head, somewhat mollified, and then left the kitchen. I took a long sip of coffee as I tapped my fingers on the report about Hannah. Once I was alone, I would pore through it and memorize every detail.

"What was that about?" Hannah asked, still clutching her robe. The thing was pale pink cotton and so thread-bare I could almost see through it—not that I minded that part. However, it was definitely a sign she wasn't living to the standard she should be, and no doubt required a full wardrobe intervention. Exactly what I had planned for today.

I reached for another mug and walked toward the coffee machine. "Do you take your coffee with two sugars and no cream?"

"I do." She said, and then her still-sleepy brain caught up. She stared at me with a healthy dose of suspicion in her eyes. "How did you know that?"

I handed her a mug and winked. "Lucky guess."

She considered a moment, her distrust clear in her guarded expression. Then she appeared to arrive at a decision. "I'm not buying that, but I'm willing to move on to get information about Brandy. As part of our deal." Her words were curt. Business-like, almost, and I appreciated her cool efficiency as I longed to make her mouth move in more sensual ways. "Did you learn something new?"

"I did." I drew my chair alongside hers, sitting possibly a touch closer than she felt comfortable with. I couldn't help myself. The desire to be near her was too strong for me to resist. "Our security cameras show Brandy left the Styx Bar downstairs with Asmodeus. He's an incubus who runs my strip clubs." I added that helpful detail and side-eyed her, awaiting a reaction.

She coughed on the sip of coffee she'd just taken. "Incubus? In your...strip clubs?"

I should have suspected she had no memory of any type of demon or supernatural entity, but perhaps I could help jog her memory. "Yes, strip clubs. I own many of them throughout the city catering to all sorts of different themes and kinks. They allow the Lilim to safely feed on humans without hurting them, and thanks to their gifts, the humans are immensely satisfied. After all—" I leaned closer to Hannah and dropped my voice. "I like all of my customers to leave my establishments satisfied. Including you."

She watched me from under her dark lashes, the suspicion in her gaze increasing as she flicked a glance between the direction of her bedroom and the main doors like she was calculating an escape. She could look around the penthouse all she liked. There certainly wasn't any escape for her. The men outside the door would see to that if she tried, and Azazel was certainly *very* good at her job.

"Lilim?" she asked after a few moments, obviously choosing to ignore my question.

Damn. Nothing I said seemed to be sparking any memories. "The collective term for succubi and incubi. They're a type of demon that feeds on lust."

"Uh-huh." She sipped her coffee, disbelief heavy in her tone like she was merely humoring the crazy billionaire. "There's only one problem with what you're saying. Brandy isn't the type of person to go to bed with a man she just met in a bar."

"She's human." I shrugged. "She wouldn't be able to resist an incubus no matter how hard she tried. Especially one as old and powerful as Asmodeus—he can enchant a human female without the slightest effort. But the problem is that he's missing too."

"Do you think he took her?" she asked, obviously ignoring the parts about the demons and focusing on Asmodeus's disappearance. There was a fierceness in her crystal blue eyes, and I had no doubt she'd try to take down anyone she thought might be a threat to her friend, even though she had no chance of actually injuring a demon like Asmodeus.

"No, I can't imagine he would do such a thing."

"Then we need to find them. We should go looking around, or question some people, or—"

She'd let go of her robe in her excitement, revealing why she'd been clutching it closed so tightly. The fabric was so frayed that the knot at her waist kept loosening, and her cleavage pressed against the edges of the collar enticingly, baring the sweet curve of her breasts. I'd barely heard what she said as my fingers itched to touch that soft, smooth skin.

"Hannah." I rested my hand on her knee, making her freeze. "There's nothing more we can do. My best people are looking for them now. I have every confidence they'll find your friend soon."

Her shoulders fell. "We can't help?"

Samael's people would find Brandy, I was sure of it. Nothing on Earth or in any of the other realms was as important to me as the woman sitting beside me, clutching her robe. We had a deal, and I'd hold up my end. I always did.

I shook my head. "If we get involved, we'll only slow them down. Let them do what they're trained to do. This isn't Samael's first time heading up a search and rescue, and the best thing we can do is go on about our lives. In fact, I have something planned for today that I think will keep your mind off of things."

"Day? I thought we were only doing nights." She blew out a long breath. "What's today's sin?"

"Greed." I gestured toward her room. "There's a fresh outfit hanging in your closet in a black garment bag. Please wear that today." I tried to keep my smile subdued, but the idea of her wearing clothes I'd selected for her sent a possessive streak of lust through me. *My* woman. *Mine.* I hadn't felt like that since... Well, since the last time.

"What are we doing?" There it was again, that suspicion threading through her tone. It was one of the reasons I liked her. She never did let me get away with anything.

"Shopping." I deliberately kept my voice casual, and she lifted her chin in question. "We'll be purchasing some new clothes for you."

She groaned. "What's wrong with my clothes?"

I stared pointedly at her threadbare robe. "Everything."

She crossed her arms. "Excuse me for not realizing I'd be playing the role of billionaire's mistress this week."

"Exactly. You need a wardrobe suiting your new position at my side." I looked back down at my newspaper, effectively dismissing her. My feigned disinterest wasn't because I was finished looking at her, but because if I continued to watch her, I'd want to touch her, to kiss her, to possess her, and she wasn't ready for that...yet.

She huffed and then turned on her heel to head back to her room, hopefully to get ready. I glanced up and caught sight of her perfect ass and the swish of her long golden hair. She looked different from before, but there was no doubt of who she was. The tug inside me, the rapidity of my heartbeat, and the twitch in my cock... Every part of me knew exactly who she was.

She must have felt it too—the pull, the longing, the need. The unbreakable connection between us that stretched back for all eternity. But it must be buried deep this time.

It was an exquisite torture to know the truth about us, and to be the only one who remembered. I wanted to tell her, but I'd wait until she was ready to hear it. This was certainly a game for a patient man, and I'd bargained on a week.

Over the next few nights I would remind her who she really was—and why she belonged by my side as my queen.

6

HANNAH

Another car whisked us out of The Celestial and down The Strip, but at least it wasn't a limo this time. Not that the sleek, silver Aston Martin sports car was any less glamorous. Lucas drove with a casual hand on the wheel, and with his eyes focused on the road, it allowed me to study him without his intense gaze staring back at me. He was too handsome to be real, like something out of a dream, and every time I looked at him I wanted to touch him to prove to myself I wasn't imagining it. He exuded a heady mix of sensual charm and dark, dangerous power that was impossible to resist. This time he wasn't in a tux, thank goodness, but his black suit was perfectly tailored and no doubt cost a fortune.

My outfit probably did too, for that matter. In my closet I'd found white shorts with a label I didn't recognize, but no doubt couldn't afford, and a sleeveless button-up shirt in lavender. I looked like I was ready to head to the country club and eat stupidly small sandwiches or drink tea with my pinky outstretched while laughing at poor people like me.

And then there were the shoes, sparkly black flats with Miu Miu on them. I'd heard of that brand and had to stop myself from getting on my phone and searching for the price. I couldn't stand the thought of walking the sidewalks of Las Vegas in shoes that cost more than my car. I chose to believe they weren't *that* expensive. I couldn't think about them any other way or I'd need to carry them and walk about barefoot. I was in so far over my head it wasn't even funny, and my gut twisted at the idea of what he'd want in return for all of this...kindness.

And how I'd probably give it to him.

At least Lucas was fulfilling his bargain to find Brandy. As we drove along The Strip, I stared out at the tourists walking past the brightly lit stores, casinos, and restaurants, while thinking back on what I'd heard this afternoon. I found it hard to believe Brandy would leave a bar with a stranger, no matter how sexy he was, and Lucas's explanation of the man being an incubus didn't make me feel any better. They had a lead though, which was more than I'd been able to get. I just had to stick through this bizarre experience for another few days until she was found and we could go back to our normal lives.

And that whole thing about Lucas being the devil? Yeah, I'd been trying hard to forget that ever since he'd brought it up last night. The only explanation I had was that he was using it as a metaphor to try and intimidate me.

Or he really believed it, which was even more disturbing.

We entered a parking garage, going down several levels until we reached an area filled with a selection of the flashiest looking cars I'd ever seen. I'd only heard of some of them—the names almost always Italian and spoken in reverent tones.

"Where are we?" I asked, as a man in a suit stepped up to open the passenger door, while a valet moved forward to park the car for Lucas. Rich people never parked, I'd quickly learned.

Lucas got out of the car and walked to my side, stepping in front of the valet to take my hand and help me out, almost like he wouldn't dare let the other man get near me. "This is a special entrance to the Shops at Crystals for their premier customers. It's a shopping center that houses only luxury brands. I own it through Abaddon Inc, which also owns thousands of malls across the world."

"You own this place? And thousands of malls?" My jaw fell open. During my short stay in Vegas while searching for Brandy I'd walked past the Shops at Crystals and marveled at them from outside, but knew there was no way I could afford anything inside.

He buttoned his jacket as he replied, "Just another of my holdings. Shall we?"

He led me down a red carpet—an actual red carpet—into a mall that was unlike any I'd ever been in before. We walked along shiny floors that had thick veins of gold running along the edges, meeting champagne-colored walls with intricate sconces every few feet to light the way. At the end of it were steps that actually looked like they were plated in gold, with lush greenery on either side. I picked out black mondo grass with pink and white periwinkles and some lilac hibiscus. I breathed in deeply as we passed them, feeling a touch of homesickness for my florist shop.

"This is a mall?" I asked in a hushed voice.

Lucas's lips quirked with amusement as he walked by my side. "This is a secret part of the mall, a special tunnel for VIP guests. Vegas brings lots of celebrities and high rollers, and they like to shop without being observed. Each of the shops has a separate entrance so we can retain our privacy."

Personally, I would have preferred to people-watch everyone else in the mall, but I supposed a man like him wanted that kind of privacy, with his darkness and obvious underworld connections—because how else would he gain that degree of power? Nothing about Lucas Ifer was like anything I'd ever known before. I'd heard about how the other half lived, but I'd never expected the difference to be so vast. It was obvious he just expected the world to bow down before him. And the world did bow.

The tunnel we were in was empty except for the two of us, but I read all sorts of signs like Gucci, Dior, Louis Vuitton, and others I'd never even heard of. Was he expecting me to buy clothes here?

I cleared my throat. "You do know I can't afford much, right? I barely had enough money to pay for gas to get to Vegas."

His hand curled around my elbow, and even that light touch made my breath hitch and my thighs clench together. "Hannah, I would never expect you to pay for any of this. It's my gift to you."

I bit my lip. "And what do you want in exchange?"

"Only the pleasure of your company."

He led me inside the first shop, where a sign over the door read Versace. It was all white, with white leather couches, white floors, white tables. The only thing that wasn't white in the whole room was the clothes we had on and the name of the shop printed repeatedly on the floor in gold.

As soon as we walked in, a saleswoman ran from the other side of the room, her pert bob bouncing in her haste. "Mr. Ifer," the saleswoman exclaimed. For a second, I thought she was going to curtsy. "It's such a pleasure to see you. How can we assist you today?"

"Please measure my companion and bring us an assortment of clothing for her to browse."

With wide eyes the saleswoman turned to rush from the room, giving me the impression of a startled deer. She was terrified of him, I realized. Was everyone in this city?

He sat on the edge of one of the couches, then patted the spot beside him for me. I shook my head, too intimidated to sit down.

Within moments, more salespeople ran in and out of the room with clothes on racks, hanging them in front of me. I could only gawk at the expensive clothes, soft fabrics, and shimmering materials. Someone handed me a bottle of ice-cold water with a fancy-looking label I didn't recognize, and I took a sip, my throat dry. I hated to admit that the water tasted better than any water I normally purchased for myself. Shit, I usually drank tap water, even when it tasted like dirt or was so sun-heated it rivaled the temperature of my coffee.

"Try on anything you like." Lucas waved in the general direction of the clothes. "It's all yours, should you desire it."

Suddenly, I felt very small and very alone, surrounded by all of these nice things I couldn't afford, under the complete control of a man who could either shower me with riches and gifts or end my life altogether, if he so chose.

"Lucas," I said, trying to speak to him around the rush of people. "I can't accept all these expensive clothes."

He stood up and crossed the room to me, then took my chin in his hand as he gazed into my eyes. "You can and you will. After all, if you're going to be seen in public with me over the next few days, you need to look the part."

I swallowed, my throat dry again, and this time from the mix of lust and fear pulsing inside me. "Is this some kind of Pretty Woman thing?"

"Not at all. I'm not paying for your body. I only bargained for your time." His thumb trailed across my lower lip, tracing sensual patterns that made me breathless. "And as part of spending time together, I demand you dress properly for the occasion. I assure you, I will not miss the money, and the gifts come with no strings attached."

I nodded slowly, hypnotized by his eyes and the low, melodious sound of his voice, not to mention the way he touched me—like he owned me already. He looked at me as if nothing else existed in the entire city, and it was hard not to want to be his completely.

I tried on some of the clothes and set aside the ones I liked, but then I found myself wanting to put some back. It just seemed like way too much, especially when I glimpsed a price tag. My monthly rent to Brandy could pay for one of the shirt sleeves and that was about it.

"She'll take it all," Lucas said in a commanding voice. "Pack it up and send it to my penthouse."

The treatment was the same at the next several stores, with the result of my head spinning and me feeling like some sort of kept woman. Or a mob boss's wife. That was probably more accurate.

We sped through Louis Vuitton, where he insisted on the rarest bag they had. Apparently, only three had been made, and I got one of them. I carried it on my arm—empty — to the next store, stiff as a corpse as Lucas wound an arm around my waist. I tried not to lean into him, but it was pretty much impossible, especially when he was so much bigger than I was and my body seemed determined to melt against him, even when my brain said it was a bad idea.

Fendi, Prada, Chanel. We got more clothes, plus matching shoes and accessories, creating a wardrobe fit for a princess, but one I could never wear in my normal life. Why would I need so many clothes for a week's worth of time? I kept trying to tell Lucas it was enough, but he ignored me. At one point I saw an outfit I loved, and he must've read my mind or something because I was *very careful* not to show any reaction. I didn't want him to think I was taking advantage of his generosity when really the weight of it left me cold, but he told the salespeople to pack it up like everything else.

The next stop was Tiffany's. I hesitated at the door, below the sign in the iconic blue. "Lucas, really. This is too much."

"I insist."

He took my hand and I didn't react quickly enough to stop him. With a short tug, he had me walking through the door and into another private showroom, just as fancy as the last five or six, or however many we'd been to at this point. As soon as we were spotted, sales people practically fell all over themselves to help us. I tried to refuse everything, even as I marveled at the jewels, but Lucas picked out several pieces, including diamond necklaces and stud earrings.

"For everyday wear," he said.

I snorted. "My everyday wear does not consist of diamonds."

"No?" He gave me a charming smile that wreaked havoc on my brain. "I thought diamonds were a girl's best friend."

"Not this girl," I muttered. "Give me books over diamonds any day, thanks."

"I can do that too, you know. But perhaps we can find something that's a bit more you." He stopped in front of a case that had a matching set including an emerald necklace, earrings, and a bracelet. The gems were exactly the color of Lucas's eyes.

I held up a hand. "They're gorgeous, but—"

"Yes, these are perfect," Lucas said with an air of finality. He looked from the jewels into my eyes. "Emerald is your favorite, isn't it?"

My breath caught. First the coffee, now this. Was he stalking me? "How did you know?"

He gave me a devilish grin. "Consider it a lucky guess."

"But where would I even wear them?"

The hunger in his gaze made my heart race. "You can wear them for me in my bed, with nothing else on."

"That's not going to happen," I said with a very unconvincing laugh.

He gestured for the salespeople to wrap the set up for him, but then he caught sight of something behind me that made his eyes narrow. "Excuse me for a moment."

He rushed past me and out the door like he was going to battle, and the swift change in his demeanor made my head spin. I watched the Tiffany employees pack up my things in cute little blue boxes and bags, wondering how this was my life.

"Should we put this on Mr. Ifer's account?" a salesman asked.

"I assume so." I glanced behind me. No sign of Lucas anywhere.

I poked my head out of the shop door, searching around for Lucas, and spotted him down the hall. He was talking in a low voice with another man with red hair, and their body language told me it was not a friendly conversation. Then suddenly Lucas grabbed the man around the neck and lifted him up into the air and slammed him against the wall.

No. *Into* the wall.

Plaster went flying and the man left a body-sized dent in it. Meanwhile, Lucas's hand was still around his neck, holding him there with impossible strength. I could only see his back, but it was enough to send a cold wave of fear through me.

Lucas dropped the man in the rubble at his feet. "Do not cross me again, or I won't be so lenient next time."

"Yes, my lord." The man kneeled on the floor and nodded, keeping his head low. He didn't appear injured, even though he'd just been sent through a wall.

Lucas brushed plaster dust off his hands and turned toward me, leaving the man kneeling there. He spotted me watching with my mouth hanging open, and gave me a dazzling smile, like everything I'd just seen was totally normal.

He joined me in front of Tiffany's and rebuttoned his suit jacket. "Sorry, darling, demon business. Now where were we?"

"How?" I gestured at the man, who got up and ran out of there as fast as he could.

"Don't worry, he's a shifter. Fox, if you must know. I barely scratched him." He took my elbow again, his fingers strong and possessive as they dug into my skin. "Shall we continue? I have one more shop I'd like us to visit."

I dimly nodded, my throat tight, as Lucas led me down the hall, leaving the plaster rubble behind, to another shop— Alexander McQueen. I had to practically pick my jaw up off the floor as we walked inside past all the beautiful clothes, shoes, and purses. There were actual runway gowns here on display in this secret back room, with capes and feathers and jewels. Real jewels, not tacky sequins. It was almost enough to make me forget what I just saw.

Lucas had picked that man up by his neck and thrown him into a wall. How did he have that kind of strength? And how had that man walked away without a scratch?

Could all this stuff about demons actually be true?

No. Impossible.

I had no explanation for it, but what I saw did confirm one thing—Lucas was more dangerous than I'd thought.

"I need a gown fit for a queen," Lucas said to the salesman. "One of a kind. In her size."

"I have the perfect thing," the smartly dressed man replied in a respectful tone. "I'll bring it out immediately."

Lucas nodded and the man disappeared. I stared at Lucas with fear trailing down my spine, wondering how he could look so casual after such an act of violence. And so disturbingly gorgeous. Fuck, maybe he was the devil. Or at least the closest thing to it.

The salesman returned carrying an ethereal ball gown that was all black except for tiny crystal stars trailing down to the different phases of the moon along the bottom hem. At the shoulders, silver moon clasps held on a long, sheer black cape with more crystal stars running down it. Everything about it was soft and billowy except for the bodice, which was low-cut and form-fitting. It was the most beautiful gown I'd ever seen in my life.

Lucas nodded. "Have it fitted for her."

I instantly reached out to touch the crystals on the gown, but then pulled my hand back. "It's lovely, but I can't imagine I'll ever have anywhere to wear it."

He pinned me with his dark gaze. "On your final night, you'll be attending the Devil's Night Ball as my guest."

I counted the nights in my head. That was the night before Halloween. "What's the Devil's Night Ball?"

"It's when the demons honor me as their King."

I had no time to process his absurd words before I was whisked away into a dressing room, where a woman helped me put on the gown. Then I stared at myself in the mirror, my face pale, my eyes scared, while I stood in the loveliest dress I'd ever worn. Was this what Persephone felt like when she was kidnapped by Hades? Did Lucas think all the glitz and glamour would hide the dark, seedy depths of his underworld?

He moved behind me and met my eyes in the mirror, then rested his hands on my shoulders possessively. "Yes, this is the gown. And when you wear it by my side, everyone will know you're mine."

"Only for seven nights," I said, my voice defiant, even though I was secretly wondering if escape was still an option.

His lips curled into a dark smile. "We'll see about that."

7

HANNAH

When we returned from our shopping trip, a whole spread of food awaited us in the apartment, with gourmet sandwiches, fancy meats and cheeses, and a salad with feta cheese. I needed some time to myself after the day's events, and grabbed some food and retreated to the guest room. But when I opened the door, my breath caught and I nearly dropped my entire plate.

Flowers and plants now packed my previously sparse guest room, and I inhaled the fresh, floral scents I loved so much. Each corner had a weeping fig tree, and flowers grew in pots along the windowsill, on the desk and side tables, and inside the bathroom. I spotted white lilies, purple violets, blue irises, and white-and-yellow daffodils. No roses, which I found curious, but I didn't mind. I'd always thought roses were overdone and overrated, especially when there were so many other beautiful plants out there.

Then it hit me. These were all my favorite flowers.

How did he know?

How did he *always* know?

Lucas's voice at my back made me jump. "I thought they might help you feel more at home."

"They're lovely," I said, trying to keep my voice steady. Between this and his earlier comments I was starting to think he intended to keep me here longer than seven nights. That was never going to happen though. As soon as Brandy was found and my time was up, I was out of here. No matter how rich, powerful, or sinfully sexy he was. Or how thoughtful and generous he was being. "Thank you."

"Try to relax and enjoy the rest of your day," his voice purred. "Take a bath, perhaps. Eat anything you like. We'll meet at nine for our evening's festivities."

I swallowed and nodded, and he retreated on silent footsteps. Once he was gone I closed the door, let out a long breath, and sat at the desk to eat my sandwich and salad. A small pot of daffodils rested on the table beside my plate, and I admired the star-like white petals circling a yellow center. Even though they were pretty common, daffodils were my favorite flower because they always lifted my spirits. Like harbingers of spring, they popped out of the ground when nothing else in the garden had yet dared to declare victory over winter. Plus, once they were cut, they secreted sap that was poisonous to other flowers, which meant you had to keep them in their own vase. They were like the plant version of introverts, except they poisoned anyone who got up in their space. My kind of plant, indeed.

The daffodil was also called the narcissus, when you wanted to sound sophisticated anyway. The narcissus was known for being the flower Persephone picked just before the earth opened up and Hades kidnapped her and took her to the underworld. At the thought, I remembered the ancient Greek vase in Lucas's library and wondered if the daffodil here was connected somehow.

I shook myself out of my dark thoughts and finished my food, while scanning my phone for any messages or updates, then resorting to glimpsing through old photos of Brandy while praying she was still alive. Then I took Lucas's suggestion and took a bath in the huge tub, luxuriating in the shampoos and soaps, losing myself in the floral scents with a richness beyond the usual cloying smells I purchased at the local dollar store.

When I got out, I discovered an entire collection of makeup lined up for my perusal, arranged like the most expensive department store counters. I stared at the pots and tubes and brushes for several minutes. It was hard to break the perfect seals and mar the powders pressed in their little dishes. Once they were used, they were used, and I couldn't shake the feeling they were all wasted on me. I was an eyeliner and lip gloss kind of gal, and I didn't even know what to do with most of these things. Did they come with a tutorial?

Fuck it. If I was being held captive by a dangerous billionaire who called himself Lucifer then I deserved all the perks that came with the situation. Like the luxurious toiletries and makeup, along with the clothes and jewelry.

Even the fancy shoes. Worst case, I gave them back at the end of my seven day sentence.

I cracked open the makeup, found a YouTube video explaining how to use it, and went at it. Sometime later, I walked out of the bathroom and found all the clothes from our shopping expedition hanging in the massive walk-in closet. While I'd been playing with eyeliner and foundation, someone had been in my room without me even knowing it. I never expected having staff would actually make me feel *more* vulnerable. From now on, I'd make sure to lock the doors.

Then, once I'd ascertained I was safe, I returned my attention to the clothes and tried to decide what to wear tonight. Lucas had mentioned in the car ride back to The Celestial that we were going to an exclusive nightclub, which was so not my normal scene. I wasn't kidding when I told Lucas I usually spent my nights at home curled up with a book.

Eventually I picked something that was bolder and sexier than I'd ever normally wear, but I had an idea for how to make the evening less intimidating. If I felt like I was in costume, I could pretend to be someone else for the night, and leave all of my worries here to come back to later.

After tugging at the tight red dress and sucking in a deep breath, I opened the door and stepped out into the penthouse's living area.

Lucas whirled, the night view of the city framing him with a neon glow, contrasting with his stylish, tailored suit and dark hair. He looked me over and a muscle flexed in his jaw, while his gaze turned hungry. "You look like—" He paused as if searching for the word, and then his lips took on a wicked curve when he found it. "Sin."

I found myself unable to tear my gaze from his mouth, as the word sin settled over me like a seductive caress on my exposed skin. If there was ever a man who embodied sin, it was him.

"Shall we?" he asked, offering his hand.

I lightly rested my fingers in his, and let out a sigh at the little shock that always ran through me when we touched. "Where are we going?"

"My rooftop nightclub, Pandemonium. There's a band playing tonight that I think you'll like."

We exited the penthouse, ignoring the guards, and entered the elevator. I didn't know if I'd ever get used to having handsome, burly men standing outside the door, but at least I only had a few more nights to deal with it. Soon all of this would be like one of those dark fairytales, a cautionary story I'd tell about how I once was a billionaire's side piece for a few nights.

"Thank you for the flowers," I said, as soon as we were inside the elevator. "But how did you know they were my favorite? And then there was the coffee this morning, and the emeralds... Are you stalking me?"

"I do my research." He raised one of those perfect dark brows at me. "I like to know who I'll be making deals with and allowing into my home. Need I remind you that you're the one who came to me to ask for a favor?"

My cheeks flushed, but I wasn't satisfied with that

answer. Nor with the ever-present feeling that he was familiar somehow. "Did we know each other before the accident?"

He tilted his head. "Accident?"

The elevator opened onto the roof before I could answer. Music and lights blasted me in the face as soon as we stepped out, and all previous thoughts died away when I saw who was playing on the small stage.

"Is that The Hellions?" I asked, raising my voice to project over the music.

Without waiting for his reply, I hurried forward to get a better look. The rooftop club had a pool on one side of the stage and a bar on the other, and was open to the night sky above us and the flashing lights of Vegas all around. It was also so exclusive that I didn't even have to push through a crowd to get to the stage. People stood around, dancing to the sound of The Hellions' newest songs, but I was able to go straight to the front.

How was this possible? The Hellions were huge, like selling out giant concert venues huge, but here they were in a tiny, intimate venue. I could almost reach up and touch the singer's black combat boot while he crooned about lost love.

As I moved in time to the beat, I noticed Lucas standing beside me, watching me with unblinking intensity. I turned toward him. "Was this in your report too? My favorite band?"

He leaned close with one hand on the small of my back, in the spot where the dress had an intricate cut-out. When his fingers touched my bare skin, I stilled, unable to focus on the music as heat rushed between my thighs. His sensual voice came through loud and clear in my ear, as if we were in a room alone. "I'm very thorough. As you'll soon learn for yourself."

"You got them to play here, in your nightclub, on such short notice?" I drew in a shaky breath. "For me?"

He let that hand trail a tiny bit lower, hovering just above the curve of my butt. "I did, yes."

I couldn't help but be impressed. I hated to admit it, but he was winning me over a tiny bit, no matter how hard I tried to resist his charms. Clothes, jewels, shoes—those felt like buying me off. But my favorite flowers? My favorite band? That was something else.

"They couldn't say no to me," Lucas continued talking as if my thoughts hadn't carried on racing forward at a million miles per hour. "They're demons, you know. Imps, actually. Their kind tends to become musicians, actors, that sort of thing. Imps always crave the spotlight. Don't worry, I paid them handsomely too."

And now we were back to the demon talk. It had to be some sort of quirky billionaire eccentricity—a way to amuse himself when he could already afford every other sort of amusement in existence, no doubt—but it was really getting old. Of course, it would explain what I saw earlier today... But no. There had to be a more reasonable explanation for that.

Lucas caught my hand and pulled me close, still laughing. "Dance with the devil?"

Maybe he was crazy, but as he drew my body flush

against his, I found myself melting in his arms. No matter how hard I tried, I couldn't bring myself to want to pull away from him. I soon lost myself in the song and the feel of Lucas's hard chest pushing against mine. Though he was much taller than me, his masculine body molded against mine perfectly, and the sense of rightness I felt in his arms was unlike anything I'd ever felt before.

His hand on my bare back led me across the floor, and for a few minutes all I knew was the pounding of the bass drum and the tingle where Lucas touched me. I couldn't deny how much I wanted him at this moment, even if getting involved with someone like Lucas was a terrible idea. Even without his obvious eccentricities, he was powerful, and it was the kind of power tainted by danger. He bargained for the things he wanted but couldn't buy, and fear as much as lust slid cold fingers down my spine as I considered my position at his side.

When the song ended and another one began, Lucas left his hand lingering on my back and turned me toward the bar. "Come, let's get a drink."

We walked toward the bar, and many people stopped to notice us, especially the way his hand claimed me. There would be no doubt in any of their minds that I was Lucas's woman, at least for tonight. For all I knew, he had a new woman on his arm every week.

As the thought of that made my stomach clench, someone in the crowd shouted. We both turned and watched as something on the stage exploded with a burst of light and a deafening boom, setting off multiple screams in the audience. One of the screams might have been from me.

The members of The Hellions ran off stage as blue flames shot into the air, quickly engulfing everything and spreading unnaturally fast along cords and into the audience somehow. People began to run toward the exit in a panic, while Lucas wrapped an arm across my shoulders and turned us away from the conflagration.

"Ignore it," he said, as he signaled to someone on the sidelines to deal with the fire. "It's all an illusion."

"What?" I glanced behind my shoulders as the flames danced across the pool's water, my head spinning and my heart pounding.

"An illusion. Imps can create them. Someone is causing a distraction, though I'm not sure why."

As he rushed me away from the burning stage, I spotted Zel running forward with Gadreel and some others, presumably to put out the fire...or whatever you did with illusions. Then the panicked crowd swallowed us up and I was bumped into by several people. In the chaos, I was separated from Lucas and surrounded by strangers, while blue flames suddenly sprouted up near us, so close that many people jumped and screamed. I took a few steps back, until I was pressed up against the wall surrounding the edge of the roof, but the flames kept coming while people around me tried to escape.

Then something hard and fast plowed into me with such force it sent me flying.

No, not flying. Falling.

The sudden force of the collision knocked all air from my lungs as I somehow went over the wall of the roof and plummeted toward my death. I couldn't even scream, because I couldn't suck in any air. Time slowed as I suffocated on my own panic, my limbs flailing, trying to grab onto something, anything, while my body dropped toward The Strip below me.

Then it hit me—I was going to die.

My life didn't pass through my eyes. There were no moments of clarity. Instead, I felt only regret for all the things I hadn't done and for not finding Brandy, along with an unexpected pang of loss for not getting to finish my seven nights with Lucas.

There was something else too. A sense of inevitability. As if I'd always known my death was coming swiftly and violently, sooner than later.

Like in my dreams.

The rush of air ripped tears from my eyes, but through the haze I saw something dark falling above me. For a second I thought a man had jumped off the edge of the roof, but that was absurd. Until the man came closer, and I made out Lucas in his black suit. I watched his eyes glint red as his determined face drew near, and I laughed, because surely this was some kind of near-death delirium. Or maybe I was already dead?

Just as he wrapped his strong arms around me, enormous, black-feathered wings erupted from his back. My stomach lurched as we stopped falling, and I sucked in a huge rasping breath of air, my heart nearly leaping out of my chest from the impact.

"I've got you," he said, as he tucked me close against his chest.

I could only stare in shock and wonder as his wings moved like shadows against the bright city lights. Darkness trailed away from each feather like smoke as we flew through the air, rising until we reached the balcony of his penthouse. He landed easily beside the pool, but didn't let me go, his arms wrapped protectively around me as I leaned against his chest. Probably a good thing, since I wasn't sure I could stand.

I looked up at Lucas's impossibly handsome face. His eyes had lost the red glow, or perhaps I'd imagined that, but the black wings were still there. They looked like they were made of night itself, and I watched the way the darkness curled around him, the shadows clinging to his body and maybe even forming the hint of horns above his head.

"Am I dead?" I managed to ask. "Are you an angel?"

"You're not dead." He gazed down at me with such fierce protectiveness it took my breath away. "And I'm definitely no angel. Not anymore, anyway."

My heart was still beating out of my chest, but I had to see if this was real. I reached up with a trembling hand to touch one of Lucas's wings, running a hesitant finger along one of the night-colored feathers. He sucked in a breath and closed his eyes for the briefest moment, and it surprised me to see how much such a light touch could affect him. How *I* affected him.

Our conversation from last night came back to me like a voice on the wind, as everything he'd told me connected with everything I'd seen in a rush of clarity.

"*I am the devil. My true name is Lucifer.*"

"*You're trying to tell me you're actually the devil. Fallen angel. Evil incarnate.*"

"*Evil? Probably. Fallen? Definitely.*"

I could no longer deny it.

Lucas Ifer really was the devil.

And I'd made a deal with him.

8

LUCIFER

With one last look at the star-filled sky I'd plucked Hannah from, and the bright lights below where everything could have ended, I cradled her closer to my chest and strode inside the penthouse to settle her on the sofa. Her blonde hair spread over the black leather cushions like spun gold, and her blue-eyed gaze watched me with a mixture of shock and something else. Fear? Curiosity?

Fire raced through my veins as I turned in a circle and raked a hand through my hair as I tried to figure out what to do. Water. That was what she needed. I headed to the bar and poured some for her, and a whiskey for me. This certainly called for a drink.

That was too close. I'd nearly lost her. How had she fallen? By the time I spotted her in the panicked crowd, it was already too late. If she hadn't screamed, I wouldn't have seen her in time. Someone must have shoved her, and hard too. Only supernatural strength could have gotten her over that wall.

Was *he* after her already? Or was it someone else? Fuck. I couldn't even keep her safe on the roof of my own building. Would it be better to send her away? Would she be safer? No. *No.* She was safest by my side. This time would be different. It had to be.

When I returned with her water, Hannah sat on the sofa in the exact position I'd left her in. She hadn't moved or said a word, she just stared off into space with her perfect lips slightly open. This was definitely shock. Falling from a roof would do that to anyone, not to mention being saved by the most infamous villain in the world.

As soon as I realized she was shivering, I waved a hand at the fireplace and it ignited, instantly. Then I snatched a velvet throw from the chair by the fire and covered her with it. As I tucked it around her shoulders, she finally moved her eyes upward, focusing on something behind me. I whirled, expecting to find someone there, but we were alone.

As I returned my attention to Hannah, I realized her wide-eyed gaze was glued to my wings. I tucked them away quickly, making them vanish.

"I was planning to show you my wings, and prove to you all I'd been saying," I said in my softest voice—the one I reserved only for Hannah—as I squashed all the fury still roiling inside me. "But not like this."

She jerked her gaze to my face, and her perfect little mouth formed an *o*. "It's true. It's all true."

"Yes, it is." I reached up to stroke her cheek, but she

flinched back from me and I stopped myself. "Do you know what happened back there? How you fell?"

She shook her head silently, her eyes still wide.

"Whoever attacked you will pay." This time, I wasn't able to keep the menace from my voice, and she recoiled again. I drew in a sharp breath and regained control of myself. "Hannah. You have nothing to fear from me."

Hannah's chest began to heave under the blankets as she took rapid breaths. "But you're the *devil*!"

Without waiting for a response, she threw her blanket to the side and kicked her heels off. Her red dress rode up her legs with the movement, revealing inch after inch of pale, soft skin. My cock twitched as I remained ever aware of how perfect she was, inside and out, even in the midst of an existential crisis. I averted my eyes.

"God," she whispered. Ah, she'd discovered the larger implications of me being...well, me. "Does God exist? What about the Bible?"

"I've known many gods in my time, and I've been a god or two as well, but I don't know if *the* God, an all-powerful and all-knowing deity, actually exists. No one does."

She jumped to her feet and scurried across the room, but she didn't leave, which was promising. I had a sliver of hope I hadn't completely scared her away. "And the other demons you keep talking about. Imps, succubi, incubi.... Those are real too? What about angels?"

"Yes, all real. Everything I've told you is true." I wanted to reach for her, to help her through this difficult realization, but I stayed back. She was still here. She knew where the door was, and she hadn't left. That was the important thing.

Hannah stopped pacing and stared at me with her jaw hanging open. "But...how?"

"Demons come from a..." How to describe it? "Parallel universe of sorts, known as Hell. Angels came from another realm known as Heaven, and fae come from Faerie."

Her eyebrows rose with every sentence I spoke. If I carried on, she'd lose them somewhere in her hair. "Fae?"

"Let's focus on angels and demons for now and worry about the fae some other time." I walked over to the bar and poured myself another whiskey. Sometime in the last few minutes I'd downed mine without realizing it. "Drink? If there was ever a time for alcohol, it's when you realize your entire view of life has been upended."

"No, thanks." She walked over to the armchair by the window and collapsed into it, completely unaware of how the dress had shifted on her frame, exposing those thighs again, not to mention most of her midsection. Another inch and I'd see the lower curve of her breasts. Not that I was complaining. "The last thing I need is for this revelation to be muddled by alcohol."

"Many humans find life preferable when muddled by alcohol. Alas, it has no effect on me." I took a sip of whiskey anyway, mainly because I liked the taste. The burn reminded me of Hell.

Hannah finally realized she was holding a glass of water and took a sip. A tiny bit of clarity returned to her eyes, and I could almost see her thoughts working inside that smart brain of hers. Her true nature would allow her to accept these revelations easier than a normal human would—some of them never recovered from learning about supernaturals. I had no doubt Hannah would be fine by the end of the night. She always was.

She turned those big blue eyes on me, peering at me from under her soft lashes. "You were an angel once."

"Archangel," I corrected. "But I rebelled against Heaven, much as the lore says I did."

"Why?"

The answer to that was too much for her to handle tonight. "Let's just say I disagreed with a few of their policies regarding Earth."

"And then you became the devil?" she asked.

"Then I left Heaven for Hell." I ran a hand down my suit, smoothing the rumpled fabric. "There I united the warring, chaotic demon tribes and crowned myself King. I've ruled the demons ever since."

I debated telling her how she played into it all, but she seemed shell-shocked enough as it was. She'd had enough for tonight. Soon she would know everything, with no more secrets between us, and I longed for that day. But she needed time to process everything first.

I stepped forward and offered her my hand. "I can tell you have more questions, but I think it's time you got some rest. You've had an...eventful night."

"But I have more questions," she said, as she slid her hand into mine.

"And I promise to answer them. Tomorrow." She

wobbled a little as she stood, and I bent down and picked her up again. The second she was in my arms, everything in the world felt right again.

"What are you doing?" she squealed, kicking her legs as I carried her across the living room.

"Taking you to your room."

"I can walk!"

"That's debatable." I kicked open her door and set her down on the bed. "You just had the shock of a lifetime, and nearly died as well. Allow me to help you get undressed."

She stood up without wavering this time. "I can manage just fine, thanks." But then she paused. "Although if you could unzip the back of this dress, that would be great. I could barely get it on by myself earlier."

A low chuckle escaped me as she turned around, and I dragged the zipper down her back, exposing her pale, perfect skin. Oh, how I longed to trail my lips down it, and to continue sliding this dress to the floor. I had to have her. Soon.

She turned around and shot me a look that reminded me of a kitten trying to be ferocious, and muttered thanks. Then she grabbed something from the closet and escaped into the bathroom, shutting the door behind her.

I lounged on the bed while I waited for her, admiring the flowers around the room. Gadreel had done a good job following my orders, as I knew he would. I breathed them in, remembering a time long ago when we'd also been surrounded by narcissus.

When Hannah stepped out she did a double-take when

she saw me on her bed. Her face was hesitant, but she licked her lips, and I knew she felt desire too. She could never resist me, no matter how hard she tried.

Her hair was loose around her shoulders, her makeup gone, and she wore a thin black nightgown with spaghetti straps. Restraining myself from slipping those straps off her shoulders was sheer torture, but I prevailed and rose to my feet.

"I'm leaving," I told her, as I unbuttoned my suit jacket. "I simply wanted to make sure you were all right before I left you alone."

She let out a long breath. "I feel like my head's been taken off, shaken about, and put back on again."

I chuckled softly. "That sounds about right. Come. Lie down."

I eased forward and took her hand, drawing her toward me. She allowed it, to my surprise, which only showed how tired she was. A near-death experience really took it out of humans, even one as extraordinary as Hannah. I drew her blankets back and when she slipped into the bed, I covered her up. When she looked up at me with her golden hair spread out on the pillow it took everything I had not to climb in bed with her. Her eyes were wide though, and I sensed her tired brain was resisting sleep, coming up with even more questions to ask me.

"Sleep. We have another big day tomorrow." With the faintest push, I added a bit of power to my words, just enough to make her yawn and her eyelids begin to flutter closed. The command wasn't very strong, but it would allow her body's own instincts to take over and help her sleep off most of the shock.

She yawned and pulled the covers up to her chin, before whispering, "Why me?"

"Because you're mine. You've always been mine." I pressed a kiss to her forehead as her eyes fluttered shut. "And you will *always* be mine."

9

HANNAH

When I woke, the sheets had twisted around me like I was being pinned to the bed by coiled snakes. A cool sheen of sweat lingered on my body, and damp strands of hair stuck to my forehead. I groaned and sucked in a long shallow breath. It wasn't enough. My body craved oxygen as though I'd spent most of the night running.

I'd always been a terrible sleeper, plagued by horrible dreams and then waking to find my body clenched tight around a pillow, my muscles aching from the tension in my limbs. But last night was especially bad.

Fractured remnants of my dreams floated through my mind. Fire and ashes, shadows and smoke, darkness curling into feathers and horns. So much fear, so much pain, so much death. And Lucas...always Lucas. His face drifted in and out of focus before being replaced by another's, though this one was blurred.

The only dream I remembered clearly was one with Lucas—no, *Lucifer*—sitting on a black throne, and the closer I tried to look at him, the more he seemed to become aware of my presence. Too late, I pulled back, but his red eyes gaze snapped to mine and he crooked his finger, beckoning me closer. That was right before I woke up, and my heart still thundered from the memory of it.

I sat up and shook my head, trying to clear it, but the fear from my dreams still lingered. I hesitated to leave the room because Lucas would be out there, with day three already planned for me. Which sin would it be today?

I swallowed the horror drying my throat. How could I possibly spend any further time with that man now that he'd revealed his secret? When I'd thought him a mob boss, I'd questioned my choices. Now I condemned them.

I moved from my bed like an old lady, slowly and carefully in case I broke. I'd nearly died last night, and my body felt tender, like it hadn't gotten the memo I was still alive. I walked to the closet on autopilot, and the hangers clacked together as I moved them from left to right. Like everything else I touched in this room, they were good quality. Expensive. And they belonged to the devil.

Did I belong to him too now?

I drew out the first outfit my hands touched—a linen, sleeveless pantsuit. I briefly wondered if it would suit today's activities but shrugged it off. I didn't care about the activities. I was only doing this for Brandy.

Once dressed, I couldn't delay any longer. I had to face Lucas.

No, not Lucas.

Lucifer.

Lu-ci-fer.

The syllables rolled around and around in my head, their sound enough to drive me crazy. Even after everything I'd seen last night, it was hard to accept it was all real.

When I finally walked into the kitchen, he was there and already dressed in another of his impeccable black suits, sipping coffee and reading a newspaper.

"Good morning." His warm voice washed over me, as if nothing at all untoward had happened last night. Except I'd all but plummeted to my death, and he'd grown a pair of wings as black as darkness itself. But then, the devil might not have a care in the world. Why should he?

"Morning," I murmured, although it was nearly noon at this point.

He looked me over, his eyes dark and unreadable. "You look lovely."

"Thank you." I couldn't look at Lucifer without memories of my dreams flickering through my head, or of the stomach-lurching jolt when he'd caught me mid-air and saved my life. Clearing my throat, I focused on the food instead.

An entire brunch buffet was laid out on the table with everything from eggs to pancakes to fruits. I picked at a couple of things, then glanced at the apples. Ruby red, juicy-looking, and tempting me like they probably once tempted Eve. Was that story real too? I shook my head, rejecting them.

Lucifer watched my progress back toward the table, and

he eyed me as I began to pick at the small scoop of eggs on my plate, but I avoided looking at him. Every time I glanced his way, my breath caught at the memory of his protective eyes looking down on me, his arms clutching me tight, his wings unfurled behind him. The enormous, shadowy, impossibly beautiful wings that had saved my life. If he had wings and red eyes—because surely I didn't imagine those either—what else did he have? Horns? A forked tail? Goat legs? My brain conjured up all sorts of horrifying images from movies and tv shows, and I shoved my food away, my hunger gone.

Yesterday, I'd been trying to humor a sexy billionaire with a devil fetish. Today, I was dining one-on-one with Lucifer himself. It was a lot to take in. I just had to get through the next few days, and then I'd have Brandy back, and I could spend the rest of my life trying to forget I'd ever met the devil.

Yeah, right. As if that was possible.

———

That afternoon, we took another of Lucifer's fancy sports cars out onto The Strip. I didn't ask where we were going, and Lucifer left me to my silence, as if he knew I wasn't ready for conversation. We left downtown Las Vegas and drove just past the edge of civilization, to the start of where the desert could swallow us up. He turned the car down a road that led to a sign for the Devil's Playground Raceway, and we soon came upon a rectangular building set against the backdrop of a large racetrack with the arid, dry mountains behind it.

"What are we doing here?" I asked, as I gazed out at the race track.

"Letting off a little steam." Lucifer gave me a wicked grin. "I thought you could use a good distraction."

He parked in front of the building and donned a pair of black sunglasses, while I stepped out of the car and under the scorching desert sun. I was used to heat after living in Southern California, but this was brutal. Another sports car pulled up behind us and stopped on a dime, and then Zel and Gadreel jumped out. Zel was wearing her battle leather and had weapons strapped to her, and she glared at everything like even the sun offended her. Gadreel grinned and ran a hand through his sandy blond hair as he checked out the place, like he was a tourist on vacation.

"We have company today," I noted.

A muscle flexed in Lucifer's jaw. "You were attacked last night. I want you protected at all times from now on."

My breath caught. "Attacked? I thought it was an accident."

"We're looking into it now." He gestured at his two cronies as they approached. "I believe you've met Azazel and Gadreel, two of my most loyal Fallen."

"Are they demons too?" I asked, lowering my voice.

"Not exactly." Lucifer wrapped an arm around my shoulder and I stiffened, while he led me into a shady area. "Fallen were originally angels, as I was, but they followed me into Hell and became...something else. Not exactly demons, but not angels anymore either."

I swallowed, absorbing this new information so casually spoken as if we were discussing the weather. "Do they have wings too?"

"They do, but mine are bigger." He lowered his shades to give me a naughty wink. "And in case you're wondering, yes, wing size does correspond directly with other body parts."

A startled laugh escaped me at that, and my guard relaxed a little. I couldn't help it. The man was just too damn charming. Not to mention that when I was around him, I felt like I knew him on some deep level. But...how?

A thin, attractive man walked out of the building carrying two helmets, and bowed his head to Lucifer. "My lord, everything is ready."

"Brilliant." He waved a hand at me. "Just the helmet for the lady today."

The man before us raised his eyebrows and glanced at me with thinly veiled curiosity. "She knows?"

"She's under my protection," Lucifer said with a hint of a growl in his voice.

"Of course, my lord." He offered me the helmet and then backed away in a half-bow. "I'll get the keys."

After the man had left, Lucifer leaned closer to me. "Another of my demons. A cheetah shifter."

"A what now?"

"Shifters are another type of demon. They can transform into animals." He gestured for me to follow, and we walked around the side of the building, where a row of sports cars awaited us. Gleaming, beautiful, aerodynamic cars in bright colors from lime green to hot pink. Some of them looked like they were right off a NASCAR racing track, with huge spoilers and stickers all over them, while others would be right at home in Lucifer's garage next to his silver Aston Martin.

"Are we going to drive them?" I asked, as Lucifer pulled the helmet over my head. I'd have helmet hair for the rest of the day, but my excitement overcame any apprehension at the realization of what we were about to do.

"We are," he said, as he led me to the first car, the lime green Lamborghini. He wouldn't let anyone else but him buckle me into the passenger seat, but he knew exactly what he was doing. Before I knew it, we were off, while Gadreel and Zel watched from the sidelines under a canopy.

Lucifer raced to breakneck speeds like a pro in seconds, zipping us around the track. The force of the acceleration threw me back in my seat and took my breath away, but I hated to admit how much it thrilled me too.

"You've done this before," I said through the helmet's speaker, but I'd forgotten he hadn't put one on. It didn't matter, though. Lucifer heard me over the engine and shot me a wicked grin. Then he went even faster.

I screamed, except it wasn't out of fear this time but exhilaration, like when you're on a roller-coaster and go down a steep drop. Even though I held on for dear life, I couldn't remember a time I'd had so much fun. Excessive speed had always made me nervous since the car accident, but Lucifer had a way of making me feel safe. Like he was in complete control, and nothing could hurt me when he was by my side.

As we finished the circuit and slowed to a halt, Lucifer looked over at me and let out a throaty laugh. It was so sexy it made me melt a little into my seat.

"You liked that, did you?" he asked.

"More than I expected."

He helped me out of the elaborate safety system and took my hand, lifting me out of the car. His touch sent an unexpected thrill through me as he pulled me close against him. He lingered there, nearly holding me, drawing me in even though his eyes were hidden behind his shades. "I knew you would."

"How?"

"I'm the devil, darling. Give me a little credit." He lifted my hand and pressed a kiss to my wrist, like he did the other night, and everything inside me turned to hot, molten lava.

He's the devil, a voice whispered in my head.

Yeah, but he's really freaking hot too, a louder voice said back.

Okay, so I was probably losing my mind, but wouldn't anyone in this situation?

We drove around the track in three other cars, testing each one out, and it was easy to lose myself in the speed and the adrenaline. Every time I glanced over at Lucifer he flashed me a smile, like he knew just how much I was enjoying myself. Like this, he was just Lucas Ifer again, a man with too much money and too many toys.

When we got out of the fourth car, Lucifer asked, "Would you like to drive one?"

"Really?" My pulse raced as I looked up at him. "You have no idea how much I'd like to drive one. Or maybe you do."

He chuckled softly. "Then choose your car."

I went with the hot pink Ferrari, not because it was pink, but because it was a freaking Ferrari. I'd probably never get another chance to drive one of those, and I wasn't missing out on that. Once again, Lucifer strapped me inside, and gave me a brief rundown of everything I needed to know. Nervous energy raced through me, and I almost talked myself out of doing it, but then Lucifer got in the passenger side of the car and nodded at me. I couldn't back out now.

I gripped the wheel, shifted gears, and put my foot to the pedal. The car shot forward, too slowly at first, but soon I grew more confident and kicked it up a notch. Pure adrenaline raced through my veins and exhilaration ripped a laugh from my lips as the car zoomed around the track, hugging the road like nothing I'd ever experienced before. My poor beat-up Honda could never compare to this.

Lucifer let me take lap after lap until a man's voice told me to come in over the intercom. I was low on fuel. When I stopped, I let out a long breath as the excitement faded away. Then I practically tumbled out of the car, halfway pulled out by Lucifer, while my body still felt like it was moving at hundreds of miles an hour.

As Lucifer helped steady me in his arms, I looked up at him with a smile. "I felt like I was flying."

Something dark crossed Lucifer's face at those words and he glanced away. Maybe it was rude to reference flying to the guy who could grow his own pair of wings at will. Or was it something else?

While I chugged water in the shade, Gadreel and Zel took a turn on the track, opting to go at the same time so they could race. Standing back, I watched in delight as Zel kicked Gadreel's ass, but then let out a startled cry as something—no, *someone*—dropped from the sky at breakneck speed. I jumped back as charcoal gray wings filled my vision as another of Lucifer's henchmen landed hard in front of us. Sam, I remembered. The one who was investigating Brandy's disappearance.

He'd obviously flown here in a hurry. Sweat gleamed on his shaved head as his dark wings tucked behind him and then disappeared completely. Whoa. I wasn't sure I'd ever get used to that.

"What is it, Samael?" Lucifer stepped forward, while Zel and Gadreel leaped out of their cars and rushed over.

"I found them," Sam said.

Now that the shock of seeing another winged man was over, I rushed forward, my heart pounding, scared to ask the question that sprang to my lips. "Is Brandy alive?"

Sam drew himself up and nodded. "Yes. And Asmodeus too."

A huge wave of relief washed over me, so strong my knees nearly gave out. Alive. *Alive!* Thank god she was alive. Although maybe I should be thanking Lucifer, since he'd done this, at least indirectly. I closed my eyes as the dread of worrying she was dead lifted from me.

"Where?" Lucifer asked.

"They're being held captive at an abandoned motel out in the desert," Sam said. "By demons. Shifters, I believe."

And just like that, the worry was back. "Is she hurt? Why did they take her?"

Sam turned his dark gaze back to me. "We haven't determined that yet."

"Well done." Lucifer clasped Sam on the shoulder with something like affection. "I knew you'd find them. We'll mount the rescue tonight. Samael and Gadreel, you're with me. Azazel, stay with Hannah and make sure she's safe."

Zel and Gadreel glanced at each other with raised eyebrows. "You'll be leading the attack, my lord?" Zel asked, obviously surprised.

"Yes, I'll be handling this personally." Lucifer cast me a quick look. "I swore I'd bring Brandy back, and I always keep my promises."

I stepped toward him. "I want to come too."

Lucifer removed his sunglasses and pocketed them. "Though I applaud your bravery, I can't allow you to do that. It isn't safe. You're human, after all."

Gadreel nodded. "Let the demons do the devil's work."

I shot him a defiant look. "None of you would even know about this if I hadn't brought it to your attention."

"And we thank you for that, but there's nothing more you can do." Lucifer rested his hands on my shoulders and pinned me with his intense stare. "Trust me, Hannah. I will handle this with all haste, and soon you'll have your friend back. I will not fail you."

I swallowed and stamped down my stubborn determination. Though it pained me not to go with them, I knew they were right. What could I do against demons? A few hours ago I didn't even know they existed, and it's not like I was a fighter or anything. I ran a flower shop, for fuck's sake, and he was the *devil*. There was no comparison.

And for some reason, I did trust him. It made no sense, but every fiber of my being told me he was telling the truth, and that he would bring Brandy back safely.

I nodded mutely and stepped back. Lucifer reached up to cup my cheek, gazing into my eyes, as his large black wings extended behind him with a rush of wind. Samael's charcoal wings snapped out next, followed by Gadreel's pale gray ones. Without further word, the three of them launched into the sky, blocking out the sun with great flaps of their large wings.

Zel watched them go, her mouth tight. "Come with me. I'll take you back to The Celestial."

But I wouldn't budge. Not until their dark forms were just pinpricks against the bright blue sky, vanishing in the distance and leaving me with only a heavy dose of fear and worry. And not just for Brandy either...but for Lucifer too.

10

LUCIFER

The ground shook under my feet as I landed outside the motel and cracks formed in the cement, fanning out into the hard-packed earth of the surrounding area. Dust kicked up around me as the wind whirled, the elements in tune with my barely constrained anger.

Dozens of my Fallen soldiers landed behind me, many of them carrying Lilim—incubi and succubi—in their arms. The lust demons had volunteered as soon as they'd learned one of their own was being held captive. Asmodeus was well-loved among his kind for running the strip clubs many of them used to feed safely, and they were incensed by his kidnapping. Though many of them were strong fighters, their race didn't have wings, and thus they were relying on my Fallen for covert transport tonight.

We were in the middle of nowhere Nevada, far enough off the main highway that no one would see us. Dim lights were on inside the motel, but otherwise it looked truly abandoned, with broken windows, peeling paint, and a sign hanging on for dear life proclaiming it the Desert Paradise Motel. An empty, cracked swimming pool sat in the middle of the courtyard, half-filled with tumbleweeds. But I knew the place wasn't as empty as it seemed.

The October night air was lovely and cool, and I breathed in the darkness, my closest companion for centuries now. Though I'd once been a soldier of the light, I was truly the Lord of the Night now. I drank in the power of darkness, letting it fill me with strength.

With Gadreel on my left and Samael on my right, I stalked toward the run-down motel with fury burning inside my veins. One of my most loyal demons was being held there, along with Hannah's best friend. They had better be fucking alive, or there would be hell to pay.

Oh, who was I kidding? There was already hell to pay, and the devil was here to collect his due.

Before I reached the door to the motel lobby, it flew open and two men ran out and began shooting at us. Guns, really? How pedestrian. I raised a hand and enveloped the bullets in darkness, fading them into the night before they could hit me or the fighters behind me.

The two men then let out a roar as their bodies grew and changed, growing fur and claws. Bear shifters. Demons of passion and wrath, who should be loyal to me.

They charged forward, and other demonic bears, wolves, and even hellhounds emerged from the motel's various doors, crawling through windows, jumping through rotten walls, and leaping off the roof. My Fallen angels and Lilim immediately charged into the fray before any of the shifters could get near me, and I growled at the sight of demons fighting demons.

"Enough," I bellowed, my voice bouncing off the surrounding mountains with a crack like thunder and echoing back to us. "Bow to me, your King."

None of them backed down, and the fight continued all around me. I gestured for Samael to go inside and he charged forward with his sword raised, with a few angry, gorgeous Lilim at his heels. Gadreel fought a huge bear beside me, using his sword and shadow magic to subdue the beast. With a great slash, Gadreel rammed his sword through the bear's chest, then wrapped darkness around his throat until the shifter slumped in defeat. Gadreel may have looked like a cheerful angel, but in battle he was truly ruthless, a rival for any bloodthirsty demon.

Other shifters foolishly tried to attack me. Their sharp claws and gnashing teeth glanced off my skin without leaving a mark. All of the anger I'd been trying to keep hidden, to protect Hannah from, spilled out of me at the complete disrespect for my power. Perhaps it was time for a reminder of who I was.

I gathered the night around me, spreading my wings wide, before I unleashed it. Like shadowy tentacles, my magic reached out and wrapped around each shifter outside the motel and carved jagged clefts right through them, ripping them apart limb from limb.

Did I need a small army at my back? No. I could destroy

everyone here with the slightest thought. I'd simply hoped to avoid bloodshed, thinking that a show of force would cause the shifters to back down and hand over the captives. But that didn't happen, and now I was really fucking pissed.

More shifters emerged from the motel, chased out by Samael and his Lilim warriors. A huge red fox decided to get brave, snapping at me. The same fucking fox shifter who'd been spying on me and Hannah while we'd been shopping.

As he leaped at me with sharp teeth, I clamped my fingers on the creature's neck and used darkness to reach inside him and crush his heart and his lungs. Then I tossed his body to the ground as the remainder of his flesh shifted back to human form. He should have heeded my warning earlier.

I looked around at the continued fighting, my chest heaving as I battled the desire to burn each of the remaining shifters to ashes. Perhaps they'd surrender now.

None of them did.

I pushed my darkness outward. As soon as the remaining shifters saw more of the twisting shadows swirling from me they ran, but they were too late. They'd forced my hand.

My darkness snaked around the throats of each of the rebellious little traitors, yanking them back. I sucked all the life out of them, drawing it back inside myself, their resistance only making me stronger.

Their lifeless bodies hit the ground and the battle was officially over. I turned toward the motel in time to see Samael emerge from the front doors with Asmodeus and a pretty Black woman. Her dark skin was dust-covered and there was evidence of blood congealing around small tears in her clothes, but her brown eyes still held a gleam of determination. This must be Brandy.

She was faring better than Asmodeus, by all appearances, and she held onto his arm, like she refused to be parted from his side. The incubus's olive skin was covered in more dried blood and dirt, as were his ripped and torn clothes. His normally vibrant green eyes were dull and exhausted, and he stumbled forward along the dirt, leaning against Brandy for support while Samael looked on with a frown.

I took a handkerchief from my suit pocket and slowly wiped off my hands. "Tell me what happened."

"They kidnapped us," Brandy said, and I was surprised she answered first. A brave one, for sure. "They tortured him, trying to get him to talk about you, but he wouldn't break."

"Did you feed on her?" I asked Asmodeus. It would be understandable given the circumstances, but humans could only handle so much of an incubus's attentions. I needed to know if he'd done any damage to Brandy before I returned her to Hannah.

"No, I didn't," Asmodeus said between clenched teeth. He obviously needed to feed, and was doing everything in his power to hold himself back.

"You heroic fool," Brandy muttered, her eyes softening as she looked at him. "I told you it was all right."

Heroic? Asmodeus? The incubus who ran my strip

clubs and went through human women like candy? I nearly laughed, until I saw the way they looked at each other. With their gazes locked, something intense passed between them, like powerful longing. It must be a side effect of his powers. Asmodeus may have refrained from feeding on her, but the lust he inspired was impossible for humans to ignore.

"I would never hurt you," Asmodeus said to her.

Samael stepped forward and took Asmodeus's arm, yanking him away from Brandy with a disapproving frown. "You need to feed, son. I'll take you now."

"Yes, go," I said, waving them off. "I'll handle things here."

Asmodeus reached out to Brandy like he was going to stroke her face, but then he dropped his hand and his expression turned grim. Samael's wings stretched out and he picked up his son, before they flew up into the sky. Unlike Samael, Asmodeus didn't have wings. He took after his mother, Lilith, instead.

Brandy watched them fly away and brushed her fingers across her eyes, wiping away tears she didn't wish me to see. Then her head snapped to me and she stared at me with something like curiosity.

"You know who I am?" I asked. As she certainly knew all about demons now, there was no sense in hiding my abilities or pretending to be other than I was.

She bit her lip and nodded, but I was impressed that she didn't drop her eyes or look away. "Asmodeus told me. I didn't believe it at first but..."

She was handling things very well, all things considered.

I could see why Hannah would practically sell her soul for such a friend. "We're going to fly you back to my hotel, The Celestial, where you can recover in safety. Hannah is there already."

"Hannah?" Brandy looked around at all the bodies helplessly. "She can't be here. This place, this world..."

Perhaps this was a bit much for a mortal to endure. I waved my arm and the night devoured the bodies, causing them to vanish. That only made her jump though, and I wondered whether I'd overdone it. It had been a long time since I'd shown my true self to humans, and I forgot how skittish they became around blood and magic.

"Hannah is the reason we found you," I explained. "She'll be relieved to see you're all right."

"Am I?" she asked with a short laugh, as she rubbed her arms and gazed at the hotel with dark memories in her eyes. Yes, she definitely needed to leave this place. After my people finished searching the motel for evidence, I'd burn it down in her honor.

I snapped my fingers. "Gadreel, please escort Ms. Brandy back to The Celestial and set her up in one of the luxury suites."

Gadreel stepped forward and nodded, his pale wings stretching out behind him. She stared at them with her mouth open, and then he said something quietly to her before picking her up. I could have carried Brandy myself, of course, but that felt like a betrayal of Hannah. Another woman in my arms? No. I only wanted the one who was meant for me.

I barked out a few orders to the remaining Fallen and Lilim at the scene, making sure they left no stone unturned in their search. I didn't know why those shifters had taken Asmodeus and Brandy, but their betrayal made my blood boil. I needed to know if this was an isolated rogue group, or if this was part of a larger act of mutiny. Hopefully when Asmodeus recovered he'd have some answers too.

I took one last look around before taking off into the sky, eager to tell Hannah that her friend had been rescued. My part of the deal was complete.

Now it was her turn.

11

HANNAH

I paced back and forth in the penthouse until my feet ached. Shouldn't they be back by now? I checked the clock for the fiftieth time but only two minutes had passed since I'd last looked at it. I groaned and turned away before I drove myself even more mad.

Azazel watched me from where she lounged on the black leather sofa in Lucifer's living room. With her rich, dark skin and black leather clothing, she looked like a panther—deadly but deceptively relaxed. While drinking a glass of red wine, she watched every single one of my movements like she had to report them all to Lucifer.

"You're making me tired, little mortal." She yawned and shifted her position, stretching like a feline.

I stopped and sighed. "I'm sorry my pacing exhausts you. Aren't you the least bit worried?"

Zel snorted. "Not at all. If your friend isn't dead already,

Lucifer won't let her be hurt. And if she is, well, it's already done."

I threw my hands up at her infuriating response. "What about Lucifer? He's your boss, isn't he?"

She laughed in response to that. "You *really* don't need to worry about him."

Maybe not, but I was surprised at how much the thought of him being wounded made my chest tighten and my heart pound. Why did I even care? He was the *devil*, for crying out loud. Should I be rooting for him at all, or was that like siding with evil? But if he was rescuing innocent women from kidnappers, wouldn't that make him the good guy? Damn, this shit was confusing.

Still, I probably shouldn't be worried. I'd only known Lucifer for a few short days, during which he'd basically held me captive. Okay, he'd also bought me a lot of nice stuff and treated me like a queen, but I'd also seen some pretty terrifying things. Not to mention, I'd nearly died too.

To say I was conflicted was an understatement.

I sucked in a breath. All I wanted was for Brandy to be safe. I would focus on that and figure out everything else later.

With nothing to do but wait, I plopped into one of the armchairs and jiggled my leg. Zel moved again on the sofa, cat-like, adjusting so she could see me better.

"So you're a fallen angel?" I asked, trying to make conversation. Mainly to distract myself from glaring at the clock once more.

"If you *must* know, I was once an Erelim."

I gave her a blank look. "Am I supposed to know what that is?"

She sighed and began to speak like she was explaining something even a child would know. "Angels have four Choirs, each with different abilities. Malakim are healers, Ishim can go invisible, Ofanim detect truth, and Erelim are warriors of light."

I shrugged. I still didn't really know what she was talking about. "So what happened?"

She pinned me with a dark gaze. "I followed Lucifer into Hell and became a Fallen, like the rest of his loyal soldiers."

My mouth fell open. "Wouldn't that make you thousands of years old?"

She idly examined one of her perfect red nails. "Yes, I've been Lucifer's blade for many years of both war and peace."

"War?" At least Zel was a good distraction from my worries. "What war?"

"The Great War." She waited for my response, but I just shrugged again, and she rolled her eyes. "The war between Heaven and Hell?"

"Oh, right." I probably should have guessed that. "Is the war still going on?"

"No, it ended a little over thirty years ago when Lucifer and Archangel Michael signed the Earth Accords, and we were all forced to leave Heaven and Hell to live in this dull realm." She sneered. "Supposedly angels and demons have been at peace since then."

"Why don't you sound happier about that?"

"I prefer war," Zel snapped.

Her words had a tone of finality, but clearly there was more to it than that. While I debated whether to let it go or ask more questions, because I still had a million of them when it came to angels and demons, the sound of windows shattering filled the room.

I screamed as shards of glass rained down on us. Zel was immediately on top of me, protecting my body with her own, pressing me to the marble floor. I managed to crane my neck up as people with demonic, bat-like wings and stony gray skin poured into the room, and I nearly screamed again.

"Gargoyles," Zel practically spat. "Stay down!"

Fine with me. No way was I getting near one of those things. If I'd had any doubts about demons existing, they flew right out the window the second I saw the winged monsters arrive.

Zel jumped up and sprang into action. I watched, mouth agape, as she whipped two daggers out of holsters at her thighs and began to mow the creatures down. She threw some incredible moves with the daggers, and they flew almost faster than I could see in her hands. One glowed with white light, while the other had a strange black glow that reminded me of Lucifer's wings. But the gargoyles seemed almost impenetrable, with skin like stone, and her kicks bounced off them. Only the glowing white dagger seemed to do much damage to them.

I scrambled back from an inhuman snarl behind me as hot, fetid breath wafted across the base of my neck. One of the gargoyles had gotten around Zel. With a panicked yelp, I crawled across the carpet on all fours, knees digging into the tiny beads of shattered glass. The gargoyle grabbed my leg, dragging me toward him with a vice-like grip, and sheer terror flooded me. I grunted and kicked at his face with my other leg, successfully connecting with his nose.

It was like kicking a boulder.

I was pretty sure I did more damage to my foot than to his face. These fuckers really were made of stone. His impossibly strong fingers dragged me toward him, no matter how much I fought back, but then Zel threw her light dagger at the beast's chest. The creature howled and released me, giving me enough time to scramble away.

The door to Lucifer's library was open and I bolted for it, running faster than I'd ever done in my life. I darted through and tried to close the door from the inside, but another gargoyle slipped his hand through and grabbed the door at the last second, stopping it from shutting all the way. He shoved the door open with inhuman strength, and I cursed and backed away.

I looked around the room frantically, searching for a weapon. Anything that would help keep this monster off me. My gaze landed on that ornamental sword mounted on the wall behind Lucifer's creepy desk. It seemed to call to me, and I was unable to tear my gaze away.

Before I could question my actions, I stood on tiptoes and jerked the sword from the wall, ripping it out of its jeweled sheath, then lurching forward when the weight of the blade surprised me. The tip nearly hit the ground before I corrected and swung it up, just in time for blinding white light to burst out of the blade as it slashed across the gargoyle's chest. The glowing sword cut through his stone skin like butter, and I gasped as he hit the ground, dead.

The impact of his stone body hitting the marble floor left cracks in it and sent rubble and dust flying. As soon as the life left him, his wings vanished and he changed, looking for all intents and purposes like a normal human. A normal, very dead human.

Holy shit, I'd just killed someone.

Before I could process what I'd done, another gargoyle charged into the library after me. By sheer instinct and some sort of survival mode I'd switched on, the sword kept moving, cutting down my attacker as I wielded it with the kind of skill I never dreamed I possessed.

I didn't have time to question it. More gargoyles poured through the door, and my hands kept moving, as did my whole body as I danced and sparred and killed. It was like I'd discovered a muscle memory I never knew I had, like I'd spent most of my life with a sword in my hand. And a good thing too, because here I was, swinging this damn sword and hitting my target every time like my life depended on it— which it totally did.

Gargoyle after gargoyle fell to the ground under the sharp, shining blade, and then Zel was fighting alongside me, her movements impossibly fast and shrouded in darkness. She'd throw a dagger, then use shadow tentacles to pull it back to her hand, and if I hadn't been fighting my own demons, I would have stopped to stare.

"You all right, little mortal?" Zel yelled, as she stabbed a gargoyle through the neck.

"I think so?" I called back, as I narrowly dodged a gargoyle's claws. With a mighty swoop, I chopped the head off of him, like some kind of bloodthirsty warlord riding a battle high. Okay, maybe I wasn't all right. But I couldn't stop either.

Zel cut down the last gargoyle, and then we were alone. Standing amid a circle of dead bodies. Panting heavily and covered in dust and blood.

I looked down at myself and the horror of it all finally hit me. The adrenaline left me in a rush, and the sword fell from my hand and clattered on the floor. I looked at my trembling hands, wondering if they were mine. How had I done all that? I'd never even held a sword before, as far as I could remember. Yet somehow I'd cut down my opponents like it was nothing. Like I'd been born for combat.

"How?" I looked up at Zel, my heart racing and bile rising in my throat. "How did I...?"

Zel leaned against one of the large bookcases, looking completely at rest as she wiped off her daggers with a small cloth. "That was some show. I have to admit, I'm impressed, little mortal."

"I killed them." My gaze flew over the lifeless bodies, knowing I'd been responsible for their deaths. "Oh god, I killed them."

She shrugged, like it wasn't a big deal. "It was you or them."

Pushing off the bookcase, she nudged the sword I'd used

with her boot, then carefully picked it up with her cloth, like she worried it would burn her, even though the bright light had faded. I felt a pang of something like possessiveness when she touched it, like I wanted to snatch the blade from her and shout, "Mine!" I stepped back instead, shaking my head to clear it. What the hell was wrong with me?

"How did I do this?" I asked, my voice faltering.

"That's not my story to tell," she said. "You'll have to ask Lucifer."

She walked out of the library, leaving me standing amid a circle of death—one caused by my own hand.

12

LUCIFER

I landed hastily on the balcony of my penthouse, taking in the destruction. The windows of the living room had all been shattered, and tiny pieces of glass shimmered in the moonlight. Panic and dread fought for control inside me as I rushed inside.

"Hannah?" I yelled.

My furniture had been tossed about and broken, and a thin layer of dust and rubble coated the floor, along with blood. No bodies though, and no sign of Hannah or Azazel either.

I ran to Hannah's room, but it was empty and untouched except for the broken windows and the glass all over the floor. Where was she? I returned to the living room and turned in a circle. My rage and fear nearly overwhelmed me. Darkness slipped from my fingertips, eager to find someone to punish for this invasion. How dare they attack *my* penthouse? Where *my* woman was?

"She's fine."

Whirling, I nearly blasted Azazel with dark magic before I reined myself in. "Where is she?"

"In your room. She's asleep, and unharmed."

Relief settled over me and I let out a long breath, then rested a hand on Azazel's shoulder. "Thank you for protecting her. I knew you wouldn't fail me. Gargoyles, was it?"

She bowed her head slightly in acknowledgement. "They were trying to kidnap Hannah."

My fists clenched at my side and filled with hellfire, waiting to be unleashed. First imps, then shifters, and now gargoyles. Were all my demons turning against me? And why attack now? They must have known we were going to be away rescuing Hannah's friend. Another betrayal against me.

"There's something you should see," Azazel said.

She led me into the library, where the gargoyles' bodies had dropped in a circle. The clean-up crew was still working here, and they all gave me a low bow before continuing their work. Even though much of the carnage was gone, I spotted some heads removed from their bodies, and there were many more attackers than even Azazel could face.

I arched an eyebrow at her. "You did all this?"

"No, I had help. From Hannah." Azazel crossed her arms and cocked her head at me. "She used Morningstar."

I glanced over at the spot on the wall where the sword

usually hung, but it was missing. Then I saw it resting on my desk, beside its jewel-encrusted sheath. I picked it up and examined the sword I'd wielded back when I was an Archangel in Heaven, now covered in traces of gargoyle blood and stone but still glowing with the white light of the angels. I'd clean it later, after I checked on my mate.

"Impressive," I said, as I set the sword back down. "She must be remembering, finally."

I left Azazel in the library and stalked to my room. The door wasn't quite closed, and I opened it silently. Hannah was passed out on the bed, curled up in a ball, clutching my pillow tightly to her chest. She'd fallen asleep tense, based on the way her brows were furrowed together, and at some point she'd thrown the sheets off herself and pushed them into a heap on the empty side of the bed.

My rage quieted, turning into a strong relief to see her alive. When I'd arrived and found the evidence of an attack, I'd feared the worst. Though Hannah's eventual death would be inevitable, I wanted to spend more time with her first.

For a few seconds I simply stared at her, watching her breathe. She wore another of those slinky little nightgowns we'd bought yesterday, and it showed off every curve of her body. Her golden hair draped down her shoulders, and one of her hands was reaching out, like it was searching for me. Intense longing to claim her ran through me, but I pushed it down, back into its dark depths.

I sat gingerly beside her and rested my hand on her shoulder, needing to feel her soft skin, to confirm she was alive. I didn't intend on waking her, but the moment I touched her, her eyes popped open and she sat straight up, like she was ready to bolt.

Tension left her the second she saw me. "Lucifer?"

I kept my hand on her shoulder, hoping to keep her calm. "It's okay. I'm here. Brandy's safe."

Hannah surprised me by throwing her arms around me and letting out what sounded like a relieved sob. "She's okay? Really?"

I held her close against me, savoring the feel of her in my arms once more. Where she belonged. "Of course she is. I promised, didn't I?"

"Thank you." She slowly sat back and wiped tears from her eyes. "Where is she?"

"She's in a suite here at the hotel, with a human doctor tending to her, along with plenty of food and plenty of armed bodyguards. I'm having some clothes brought up for her too, and I sent someone to let her family know she's all right."

"You did all that?" Hannah asked, tilting her head as she studied me.

"It's the least I could do. She was kidnapped from my hotel, after all."

"Can I see her?"

I shook my head. "Your friend has been through a traumatic experience and is exhausted. Right now she needs sleep more than anything." Her shoulders slumped in disappointment and I quickly added, "However, I booked you both a spa day tomorrow. A slothful day, if you will."

"A spa day sounds good." Her eyes focused on my white shirt, and she reached out to touch a spot on it, her palms resting against my chest. "Are you bleeding?"

My muscles clenched under her touch. "I'm fine. It's not my blood."

"I guess tonight was wrath." Her words were barely above a whisper and she looked away, her face twisting to a grimace. "For both of us."

I sensed the turmoil inside her and guessed it had something to do with the attack. "Do you want to tell me what happened?"

She looked at me with wide, shocked eyes. "These... gargoyles flew in and attacked us. Zel fought them off, but there were so many of them. I ran to the library and got that sword off the wall, and it was like I'd been trained in how to use it. My body moved and worked on its own, without me controlling it. It was like..." She hesitated and frowned. "Muscle memory or something."

She looked at her hands, shocked and maybe a little excited. Of course, there was no mystery as to how this had happened, her being able to handle a sword. Not for me, anyway. But was it the right time to tell her?

"Perhaps you tapped into some deeply repressed memory?" I suggested, hoping my words might create some recognition.

"Maybe," she murmured, but nothing changed in her expression.

"That sword was mine when I was in the Angelic Army, created to cut through demons using heavenly light. Few others can wield it without it burning them." I reached up and stroked her cheek softly. "I'm glad it protected you tonight."

One bare shoulder lifted in a shrug. "Zel did most of the hard work."

"From what she said, it sounded like you held your own against them." I slid my fingers into her soft, golden hair. "Are you all right? You weren't injured?"

"I'm okay. Physically anyway. Emotionally... I'm pretty shaken up." She drew in a long breath, but then smiled weakly at me. "At least Brandy is okay. I'm so grateful to you for everything you've done for her. And for me."

"It's my pleasure and my duty." The way she looked at me made my chest tighten with longing. "I would do anything for you."

She raised her eyebrows at that. "Maybe the devil isn't the bad guy everyone thinks he is."

I laughed darkly. "I assure you, I'm every bit the villain they think I am."

"I don't think that's true."

"Shall I prove my point?"

I took her chin in my hand and turned her head to the side, then leaned in close, breathing in her sweet scent. I wanted to fill my lungs with her, to drink her in until she suffused my empty, dark heart with her light. My soul ached to consume her, but it settled for me pressing my mouth to the spot just below her ear. The slight taste wasn't nearly enough to sate me, especially when I felt her pulse race faster and her breathing grow shallower. Was she growing wet for me? Did she crave me as much as I craved her?

I ran my thumb across her soft lips, imagining them wrapped around my cock or shouting my name as she came. Her eyes fluttered shut at my light touch, her breasts rising and falling in time with her heavy breathing, her nipples straining against the thin fabric of her nightgown. My mouth trailed down her neck ever so slowly and she arched her back toward me, unable to help herself.

"Lucifer," she gasped softly as my lips reached the curve of her neck. Her fingers grasped my shirt, digging into my arms, though not to stop me, but to pull me closer. Her desperate need matched my own, and a low groan of masculine satisfaction hummed deep in my throat. This woman would be my undoing and my absolution, as she always was.

I turned her face toward me and met her eyes, then captured her lips and claimed the kiss I'd long awaited. For years I'd dreamed of this moment, but the reality of it was even better than I'd imagined. As my mouth captured hers, time stood still. For the first time in an eternity, I felt *alive*. Whole. Complete. Blood pounded through my veins, and my senses sharpened, while darkness swirled around us. I deepened the kiss, wrapping my arms around her and probing her delicate mouth with the tip of my tongue. Her fingers slid around my neck, pulling me closer, kissing me back with as much passion as I felt. Even if she didn't remember the truth about us, her body did, her instincts telling her that she belonged to me.

When I pulled back, she licked her lips and stared

hungrily at my mouth, eager for more, and fuck, how I wanted to give it to her. Everything inside me surged with the need to possess her body again, and I knew she'd let me do anything I wanted to her. Within minutes I'd have her begging for me, until she knew deep in her soul that she was mine, and mine alone.

But I couldn't do it.

Not yet.

Those crystal blue eyes were hazy with sleep and desire, but something held me back from making her mine. A slight hesitation in her gaze, a small tremble in her touch. She wasn't ready for this. Not after the night she'd just had. The act of restraining myself nearly undid me, but I told myself it would only make my claiming of her even sweeter when it did occur. I pressed one last hot kiss to the hollow of her throat, and then relaxed my hold on her.

She looked confused for an instant, but then footsteps sounded outside the door. Rage threatened to bubble up inside me again—who dared interrupt me with my woman in my bed?

Gadreel strode purposefully inside and then paused when he saw Hannah in my arms. She looked a little stunned as she touched her lips, like she was still dazed from the way I'd kissed her. I couldn't blame her.

"I'm sorry to interrupt," Gadreel said, averting his eyes. "I'll come back later."

"It's fine." I let go of Hannah, though it pained me to do so. "You have a report for me?"

"Yes, we managed to capture one of the shifters at the motel. We're holding him for questioning now."

"Very good. Did they find anything else at the motel? Any indication of who was leading them?"

He kept his head bowed. "No, my lord."

A low growl rumbled in my chest. Imps, shifters, and gargoyles had all acted against me or Hannah in the last few days. Ever since she came into my life, demons who were once loyal to me were turning against me. Was it a coincidence or part of a larger conspiracy? The Fallen and the Lilim still seemed loyal, but what of the dragons and vampires? I needed to question that shifter tonight and find out the depth of this mutinous plot. Either way, I would have to deal with this problem before more demons got any ideas about defiance.

I ran a hand through my hair, the anger and pent-up lust making my movements sharp. "Thank you, Gadreel. I'll meet you in the war room soon."

He bowed and then departed, and I turned back to Hannah, who'd watched the conversation with questions shining in her intelligent eyes. Damn it. I needed to tell her who she was, but first I needed to deal with this insubordination problem. Besides, she wasn't ready for any more surprises tonight.

"Sleep," I told her, easing her back into the bed, putting a touch of power in my words once more. "Stay here in my bed, where you belong. I'll make sure you're safe."

She nodded slowly as she settled down, her eyelids growing heavy. "Don't leave just yet."

My heart twisted at the soft plea. "I'll stay until you're asleep."

That seemed to satisfy her, and I stroked her head softly as she relaxed, no longer tense like before. I longed to crawl in beside her, to curl up behind her and wrap my arms tight around her small frame, but I had matters to attend to tonight.

Tomorrow. I'd tell her the truth tomorrow.

13

HANNAH

Sleeping in Lucifer's room was like an extra level of decadence. I'd escaped there because it was the only untouched room in the penthouse after the gargoyle attack, and sheer exhaustion and lingering shock had made me pass out in his bed, amid black silk sheets that smelled like him. When I awoke to his touch and his news that Brandy was alive, I'd never felt such overwhelming relief and gratitude. He said he was a villain, but last night he'd been my hero.

And then there was that kiss, and the way he touched me like he already knew every inch of my body. I grew wet again just thinking about it, imagining him here in bed with me now as I stretched out upon his soft sheets with morning sunlight filtered through sheer black curtains. I had no idea where he'd slept last night, or if he'd slept at all. The last thing I remembered was him stroking my hair as sleep overcame me.

Lucifer wasn't in the kitchen either, I discovered with a pang of longing. I was sure he was dealing with the aftermath of last night's events, and I wanted to go see Brandy anyway, but I still felt his absence in the big, empty penthouse. I quickly downed my coffee and ate a muffin, then threw on some yoga pants and a t-shirt from my own wardrobe.

Once I was ready, I hurried down to The Celestial's day spa to meet Brandy, with Azazel and a few other guards surrounding me. It was no surprise that The Celestial had its own luxury day spa. There seemed to be nothing that Lucifer's resort and casino lacked. I even saw a champagne vending machine on my way down the marble halls. I could probably live my entire life in this hotel without needing to ever step outside again—especially if Lucifer continued to bring the world to me. Memories of his kiss flooded back to me at that thought, practically setting my panties on fire. Maybe being the devil's captive wasn't so bad in the end.

I stepped inside the Diabolique Day Spa and marveled at the large, relaxing fountain in front of me. Everything was white marble, shining blue glass, and smooth, curved lines.

"Ms. Thorn," a beautiful woman said, stepping forward to meet me. I briefly wondered if she was a demon, and if so, what kind? "We've been expecting you."

"Is my friend here yet?" I asked.

"No, but we will bring her in as soon as she arrives." She gestured down the hall. "Follow me."

I was led down shimmering floors and through a frosted blue door into a room with two massage tables. Another woman approached with a glass of champagne, and I waved her away. "No, thank you."

They left me alone in the room. To change, I supposed. I'd never actually been to a spa, at least, not that I remembered, and wasn't exactly sure what all it entailed. Instead of getting undressed, I paced the room with butterflies in my gut. Brandy was supposed to be here any minute.

When the door opened again, I rushed toward my best friend. She looked too thin, and bags stained the skin under her dark brown eyes a purple-gray color, but she was alive and safe and that was all that mattered.

"Brandy!" I threw my arms around her. "I've been so worried!"

Brandy hugged me tightly. "Thank you for coming to Las Vegas to look for me."

"How could I not?" We didn't let go of one another for several moments, neither of us entirely steady. Tears filled my eyes, and I heard her sniffing too. "I'm so glad you're okay."

I pulled back and examined her again. I was right—her face was just this side of gaunt and her normally glowing dark skin looked ashy. She mustn't have eaten well in captivity, if at all. Thank goodness Lucifer had rescued her when he did. There was a darkness in her eyes too that hadn't been there before, like she'd seen and learned things that had shaken her to the core. I wondered if I had the same look in my eyes.

As we hugged and cried, the masseurs kept checking into the room to find us still clinging to one another, and it took us several attempts to separate and lie on the tables for our first appointment of the day. But full body massages waited for no one, and Brandy looked like she really needed the care and attention.

"We better let them do the massage before they combust," I said.

Brandy managed a ghost of a smile and nodded. "I could definitely use a good massage."

We stretched out and tried to keep the conversation vague while the women were in the room. I told her about her mom and son, how worried they'd been, and we discussed what we'd seen of Vegas, but the conversation made me prickle with an urgency to know more, and I could hardly wait until the massages were over so we could talk properly.

Once our massage was finished, the women led us to another room. It was dimly lit, with a long, expensive-looking counter and two reclining chairs, similar to those usually found in a salon. Various pots and machines sat on the counter. The tools of the trade, I assumed, although I couldn't begin to guess what some of the machines did. One of them offered us champagne, which Brandy gladly took.

"Your facialist will be here soon," the woman said. "Mr. Ifer instructed us to give you at least a half-hour break between each session. He said you'd be eager to catch up."

I thanked her with a smile, though I wondered if I should be thanking Lucifer. Again. How could he be the actual devil, with all the wickedness and darkness that brought, and still melt my heart with his small gestures of consideration? But my smile quickly disappeared as I looked at Brandy once we were alone, and I shuddered at the thought of the things she must have gone through.

I sank into one of the chairs. "Tell me what happened."

"This is some high-class shit," Brandy said, before she downed the champagne. I got it—it was easy to be distracted by the trappings of Lucifer's life, especially when the other subject might be more difficult to address. She stared into the empty glass. "I guess you deserve to know, more than anyone."

"If it's too painful to talk about, I understand."

She sat beside me and shook her head. "No, it will help to talk about it. It's so crazy I have to share with someone." She drew in a sharp breath. "Well, you know I came to Las Vegas for a librarian conference, right? But when I got here, there was no conference."

I nodded. I'd learned the same thing when I'd started poking about.

"I didn't know what to do. I mean, I was in Vegas, by myself, with nothing to do. In the end, I went to the bar to get a drink." Her face took on a far-off, dreamy look. "That's where I met Mo—Asmodeus, I mean. He was probably the hottest guy I've ever seen, and charming as all hell. Before I even got my drink, I wanted to take him back to my room and do naughty things to him."

My jaw dropped. Brandy had never been the hooking up in a bar sort of girl. Maybe that was his incubus powers at work? "What then?"

"He convinced me to go out to dinner with him. While

we were leaving the hotel, we were attacked. By these... monsters." She shook her head like the disbelief was still real, and I gripped her hand as horror showed again in her eyes. "Giant wolves and bears. It's such a cliché, but it all seemed to happen so fast, and it was totally unbelievable at the time. Then I got knocked out."

"That had to be a big shock." From what I'd heard, it was shifters who had captured her. I'd never seen one in animal form myself, but I'd seen gargoyles and Fallen angels, and they were scary enough, thank you very much.

"I'll say." Brandy snorted before reaching over to grab the champagne bottle and pouring herself another glass. "When I woke, I was with Asmodeus in a small concrete room—some kind of basement I guessed, because there was a tiny thickened glass window at the top of the wall. It didn't open and there was no point banging against it." She laughed a little. "I mean, I tried. But it just hurt my fists and barely made a noise. We couldn't even see through it." Her eyes took on that distant look again. "Asmodeus was with me the entire time, and we talked a lot. There wasn't much else to do. He...filled some things in for me."

I looked at her, trying to figure out what she and Asmodeus had spoken about. I didn't want to dump a load of information on her that she didn't need. Being taken hostage was probably traumatic enough *without* learning all about Lucifer and associated paranormal beings. I could hardly believe it myself still—and that was after all the things I'd experienced. "What things?"

"Things I still find hard to believe," she muttered.

She knew. She had to know. I was just going to come right out with it. She was my oldest friend—we didn't have secrets. "He told you about demons, didn't he?"

Her shoulders dropped and a huge sigh of relief rolled from her. "So, you know? Please say you know."

I pulled Brandy into a hug and tried to reassure her, but what could I really say? She hadn't said what exactly Asmodeus had shared with her. I probably *did* know, but she didn't need to hear any kind of uncertainty from me. "Yes. I know. You can be totally open with me. Of all people, I'll understand."

"How?" Disbelief rang in her tone.

"You know the guy they call the devil of Las Vegas?" I asked. "Turns out he's the *actual* devil. Not just of Las Vegas."

"Asmodeus told me he worked for the devil. I didn't believe it at first, but..." She nodded slowly. "I met him last night. He was fine as hell, but...intense. You should have seen what he did to those demons who kidnapped me."

I sat up a little straighter, curious what he'd done. "Did he kill them all?"

"He sure did."

"Good." The word slipped out of my mouth, surprising us both. I'd never wished anyone dead before, but all I felt was a deep sense of satisfaction knowing the people who hurt Brandy had been punished.

"He saved us." Tears filled her eyes again. "And he said he found me because of you. Thank you."

I still hadn't let go of her hand, and I let her hold onto

me as tightly as she needed. "Of course. You would have sent the devil himself to save me, too."

She flicked her tears quickly away, but her sadness hurt me, squeezing my chest. "I didn't think we'd get out. I thought we'd die in there."

"Do you have any idea why you were kidnapped? Did Asmodeus know?" Maybe she'd have some answers that could help Lucifer figure all this out.

"Not really. Asmodeus said he was investigating a conspiracy against Lucifer, but he also said he got a text from his dad, ordering him to seduce me, but he didn't know why. The library conference seems like a setup too, but why would demons want to kidnap me?"

"Seduce you?" I asked. There was something about the way Brandy said his name. "Did he succeed?"

She opened and closed her mouth several times. "Before I tell you everything, I should probably say that Asmodeus is an incubus, a demon of lust. He only needs to look at someone to seduce them, and he needs sex to survive. He requires a steady stream of lovers to feed on, and humans can't survive sex with an incubus more than once, which means the two of us... Well, it's not possible."

She spoke so matter-of-factly about the things I was only just starting to come to terms with. How much more did she know? And just how far had she and Asmodeus gone in their basement prison?

She looked at me like she could read my thoughts. "But to answer your question, no, he didn't seduce me. We kissed once, and frankly, it was better than any sex I'd ever had, but that was it. Mostly we talked a lot and learned about each other. There was nothing else to do."

"So, you *didn't* have sex?" I asked. Given that Asmodeus was an incubus, that seemed almost impossible.

"No." She shook her head. "The shifters tortured him, trying to get info on Lucifer, but Mo wouldn't break. Even when they tried to get him to feed on me, he held back. At times, it was obvious how painful it was for him to be in the same room as a woman without feeding, especially when he was injured. But he was so strong." Her eyes took on that faraway look again, before a small frown forced the fledgling happiness away. She definitely had a thing for him. No doubt. But she also believed there was no way to work it out. I wished I had the answers for her, but there was still so much I didn't know about this world.

She shook her head and blinked rapidly. "How *did* you get the devil to rescue me? And this?" She gestured around the room. "This is so far above either of our pay grades."

As I explained how I came looking for her, and the deal I'd made with Lucifer, she grew somber. And then downright pissed off.

"You sold yourself to him for seven nights?" she practically yelled. "Like some kind of sex slave?"

I held up my hands, feeling the urge to quickly defend him. "He swore he wouldn't force himself on me, and so far he's been a perfect gentleman. I don't know why he's interested in me, but there's something there. Something I can't explain." I paused and tried to find the words. "I know I'm in a dangerous situation, but I made a deal, and he's delivered on his end. That just leaves my side of it." I sucked in a breath. "I have to see it through."

"Hannah, we can go. We can leave now. Nobody is here to stop us. We'll go straight back home and forget any of this ever happened."

I shook my head. "I can't do that."

Brandy looked at me, her gaze steady as it met mine. "I'm going home to my mom and son as soon as I can. I have to. You understand, right?"

I leaned forward and threw my arms around her. "Of course, I do. I wouldn't expect you to stay. I don't even really want you to—this whole trip has been about getting you home safe. That's all I want. We don't even have to do this spa day if you want to go now."

She shook her head. "No, Lucifer arranged a car to drive me back to Vista as soon as this is over. I can wait until then. Besides, I think I probably need the pampering. If I arrive at home looking like this, Mom will flip."

The facialist soon came in and gave us a treatment that was more massage than anything, but both of us moaned our way through it, so we didn't complain. When it was over, my skin felt like a baby's and practically glowed. Brandy looked about a thousand times better too.

Next, we were fed a ridiculously huge, fancy lunch, which Brandy devoured. Then we hit the salon and had mani-pedis while the experts did whatever they wanted to our hair. We gave them permission to do their thing, and they managed to give us both luscious waves that made us look like we were about to walk onto a movie set.

After we'd had lunch and another round of appointments, the day came to an end much faster than I wanted. Brandy had to get back to her family, and I couldn't go with her, and that was fine. But I'd just found my best friend, and I didn't want to say goodbye to her already. Plus she'd been my entire purpose for being in Vegas. With her gone, all I had was my deal with Lucifer. The thought made my pulse race.

Brandy and I stopped in front of a limo in the private parking garage and I pulled her into a fierce hug. Emotions flooded me—thankfulness that she was safe, pleasure that she was with me, and sorrow that she had to leave, even though it was what I wanted most in the world. "I'll see you soon. I promise."

She stared into my eyes. "I meant what I said. Just get in this car with me, and we can both leave."

"I can't. I promised Lucifer I'd be his for seven days and nights, and this is only day four. I owe him three more nights. I can hardly break a promise to the devil, can I?" My heart hammered with both lust and unease when an image of his face, all dark shadows and focused masculinity, flitted through my mind. Besides, there was obviously something strange happening with me, and I needed to know the truth.

"I don't know," Brandy said, eyeing me with brows furrowed. "You're hung up on him somehow. Has he seduced *you* yet?"

Heat filled my cheeks. "We kissed. That's it."

She let out a hoot. "I knew it!"

"It's nothing more than you and Asmodeus did!"

"That's all well and good, and maybe you'll get some good sex out of this, but be careful. Remember that these people are all about temptation. Guard your heart." She shot the driver, who waited with the limo door open, a look and lowered her voice. "I've seen what they're capable of, Hannah."

I remembered last night, and how I'd cut down the gargoyles who'd come for me, and I swallowed hard. "I've seen some things too, but I'm handling it. Trust me." I hugged her again. "Give my love to Jack and Donna."

"Will do. Come home when you can." She stepped back with a sad smile and then slipped into the limo. The driver shut the door, and the windows were tinted so dark the car seemed to swallow her up.

I waved as the limo pulled away, thinking about what she'd said.

She was right. I had to guard my heart. But with a man like Lucifer, was that even possible?

14

HANNAH

I headed back to the penthouse, completely deflated after saying goodbye to Brandy. When I arrived, with Azazel at my side, I looked around feeling at a loss. The mess from the gargoyle attack had been cleaned up while I'd spent the day at the spa, and even the windows had already been replaced. It was like it never happened. There was no sign of Lucifer though, and I wasn't sure what to do. I considered spending some time in the library, but in the end, exhaustion claimed me, and I headed to my room for an afternoon nap. Today was about sloth, after all.

Sleep came easily for a change, but it wasn't peaceful. I woke up curled in a ball and wrapped tightly around a pillow, as I often did. Tense, with my muscles sore and stiff, like I'd spent the day in the gym rather than at the spa. And the dreams... I never remembered specifics, just fear and darkness, pain and death. Only snippets, but always violent and tinged with terror and grief.

This nap was no exception. I was fairly sure my inability to sleep peacefully had gotten worse since I met Lucifer. It was probably being out of my element, in a strange place and a deeply unsettling situation, but I longed to just close my eyes and wake up hours later with no memories of anything at all.

Sometime during my fitful sleep the sun had set, and I sat up to look out my window at the night sky lit up by all the Vegas lights. The sound of piano music drifted through the crack under my door, luring me toward the living room like a siren's call. Where Lucifer was no doubt waiting for me.

I checked my spa-teased hair and makeup in the bathroom, glad to note they had survived my nap pretty well. I fluffed my hair and dabbed on a bit of lip gloss before stepping inside my walk-in closet and marveling at all the gorgeous clothes inside. It was still hard to believe they were mine, at least temporarily. I wasn't sure what Lucifer had planned for tonight, but I guessed my yoga pants and t-shirt weren't going to cut it. Instead, I selected a long black dress, the fabric soft and airy and with a gentle shimmer. Then I grabbed the first pair of black heels I put my hands on, and there were many, as if they were breeding in there. As I buckled the straps, the music escalated into a crescendo. Was Lucifer the one playing?

Curiosity drove me out of the room. Not just about the music, but about a dozen other things. Demons. Brandy's kidnapping. The attacks on my life. And most of all, how I'd swung that sword around like the world's mightiest warrior instead of a florist from Nowheresville.

Okay, and a big part of me wanted to continue what we'd started last night too.

Peeking into the living room, I watched Lucifer from behind as his fingers flew over the ivory keys of the grand piano. He seemed to be one with his music, and the effect was pure magic. I was completely entranced by the way he played, not to mention the slant of his shoulders in his black suit and the way his dark head bent over the piano. I'd never seen a man more gorgeous in my life, and I'd never wanted anyone more.

I didn't recognize the piece he played, but it was haunting, full of minor keys and slow melodies. The room was lit by dozens of red candles, and the ambient lighting turned low so the city's neon backlit the flickering flames. The shadows created by the effect were beautiful rather than scary, and I was drawn to them.

And to him. Always. Impossibly so.

The question was...why?

Lucifer must have sensed I was there because he cocked his head. "Please, come in."

"What's all this?" I rounded the piano and gestured at the candlelight.

"I thought we could stay in tonight. Nice and quiet. Safe." The music faded as Lucifer reached the conclusion of the song. He nodded toward the windows. "I've posted guards everywhere to ensure your protection."

I turned my gaze to the tall windows and focused on the darkness around the Vegas neon. It was almost like looking with my peripheral vision, but eventually I saw them. Dark-winged Fallen, circling the building, with shadows clinging to their feathers. I had no doubt Azazel was out there, and probably Gadreel too.

"All to protect me," I said slowly, still finding the situation unbelievable. "Why?"

"I won't let anyone harm you."

I nearly replied that he hadn't really answered my question, but then he rose from the piano bench and took my breath away. The flickering candlelight played across his face and only made him more alluring. A mixture of dark and light. A reminder that the devil was once an angel.

Lucifer stepped toward me and offered his hand. "I hope you're hungry."

I hesitated, not because I didn't want to take his hand, but because I so desperately did, and because I knew I'd feel that familiar rush of desire the second we touched. Eventually my resistance crumbled and I slid my hand into his. "Yes, I am."

"Excellent. I made your favorite meal." He led me around the bar to the kitchen and dining area, where a pristine white tablecloth had been laid out on the table, along with the finest silverware. All chairs had been removed except for two, and the red candles made the setting intimate. A single narcissus flower sat in the middle of the place settings.

Lucifer helped me into my seat like a gentleman, letting

his hand linger on my back for a moment, before he stepped behind the kitchen island. There he began to serve something on two dishes, while steam rose into the air. The tantalizing scent of herbs and tomatoes drifted toward me, increasing my hunger.

"You cooked?" I asked, unable to hide the surprise in my voice.

"I'm a man of many talents. As you'll soon learn."

He set down a steaming bowl of spaghetti and meatballs in front of me, then laid out some garlic bread and a side salad. Finally, he poured some sparkling water into my wine glass, before sitting across from me at the table. I wondered how many other women had ever been served food by the devil. Or been cooked their favorite meal by him.

"How did you know this was my favorite?" I asked, as I breathed in the scent before picking up my fork.

He gave me one of his devilish grins. "I have a whole file on you, my dear Hannah. You'd be amazed at how much one can find online."

I flushed, thinking of him scouring my Facebook profile. That couldn't be all of it though. He knew too much, things that he couldn't have found from stalking me on the internet. Tonight I intended to get answers from him—after I bolstered my courage with some food.

My lips closed over my fork, and I moaned in delight. The sauce was perfectly spiced. Most people thought spaghetti was a little kid meal, but I didn't care. It was my favorite, and this was sheer perfection. "Wow, this is amazing. Did you make the sauce yourself?"

"I did." He arched a dark eyebrow. "Why are you surprised?"

I tore off a piece of garlic bread next. "I never thought you'd be the type to cook, let alone be a master chef."

His eyes danced with amusement. "Well, I have had thousands of years of practice..."

I nearly choked on my garlic bread at his words.

Thousands. Of. Years.

Sometimes I forgot he was so old, and then he just sprung it on me in casual conversation like that.

He took a sip of red wine. "I'll have you know I'm an expert chef of many cuisines, some of which you've never even heard of, since they've long faded from history."

Another reminder of how ancient and unfathomable he was. Why would he be interested in a normal human like me?

While I was contemplating his immortality and my mortal existence, he asked, "How was your day? Has your friend recovered from her ordeal?"

"She seems a bit shaken by what happened, but she's tough. She'll get past this." I twirled my spaghetti on my fork. "Although I think she has a thing for Asmodeus."

"Who wouldn't?" Lucifer smirked. "I'm lucky you haven't met the man yet. Let's just say he makes me look ugly."

"I don't think that's possible," I blurted out, then awkwardly changed the subject, answering his other question. "I think the spa day was exactly what she needed. Thank you again. For everything."

He inclined his head. "It was nothing."

"Did you learn anything about why she was kidnapped?"

"No. Not yet. It seems there may be a rogue group of demons conspiring against me, but I don't know who is leading them yet." He stirred his glass, swirling his wine around. "Have no fear. It will all be dealt with soon."

"Okay, it's just..." I chewed my lip, summoning the courage to voice my thoughts out loud. "It's going to sound crazy, but I'm starting to wonder if Brandy was brought to Las Vegas and kidnapped on purpose to bring me here. To you."

He pinned me with an intense stare. "Why would you think that?"

"It makes no sense otherwise. Why would someone set up a fake librarian conference to lure her here? And then there were those attacks on my life. I could have believed the roof attack was an accident, but there was nothing accidental about gargoyles coming after me. Or how I cut them down." My hands trembled as I laid out all the thoughts that had been whirling around in my head over the last few days. "There's something going on here, something you aren't telling me. I think it's connected to how I wielded your sword like some kind of ninja. And why I find you so familiar and...comfortable, even when I should find you terrifying. And why I always have horrible dreams full of death and violence, which have only gotten worse since I met you. I thought the dreams were related to the car accident when my parents died, but now? Now I don't know."

I fell silent, and my words seemed to echo between us as Lucifer gazed at me with an unreadable expression. The seconds ticked by, and neither of us moved, our food forgotten.

Finally, he sighed. "Oh, Hannah. Answering your questions is like opening Pandora's box all over again. Once you learn these truths, there is no turning back from them. Are you sure you want to go down this path?"

I'd never been more certain of anything in my life. "I need to know."

He nodded, his mouth twisting in a grimace. Then he rose to his feet, making me look up at his tall height. "Let's adjourn to the other room for this conversation."

I stood and he rested his hand on my lower back, the slight pressure sending heat between my thighs. Together we returned to the living room and I sank into one of the leather couches, while he perched beside me, his hand lingering on my knee.

"We've had this conversation hundreds of times, and yet it never gets any easier," Lucifer mused to himself. "You'd think I would have a script by now, wouldn't you?"

My brow furrowed. He wasn't making any sense. "What do you mean?"

Lucifer took both my hands in his and gazed into my eyes. "I told you I once had a great love, but I lost her. That love was you."

"Me?" I asked, even though his words rang with truth inside me. "Was it before the accident? Is that why I don't remember you?"

He shook his head. "No, it was before even that. Before this life."

I blinked at him. "I don't understand."

"Hannah, you have lived many lives, going back thousands of years."

"Like...reincarnation?"

"Exactly. And in each life, you're my mate. My destiny. My heart."

My pulse raced fast as he talked. I looked deep into his emerald green eyes, and I couldn't stop the feeling of falling. "Your mate?"

"Yes. Demons sometimes have fated mates, as do a few select angels, including Fallen. It's rare, but it happens."

"Like a soulmate..." I said slowly, feeling the rightness of it deep inside me, even as it sounded too impossible to be true.

He leaned closer, close enough that my gaze dropped to his lips, wondering if he would kiss me again. "We're meant, through all eternity, to be together. It is our fate. Our destiny. And our curse."

His words stirred something within me, something primal and true. The feeling of falling increased, and I gripped tighter to his hands, knowing he'd catch me. Everything he said was unbelievable, but then again, I'd thought the same thing about demons a few days ago. And with each word, it felt like a light was going off inside me, like something old and powerful finally waking up.

I closed my eyes and breathed in, searching deep in my soul. I always trusted my gut, and it told me that Lucifer wasn't lying. That everything he said, about reincarnation and destiny and mates, was all true, no matter how insane it sounded. Of course, that only brought up more questions.

"Is that why I was attacked?" I asked.

"Yes—because they know you're important to me. And why you could defend yourself so easily."

I stood up and began pacing as his words sank in, resonating inside me. "How many lives? How many times have I died and been reborn?"

"Hundreds. Sometimes we only get a few days before I lose you again. Sometimes we get many happy years together." He stood, but didn't come any closer, like he sensed I needed space. "I'm hoping this will be one of the better lives."

"And we're together in all of them?"

"Yes, Hannah. Every time you die, I wait for you to be reborn. Those years without you feel endless, and my heart withers and dies, only to return to life once I find you again. And I always do. I find you, I claim you, and I love you, in an endless cycle."

"Why?" I asked, the only word that came to my lips. "Why me?"

"Because you're mine." He stepped forward and took my face in his hands. "You've been mine since you took your first breath, and you'll be mine after you take your last. We are inevitable."

The truth settled over me like a warm blanket. I still didn't remember anything from before the accident, but everything he said felt...right, somehow. Like a truth I'd always known deep inside me. Some part of me had recognized him from the first time we'd met, and even though I should be terrified of Lucifer, I wasn't. Not anymore.

"You find me." It wasn't a question. My soul knew it was true. "Every time."

"Always." He looked at me with such longing, it cracked a piece of my soul. Something kept me from remembering him, a bitter torture that wouldn't clear from my mind. Maybe this would do it.

Pushing my mouth against his, I kissed the devil with everything I had in me. I was ready to give it all to him. He cupped a hand around the back of my neck and drew me in close, taking control of my mouth. His tongue slipped past my lips, and I knew the feeling. I'd felt it before. Not from another man, but from him. Always him. *Lucifer*.

My mind might not remember him, but my body sure did. And it craved more.

15

HANNAH

Need pulsed inside my veins and heat pooled in my core as Lucifer's kiss dominated me. His arms shifted around my waist, and he lifted me with an ease I still couldn't believe. My nipples ached as they pressed against his hard chest, and he carried me across the room while plundering my mouth with his tongue like he owned it.

He set me on the very edge of the large, black piano and finally broke the kiss to look at me with his infernal eyes. His hand found the thigh-high slit on my long dress, and he dipped a finger under it, stroking my skin. Teasing me. A master of temptation.

Then he grabbed the slit and tugged the fabric, grunting in pure male satisfaction as it ripped easily in his strong hands. The act was so surprising and carnal, I gasped. Then he removed his own jacket with quick, determined motions, like a man about to get down to business. The business of claiming me.

With strong hands he gripped my thighs and spread them apart, flashing him a peek of my dark red thong. I reached out and grabbed his expensive white shirt, the buttons digging into my palms as I pulled him close. The piano was the exact right height for him to fit between my legs and press his hard bulge against my core. I wrapped my legs around him, and his reaction was visceral as he let loose a low growl.

His lips brushed my ear. "I can't hold back if you do that."

I ground myself against him slowly, looking up at him with a challenge. "Don't hold back."

That glorious fire glinted in his eyes again, a turn-on even now that I knew what it was, and he pulled me closer, lifting me from the piano. I tightened my legs and twined my arms around his neck, running my tongue over the dark stubble along his jaw as he carried me toward his bedroom. Need pounded through my body. I couldn't remember ever being this desperate to be with someone.

When my mouth reached Lucifer's ear, I bit it—perhaps a little bit harder than I would've if I hadn't known he was the devil. His growl returned, and the next thing I knew, my back hit his plush mattress hard. Lucifer stood above me in the low light of his room, radiating power and control in his black suit, his face dark and his eyes hungry. For me.

With slow, measured movements, he yanked at the tie

on his neck and removed it, while his eyes never left my face. My mouth watered, and I hoped he would continue removing his clothes, but he only stared down at me like the predator I instinctively knew he was.

And tonight, I was his prey.

He grabbed the hem of my already ruined dress before tearing it in half in one quick motion. The sound of the ripping fabric filled the room, and cool air rushed over my bared skin, heightening my desire. My pulse raced faster as I lay before him in nothing but my red lace bra and panties with my black heels. I waited for him to do his worst.

"So lovely," he said, with that sexy accent that drove me wild. "In every life, you manage to stun me with your beauty."

Heat rushed through as he finally lowered himself over me, then claimed my mouth again. His kiss was hot and desperate as his hands trailed down my naked skin, and then his lips followed, moving from my neck to my collar, then even lower. I tangled my fingers in his dark hair as his tongue glided along my skin over the top of my bra, my nipples so hard it was almost painful. Then he gripped the edges of the red lace and yanked the bra in half too with a loud rip, making my breasts spill out. I was losing a lot of clothing tonight to Lucifer's lust, but he'd paid for them, so I supposed he could do what he wanted to them.

Lucifer looked up at me with a devilish grin, then lowered his head again to my breast. His mouth enveloped one of my already-peaked nipples, sucking eagerly as lightning shot to my core. I arched my back and moaned, needing more.

"Lucifer." I gasped as his tongue swirled around my nipple. "Please."

He let out a low, sensual chuckle. "I did say you'd be begging for me."

Then he captured the other breast with his mouth, while his hands slid along my thighs, so close to where I needed him, but not close enough. His fingers brushed against my lace thong, but only for an instant before retreating again, just enough to make me wetter for him.

He really was the devil, and this was his way of torturing me.

"Please," I begged again. "Let me touch you."

"Tonight is all about you," he replied, his voice husky. "Always you."

I trembled as his words only increased the need inside me. My body built toward orgasm just from the tone of his voice and the touch of his tongue and mouth on my skin, but it wasn't quite enough. I felt like I'd been waiting for this moment my entire life, and only when he entered me would I be complete.

He lifted his mouth from my other breast, where he'd been teasing my nipple with his tongue, and then trailed hot kisses down my skin, which tingled with every brush of his lips. His mouth moved across my stomach, down my hips, and finally lower, his teeth nipping lightly at the lace between my legs. I gasped and lifted up slightly, and he used that movement to hook his fingers in the sides of my thong and tear it off me.

He gripped my knees and spread me wide for him. "Look at this beautiful pussy. Sheer perfection, and all mine. Forever mine."

He was so close to my core, his hot breath dancing across my slick, eager folds. I was writhing with delirium already and he hadn't even touched me where I needed him most. Then his tongue slid inside of me, and I nearly leaped out of my own skin.

He darted in and out, tasting me with a low hum of approval that vibrated through me. Then he licked upward, and the tip of his tongue touched my clit seconds before he sucked it into his mouth. I cried out at the sudden burst of pleasure, fingers digging into his silken sheets, while his lips and tongue consumed me.

His fingers joined in moments later, sliding inside of me, fucking me slowly in time with his other movements. With his other hand, he gripped my ass, using it to drag me closer to him, lifting me up like an offering to his greedy mouth.

And then I came apart. My hips bucked, pressing my wet pussy into his face as my inner muscles clenched over and over. Lucifer kept licking and sucking through my orgasm, pumping his fingers into me while I writhed on the bed and moaned, unable to control my own body anymore. It was his now, completely and utterly his.

"It's been far too long since I tasted you." Levering himself up on his elbows, he licked his lips as if savoring his favorite meal. "And far too long since I felt you come. But now I want you to come around my cock. Do you think you can do that?"

I nodded, unable to speak, unable to do anything but tremble with pleasure and anticipation. He rose up above me like a dark god, still fully dressed, and I could only stare as he slowly unbuttoned his shirt, reveling in each inch of skin he exposed. I'd seen him shirtless the other day and the sight had soaked my panties and fueled my dark fantasies when I was alone. Lucifer's chest was hard and muscular, a warrior's body hidden under a three-piece suit. I wanted to run my tongue along the valleys and ridges of his abs, then tease his dark nipples the way he'd tormented mine.

He removed his belt with a sharp snap, then unzipped his black slacks. I held my breath as he shoved them down, revealing his enormous cock. I'd thought he was bragging before when he joked about his size, but no. It really was that big, hard, and glorious.

He slowly slid up my body and then his mouth came down on mine again, his strong hands gripped my aching thighs, settling himself between them. That hard length brushed against my sensitive skin as he grabbed my wrists and pressed them into the bed, holding me down.

"I've waited far too long for this," he said, as the head of his cock slid inside me, just enough to tease me. "Now I'm going to take what's mine."

My core clenched at his words, my body eager for him to fill me completely. I flexed my hips, pulling him deeper inside me. His name fell from my lips on a soft moan. "Lucifer."

That seemed to push him over the edge. His control slipped and his cock thrust into me, hard and fast. Completely filling me, stretching me around his size. I gasped at the sudden intrusion, and at the way it made me feel whole.

"You were made to take my cock." He punctuated each word with hard, deep strokes. "We always fit together just like this. Perfectly."

His words were like a drug to my libido, spiking my desire into a desperate, ravenous need. My hands were still pinned down by him, but I hooked my legs around his hips, drawing him closer. He set a relentless pace that gave me exactly what I needed, as he rocked into me with impressive force. Each thrust felt like he was laying claim to me, marking me as his own, erasing any doubt that I belonged to him.

He found a rhythm that made my body quiver. Fire danced in my veins with each delicious stroke of his cock. He yanked my arms up above my head, his hard, masculine body pressing me down into the bed, his fingers tight on my wrists. I surrendered to him completely, crying his name as another orgasm slammed into me. Pleasure broke me like a hammer against glass, and I so desperately wanted to be shattered.

"That's it," Lucifer groaned. "Come for me. Take me with you."

I lost all control of my body as it trembled and tightened around him, my hips rocking against him in a wild rhythm that he matched, stroke for stroke. Then he drove harder into me, throwing his head back, exposing his perfect, masculine throat as he erupted inside me. Together we rode out the waves of pleasure, unable to stop ourselves, until we were both completely spent.

Lucifer released my wrists and pulled me into his arms, tucking me against his strong chest. My body was weak and languid, tingling with the after-effects of pleasure, and all I could do was curl against him.

It made no sense, but here in the devil's arms, I felt like I'd finally found home.

16

LUCIFER

Before I opened my eyes, I felt it. A lightness that hadn't been there the day before, the warmth in my chest that I only had when she was close to me. As the rest of my body caught up to my mind, the pure pleasure of waking with Hannah in my arms spread through me, and I lay still for a moment, just savoring it. Unlike the other times I'd seen her sleeping, she was relaxed and calm. I stroked her golden hair lightly, trailing my hands along her soft skin, marveling at the way she fit perfectly against me.

She stirred and pressed back toward me, waking my cock, while using my upper arm as her pillow. She had to know what she was doing. Had to feel my own arousal pressing against her from behind. Seeking out what was mine.

I skimmed my fingers along her side, along her naked skin, then dipped down, between her thighs. Finding her already soaking wet for me. She moaned a little, her voice still heavy with sleep, and that was enough for me.

I slid my cock into her tight pussy from behind, while my fingers teased her clit. She gasped at the sudden invasion, her back arching, which only pushed her ass harder against me and sank my cock in even deeper. Fuck, she was perfect, her body made to respond to me. She fit me like no one else ever could.

I slowly began to thrust in and out of her, taking my time, without the urgent need to claim her I'd felt last night. Early morning sex was meant to be leisurely, at least at first. She moaned and rocked back against me in time to my movements, while I teased her clit with my fingers. I bent my head over her neck and pressed hot kisses there, unable to get enough of the way she tasted.

In this position, all she could do was take what I gave her and follow my lead. I drew out the moment together as long as I could, until her hips pressed back harder, and I sensed she was growing close. Although I was tempted to delay her pleasure and torment her a bit, there would be time for that later. With a few hard strokes of my cock with my fingers on her clit, she began to tremble and moan, her pussy clenching around me, which sent me over the edge too. My hot seed filled her core as I crashed down with her into the abyss.

She turned in my arms and looked up at me with eyes heavy from sleep and the after-effects of pleasure. "That was a nice way to wake up."

"Good morning," I whispered into her ear before nuzzling the soft spot underneath. "I hope you slept well."

Hannah stretched, her lithe body pressing along the length of mine. I resisted the urge to repeat what we'd just done. As much as I wanted to spend the day in bed with my reunited mate, I had some answers to find.

After her long stretch, she nuzzled back into me and suppressed a yawn. "You know what? I slept better than I have in as long as I can remember."

She tucked her arms in between us and idly stroked my chest. She probably didn't realize it, but it was a position she'd preferred for countless millennia—with my arms enveloping her and her face in the hollow of my throat.

I sighed and hugged her close for another long moment, stretching out our time together and committing the very feel of her to memory, before rolling back. "I slept better than I have in a very long time as well." Since the last time I'd slept with her in my arms, at least.

"What's planned for the day?" she asked as I climbed out of bed. Her gaze followed me, roaming over my naked body in a way that made it exceedingly difficult not to climb right back into the bed with her. I might have preened a little, but I would have denied it if anyone asked.

I grabbed my phone to check it, and had a few messages from Samael. He wanted to meet immediately. "I have some devil business to attend to right now, but you're welcome to do anything you'd like today. Stay here and relax in the penthouse, or go out somewhere else with Azazel. Use my credit cards and take one of my cars. Everything that's mine is yours."

She sat up. "I can leave?"

"You're not a prisoner here, Hannah. You're my guest. Enjoy yourself."

I took a quick shower, leaving the door open in case she wanted to join me, but she didn't move from beneath the covers. Probably a good thing, because we both knew where that would lead.

After I'd wrapped a towel around my waist and walked back into the bedroom, I pulled a suit out of the closet and began to dress. She put her hands behind her head and continued watching me as I looped a tie around my neck. The comforter dipped to her waist, baring her naked breasts, and I averted my gaze before my cock thickened too much to ignore.

"Have you decided what you'll do today?" I asked. Knowing Hannah, she wouldn't spend much, but if she wanted to, she could.

"I don't know." She tapped her lips mischievously like she really did know. "Maybe I'll drag my favorite Fallen bodyguard out to do something touristy and fun. Like ride the roller coaster at New York-New York or something."

I laughed heartily as I sat on the bed and drew on my socks and shoes. Perhaps she had some of my predilection for torture after all. "That sounds perfect."

Then I leaned over and captured her mouth for a long kiss that I hated to end. Too many years had passed with a hole in my heart, but for the first time in ages I felt alive. I only ever felt this way when I was with her. The rest of the time, during the many long years alone, I was empty, a husk of a man simply waiting for the next time I would be with her. When she brought me back to life again.

But this happiness wouldn't last. It never did. I had to do whatever I could to defend what we'd just reclaimed. To stop her from being lost again.

I had to somehow delay the inevitable.

Damn this curse.

I touched her cheek lightly as I pulled away. "I'll see you after your adventures with Azazel."

She sat back against my pillows. "Have fun doing... whatever it is you do. Things I probably don't want to know about."

I gave her a wink. "Oh, I definitely will."

In the kitchen, I poured myself a cup of coffee, as strong and dark as my soul. Azazel was already there, and she gave me a salute as she drank her own black coffee.

On the way out, I found Gadreel perched outside the penthouse door, guarding it. He straightened to attention as soon as I approached.

"Good morning, my lord."

I paused a moment as I took a sip of my coffee, then addressed him. "Please stay with Hannah today. I want to make sure no harm comes to her."

He bowed his head in submission to me. "I will protect her with my life."

As I knew he would. I nodded in acknowledgement and headed straight for my war room to find Samael. Last night Gadreel had mentioned a captured shifter, and by now

Samael should have questioned Asmodeus too. Someone had better have some fucking answers for me.

"Report," I barked as soon as I walked in the room.

As always, lights flickered over giant screens and cameras showed various views of the city, but I wasn't interested in any of that. Demons and Fallen scurried all over the place, some to get out of my way, and others simply to showcase how busy they were.

Samael walked toward me and gestured for us to enter the conference room, then shut the door. "Good morning."

"You have news?"

"We've captured an imp, a shifter, and a gargoyle, all of whom we believe were connected to the attacks."

I sat at the head of the conference table. "And?"

"Nothing. They won't talk." He drew up a chair, joining me as he spoke again. "Perhaps you can persuade them."

I steepled my fingers. I could be *very* persuasive. "And Asmodeus?"

Tension tightened around the corners of Samael's mouth, the only sign he was angry. "My son knows very little, unfortunately. He was investigating rumors spreading among the Lilim about some demons turning against you, and he thinks that's why he was kidnapped. The shifters tortured him for information on you while he was being held hostage, but he doesn't know who they're working for."

"How is he doing now?"

"He is...refusing to feed completely." Samael shook his head with a hint of disgust. "I think he has feelings for that mortal woman."

My eyebrows shot up as I leaned back in my chair. "That won't end well for either of them."

"Obviously." Samael grimaced, but then he returned to being all business. "He also claimed to receive a text from me ordering him to seduce this woman, but I never sent it. I suspect someone is trying to overthrow you again. Possibly one of the Archdemons."

"I suppose we're overdue for another attempted coup." This happened every century or so, but I'd been the King of Demons for thousands of years for a reason. It would take more than a few pathetic attacks to overthrow me. The only reason this was a problem now was because it put my mate in danger.

Perhaps that was the point.

"The timing of this coup is suspicious," Samael said, echoing my thoughts. "I believe Brandy was deliberately kidnapped to lure Hannah here and distract you. They likely think Hannah will weaken you, or divide your focus."

"Nothing weakens me." I drummed my fingers on the table. "I've been thinking the same thing though. Something about this situation seems like a set-up, meant to bring Hannah to me and then take her away again."

"Do you think it could be her first husband?"

"I'm not sure yet." Red hot hatred filled my veins at the thought of that monster, but this didn't seem like his actions. "I want him found though. And we'll need to set up extra precautions around Hannah either way."

"I'll handle it." Samael paused, his dark eyes judging me silently. "Does she know yet who she really is?"

"I told her some of the truth last night. Not all of it. She isn't ready to know about the curse yet."

Samael's lips pressed into a tight line. "I don't like this. She is making you weak, even if you don't see it. The moment she came back into your life, your focus changed."

I slammed my hands on the table and stood, glaring down at him. "You're wrong. Hannah makes me strong. I need her by my side."

He bowed his head. "Where is she now?"

"Last I heard, she was taking Azazel to the roller coaster at New York-New York. I sent Gadreel with them too."

Samael chuckled low in his throat, the rich sound a welcome relief. "Azazel will hate every second of that."

"I'll speak with the prisoners now." I started to leave, but then paused at the door as my hands tightened into fists. "One last thing. Make sure all the Archdemons are at the masquerade ball on Devil's Night. I have something special planned for them."

"As you wish," Samael said.

I strode from the room to find the prisoners and make them talk. If torture wouldn't work, my special powers of coercion would.

The devil's work was never done.

17

HANNAH

I spent the day with Zel and Gadreel—who I'd started to call Gad—doing all sorts of touristy things on The Strip I'd never get a chance to do otherwise. Zel grumbled and complained the entire time, saying things like, "Roller coasters are for people who don't have wings," but she stuck by my side. I just knew there was a gooey center underneath that hard exterior, and I was determined to find it. Gad, on the other hand, gleefully joined me on every ride and for every silly photo shoot. We rode gondolas at the Venetian, stood at the top of the Eiffel Tower replica at Paris Las Vegas, saw the white lions and dolphins at the Mirage, and so much more. Anything that had a ride? We did it. At least once. Sometimes twice, just to annoy Zel.

I also lost a lot of Lucifer's money on ridiculously-themed slot machines, but somehow I didn't think he would miss any of it. Soon most of the day had gone by, and there was still so much more we could have seen and done in Las Vegas, but it was time to meet Lucifer. I'd have to take my two Fallen bodyguards out for another tourist excursion soon.

I met Lucifer at a helicopter pad on the roof of a building that was part of The Celestial's sprawling resort. When I saw him, standing in another black suit beside the Abaddon Inc helicopter he owned, his face was dark, his mouth set in a grim line, and I guessed his day hadn't been as fun as mine. Then his eyes landed on me and everything changed, the darkness parting like a curtain to allow the light to shine through, and a devastatingly gorgeous smile spread across his sensual lips.

I had that effect on him. Me.

It was a powerful feeling, knowing I could make the devil smile with my mere presence. I couldn't help but smile back as I approached. Then his smile shifted, becoming naughty, and he winked. Memories of last night and this morning flooded me, and my thighs clenched with desire, which was probably his intention. The man really was sin and temptation.

Lucifer swept me into his arms and gave me a kiss that ignited every one of my nerves and sent lust racing through my veins. According to him, we were destined to be together, and when he held me like this I began to believe it. The past lives thing? That was a lot harder to accept.

"How was your day?" he asked, as he led me to the helicopter.

"Fun." I glanced behind me at my two bodyguards, who

trailed behind us. "Zel hated every second of it. Or at least, pretended she did."

That got a sexy, low chuckle from him. "Good. She could use some fun in her life."

"Where are we going?" I asked.

"I'm taking you on a helicopter tour of the Grand Canyon."

My eyes widened at that, and then he helped me inside the helicopter, which was another new experience for me. At least, I assumed it was. Then he got in the pilot's seat and we both put bulky headphones on so we could talk over the roar of the helicopter. Zel and Gad got in the seats behind us, but they didn't bother with headphones.

I was truly impressed when Lucifer guided the helicopter into the air. I supposed when you were as old and rich as he was, you could pick up some expensive hobbies. First we flew over the city, and I marveled at the view of The Strip from above. Then we set out over the seemingly endless desert, and excitement nearly spilled out of me at the sight of the world laid out before us.

I turned to watch Lucifer, who exuded masculinity and power as he flew the helicopter with practiced ease. "How was your day? You looked...troubled earlier."

He shook his head slightly, as if surprised by the question. "You always did catch everything. Yes, troubled is a good word for it."

"What happened?"

"We managed to capture some of the demons involved in the kidnapping and the attacks, but we couldn't get them to tell us anything. Not even when I questioned them personally..." His eyes burned with dark fire. "And I can be *very* convincing."

"Did you..." I drew in a breath and tried again. "Did you torture them?"

"Not physically." He glanced over at me as if considering something. "One of my powers is...coercion, you could say. I can convince people to tell me anything, or do what I wish."

A memory sparked in my mind of Lucifer telling me to sleep, and cold fear trickled through me. "You used it on me, didn't you?"

"Only to help you sleep. That was all."

I bit my lip. "But you use it on others?"

"Now and then, yes. It's a useful tool, but one I use sparingly."

I had a sudden realization and gasped. "The devil made me do it. That's really a thing, isn't it?"

He let out a low sound of discontent. "I can't *make* anyone do anything. That's more of a vampire power. What I do is tempt. Coerce. Sway. If someone is at a crossroads, I can nudge them down a path I choose."

"The darker path, no doubt," I muttered.

"Perhaps, but is darkness always evil? Or is it necessary for there to be light?"

I shook my head, unsure about his justification for what he did. Maybe to an ancient being like himself it seemed normal, but to me it sounded like mind control—and made me wonder what other powers he had that I didn't know about. And how many stories about the devil were true.

I sighed and turned back to the view, as we flew along a river that eventually led to a big bridge and a white dam behind it. Lucifer informed me it was the Hoover Dam, and I leaned over to get a better look at the impressive structure nestled between the arid mountains. At the entrance, two huge green statues with tall wings stood guard. When Lucifer caught me looking at them he explained, "I helped fund the Dam, long ago."

More conflicting feelings warred inside of me. Was he good or evil? Should I be worried about the feelings I was developing for him? And how right it felt to be by his side?

I stared out at the view to distract myself, which was easy when the sunset set the Grand Canyon ablaze with color. The immense size of it left me awestruck, as did the raised plateaus and steep canyons, with winding rivers cutting through them. My inner nature lover longed to be out there hiking the trails, checking out the plants that grew here and breathing in the wild scents.

Suddenly the helicopter swung low over the canyon, making my stomach drop, and impulsively I grabbed Lucifer's hand. He gave it a squeeze as he prepared to land the helicopter on top of one of the plateaus, and I spied a table with a white tablecloth with rocks holding it down so it didn't get completely blown away by the chopper wind.

When the blades quieted, Lucifer helped me step out onto the rocky terrain. Zel and Gad exited behind me and took flight, quickly disappearing from view somewhere among the crags of the steep walls.

The sun had just sunk behind the cliffs, leaving us in a glow of orange and red. Lucifer kept my hand as we walked across the hard, rough landscape over to the small table. He helped me into my seat, because if nothing else, the devil was always a gentleman. Then he opened a large black container, which he'd carried from the helicopter. A super fancy picnic basket. He quickly set the table with red candles, real plates, and silverware. No paper for this picnic. With a snap of his fingers, he lit the candles with pale blue fire—another of his powers, it seemed—and I tried to hold in my gasp.

Lucifer poured drinks for both of us, and when I was about to protest, he winked and showed me the label. It was a fancy sparkling cider. "Non-alcoholic, of course."

Warmth filled my chest knowing he'd remembered and respected my wishes, and that he'd set up all of this for me. I took the glass and gazed out at the incredible view, while the cool wind softly teased at my hair.

"What sin is tonight?" We'd done gluttony, greed, wrath, and sloth so far. That only left three more.

"I'm not sure." He raised his glass in a toast. "Let's see how the evening goes."

He opened a basket and set out fancy sandwiches, an impressive cheese plate with tapenade, and artisan chips. I had no doubt everything would taste amazing, because with Lucifer it was nothing but the best.

The light reflected in his eyes, bringing out that flash of

flame even more as he bit into a piece of cheese. As I picked up a sandwich, I blurted out one of the many questions always rolling around inside my brain. "Do you really need to eat?"

His eyes danced with amusement. "Of course, all things need sustenance."

"But you said Lilim feed on lust. Do you need something else too?"

He raised his eyebrows like he was impressed. "A very attentive question. Yes, all supernatural beings must feed on energy of some kind. The fae, for example, feed on nature itself, while angels feed on light. Demons vary in what they feed on depending on their type, but generally speaking, they feed on the emotions of others. And Fallen are the inverse of angels. They need darkness to survive and fuel their powers."

"Including you?"

He leaned in close and lowered his voice. "I'll tell you a secret. I can feed on both light and darkness. It's one of the reasons I'm the most powerful being walking the Earth right now."

"Wow, cocky much?" I asked, with a sharp laugh.

He settled back and lifted a casual shoulder, giving me one of his devilish grins. "Is it cockiness if it's the truth?"

I grabbed a fancy chip from the bag. "So there's no one else as powerful as you?"

"Oh, there are a few. The High King of the fae, for example, but he's in Faerie and knows better than to set foot here. The Elder Gods certainly, but they're all banished or sealed away." His smile widened, showing teeth. "But on Earth? I'm the big bad, darling."

Well, shit.

I decided right then that when confronted with impossible, terrifying things that were hard to accept and understand, one could either run, or make a joke. I chose the latter.

I raised my glass and grinned. "Tonight must be pride, because you're certainly full of it."

He let out a deep laugh that was pure sex. "You're probably right. Pride is my sin, after all."

18

HANNAH

W e continued eating as the sky darkened around us and the candles flickered in the soft breeze. Finally, I worked up the courage to breach the topic hovering in the back of my mind all day. "Tell me about my past lives."

"Which ones?" He poured us both more cider. "There's no way we could discuss all of them tonight. I have a better idea. Tell me about your life now."

"Don't you have everything about me stored in a little file somewhere?"

"I'd rather hear it from you." He passed me the cheese plate. "Last night you mentioned your parents died in a car accident. That was five years ago, wasn't it?"

I swallowed and stared down at my plate, wishing I didn't have to discuss this, but knowing it had to come up sometime. Better to get it over with. "It was a drunk driver."

"Ah. Hence the reason you don't drink."

I nodded and breathed deeply, trying to force myself to be calm as the emotions welled up inside me. "I was in the car with them, but I was the only one who survived. I lost my memory at the same time. I don't even remember them."

He reached across the table and took my hand. "How awful that must be for you."

My vision blurred, and I blinked back tears. "I wish so much I could remember them but there's just...nothing. My earliest memory is waking up and my sister telling me what happened."

His thumbs rubbed back and forth over my knuckles slowly. "Your sister... Jo, isn't it?"

I had a hard time believing he didn't already know everything about me, but I humored him. "Yes. She lives in San Francisco and runs a tech company there. She helped me get back on my feet after the accident, and then I started working in the florist shop we inherited from my parents. Not long after that I met Brandy where she works at the local library, and we became friends. She ended up getting a divorce, and I moved into her house after that."

He leaned back, releasing my hand, and began to swirl his cider as if it was wine. "Do you ever want more from life than working in a flower shop? Or is that your heart's desire?"

I bit my lip and looked away, his question touching something deep inside me, something I tried to ignore. I did want more. Desperately. But I also had a duty to run my parents' shop, and I couldn't run away from that. "I've taken a few online classes here and there, and sometimes I wish I could go to college and get a degree, but I don't really have time. I have to run the shop and keep my parents' legacy alive. That's enough. It has to be."

"Hmm..." He sounded as if he didn't believe me. "When you dreamed bigger, what did you want to do?"

"I don't know. Sometimes I dreamed of becoming a landscape architect and designing outdoor spaces for people." I shrugged and wiped my mouth on my napkin. "It doesn't matter, since it will never happen."

"A job involving nature and plants. Seems like that would suit you."

I glanced around at the amazing view with a small smile. "I love being around plants. Always have."

He nodded like he'd expected as much as he pulled a big, red pomegranate from the picnic basket. He held the fruit toward me. "Would you like some?"

I nodded as I inhaled the delicate, powdery fragrance. Just a touch of sweetness that hinted at the luxury within. He must have known it was one of my favorite fruits. I wondered if he knew my trick for cutting into one.

With a small knife, he sliced off the stem, revealing the center and the parts of the pomegranate that didn't have seeds. After turning it on its side, he scored down the fruit, following each section. With his hands, he broke the pomegranate into sections, the seeds both beautiful and bountiful on each one.

My eyebrows shot up. "Did you teach me that trick?"

"Actually, you taught me." He picked up one of the sections and held it close to my mouth. I bit into it and the tips of his fingers brushed my lips, sending tingles through me as juice exploded over my tongue.

His eyes stayed fixed on my mouth as my tongue darted out to gather the stray juice off my lips. "In one of our past lives, they called me Hades. You were named Persephone."

I nearly choked on the delicious fruit and stared at him in shock. "The goddess?"

"Angels, demons, and fae were often portrayed as gods in mythology. You were actually a fae of the Spring Court in that life." He winked, a naughty grin slanting across his mouth. "I snatched you away from Faerie to live with me in Hell, much to your parents' dismay."

I shook my head in wonder, trying to absorb his words. The vase in his library made a lot more sense, along with the narcissus flowers in my room. Was it my favorite flower because it subconsciously reminded me of my past life? What other things from my previous lives influenced me now? Favorite food, favorite color, even the way I drank my coffee—how much of that was from my current life and how much was from before? Having so much knowledge just out of my reach was maddening.

"It was a time of relative peace between the supernatural races, where we all moved freely between Earth and the other realms." Lucifer kept feeding me the pomegranate seeds, holding them to my lips as he spoke. I let my tongue touch the tip of his finger, watching as his eyes flared, but he didn't miss a beat. "You ruled alongside me in Hell for many years, though your mother made you spend part of your time in Faerie too."

That did align with the myths about Hades and Persephone. I closed my eyes and searched my soul for some memory of this, but found nothing. "What happened to us?"

"All good things must come to an end." Something dark lurked in his expression, something that made me wonder if my memories were repressed for a reason. He stood and held out his hand, as his shadowy black wings erupted from his back. "Come. Let me show you the Canyon the way it's meant to be seen. At night, in my arms."

I couldn't refuse him, even though the thought of flying again made my hands tremble. All I could picture was my terrifying fall off the edge of The Celestial, and the way he'd caught me mid-air with a jolt. But he hadn't let me fall then, and I knew, deep down, he wouldn't let anything happen to me now either. The devil was dangerous and deadly, but he would never hurt me.

He lifted me up in his arms, carrying me like he did the other night, as though he was rescuing me from something. I squeezed my eyes shut and clung to his neck as his great wings flapped, sending a rush of cool air all around us, and we launched straight up. He held me close to his chest as we flew higher, and I tucked my face against his neck, afraid to let go.

"I've got you, Hannah. Open your eyes."

His wings kept us steady, and I dared a peek over his shoulder. The sun was very low on the horizon, just peeking above the mountains in the distance. Dusk had never been so beautiful before, as a rainbow of colors reached across the sky, painting a canvas over the entirety of the Grand Canyon. I relaxed my hold on him as I gazed around us, soaking in the wonder of nature.

"It's incredible."

He nodded, but his eyes were distant as he took in the moment when the sun vanished and the sky turned indigo. "This is what day looks like in Hell."

His voice held so much longing, and I wondered if he missed his other home. I wanted to ask him why he lived here and not there, but then we were flying and all thoughts rushed out of my mind. I tightened my hold on his neck as he flew along the cliff walls, through the winding valleys, and dropped down to skim just over the river. His grip on me never once faltered and he was always completely in control. Even when the gusts were strong, he used them to lift us up instead of being buffeted. I trusted him, in a way I'd never trusted any other man.

I shifted myself in his arms to see better as he flew up and spun around, before diving back down. Fear no longer seized my muscles and gripped my throat, and instead something new had taken over. Elation. Adrenaline. Joy. It was a lot like when we'd been in the race cars. It felt...natural.

As night fell, it got harder for me to see, though the myriad of stars above us made for a gorgeous backdrop. Somehow Lucifer's wings were even darker than our surroundings, like they were blacker than night itself. My focus shifted to the man holding me instead of my surroundings, since I could still make out the features of his face. I slid my hand along his neck, up to his stubbled jaw, then to his sensual mouth. "How can you see where you're going?"

"All demons and Fallen can see in the dark," he said, his voice easily carrying over the wind.

He flew around a curve in the canyon, but then something shot toward us from out of nowhere. Something huge. Lucifer suddenly dropped, plummeting down to avoid the thing hurling toward us, and my stomach lurched as I clung tightly to him again. There was a huge rush of wind as the thing flew past us, and then Lucifer turned to face it.

Then there was light—no, fire. Coming out of a huge mouth. With giant fangs.

Holy shit. Was that a fucking *dragon?*

The fire illuminated a winged, reptilian creature the size of an SUV, before flames hurled toward us. Lucifer stretched out a hand and darkness, even blacker than night, shot out and consumed the flames, until the light faded.

"Hold on tight to me!" Lucifer yelled, as he flapped his wings and hurled us toward the dragon.

With a shaky breath, I tightened my grip around his neck and tucked my legs in as close as I could. There was nothing else I could do, and I felt so damn powerless and terrified.

The dragon roared, sending shivers of terror through me, but it was hard for me to see him in the darkness until more fire emerged from his mouth. Before he could unleash it, tendrils of magic so dark they blended into the night erupted from Lucifer's hands and shot toward the dragon. The dark tentacles circled the dragon all around, coiling over it and tightening in place like a net.

But then Lucifer swore under his breath in a language I didn't recognize, his gaze on something to the right. I turned and spotted more fire emerging from two other dragons' mouths, as they loped toward us on reptilian wings.

Lucifer turned and flew faster, arms tight wrapped around me, toward the helicopter. As we shot through the air at breakneck speed, the other dragons chased after us, moving just as quickly. Lucifer moved instinctually, avoiding the bursts of fire that blazed hot trails toward us, and I tried not to scream when one came dangerously close.

Azazel and Gadreel descended on the dragons, and I watched in awe as they whipped, whirled, and surged around the enormous creatures, wielding glowing white swords. But then we turned a corner of the canyon, and in the darkness of night it was impossible for me to see what happened next.

Lucifer reached the helicopter and landed hard on the rough stone, the ground trembling under the impact. I glanced back, but didn't see any hint of the battle going on out there.

"Get in!" he yelled, as he helped me into the chopper. The very rock behind me shuddered with the rage in his voice, and I scrambled inside the cockpit.

He slammed the door shut and then vanished, literally just...disappeared into the night. A second later darkness surged into the cockpit with me and coalesced into his form, while my jaw dropped to the floor. Damn, how many powers did he have?

"What the hell was that thing?" I asked, as I hurried to buckle myself in to the seat.

"A dragon shifter. A demon of greed."

Shit, I really had seen a dragon. I'd started to doubt myself as soon as we were out of sight, like maybe it had been a trick of the light or something, but no. A fucking dragon! Breathing fire at us!

"How dare they attack us?" Lucifer growled, as he started up the helicopter. He was beyond furious, but also something else. Terrified, I realized. For me. "You're my mate. They know better than to hurt you. If they'd harmed a hair on your head, I'd wipe the rest of the fucking dragons off the face of this world."

The helicopter lurched into the air and my stomach plummeted as it rose higher and higher. I held my breath as we zoomed off, and in the distance I saw the flash of bright lights and burning flame, and prayed my two bodyguards would make it out alive too.

When we got back to The Celestial, Lucifer was still furious. He immediately summoned some Fallen guards to watch over me, and then he gave me a hasty kiss. "Now that you're safe, I have to go back."

I nodded, my hands trembling a little, my stomach twisted with worry for Zel and Gad. This time Lucifer took off on his wings, flying faster than he'd done with me, and then vanished into the night. With a sigh, I realized he would have stayed to fight the dragons if not for me. He probably could have defeated them easily, but he'd run because he was worried for my safety. My mortality was holding him back. He feared losing me again so soon.

I was the devil's weakness.

19

HANNAH

I fell asleep in Lucifer's bed alone, curled in his black silk sheets. He joined me late in the night, murmuring softly that both Zel and Gad were all right. The three of them had killed one dragon and captured another, but the last had escaped. Then he tucked himself around me and held me close as I fell asleep again, feeling safer in his arms than anywhere else in the world.

When I woke in the morning, he was already gone. A note told me he was investigating the attack and that he'd prefer it if I stayed in the penthouse today. Fine with me. I had a library to explore anyway.

After a front row seat at an epic dragon battle last night, plus all the mind-bending discoveries of the last few days, I was ready for some quiet time to myself. I took a long, hot shower in Lucifer's bathroom, which was even more luxurious than mine, and found it was already close to noon.

Lucifer had ordered an enormous spread of food from room service for me—from colorful tropical fruits I'd never even heard of, to smoked salmon and pre-massaged beef, artisan breads and tiny egg omelets with flakes of truffle. Then there were exotic chocolates dotted with gold and cheeses flown in from all over the world. It was probably the most expensive buffet I'd ever been to, and there was no way I could eat all of it.

I noticed Gadreel standing by the door, acting as my bodyguard today. He wore jeans and a faded t-shirt, showing off his impressive arms, and with that golden hair and those blue eyes, he looked like a college football player more than a Fallen angel.

"Where's Zel?" I asked, while I began making up a plate of food.

"She got hurt last night and Lucifer made her take the day off to heal." He smirked. "There was a lot of arguing. She takes her duty to protect you seriously."

My chest tightened at the thought of her getting injured. "Is she all right?"

"Yeah, just a little dragonfire on her legs. Nothing she can't heal herself in a day or so, but hurts like hell in the meantime."

I tilted my head as I popped a piece of cheese in my mouth. "Heal?"

"All supernaturals heal faster than humans. One of our many gifts. There's also a type of angel called Malakim that can heal others, but we prefer not to ask them for favors if we can avoid it. Old rivalries, and all that."

"Right," I said, nodding slowly. My plan today was to scour Lucifer's library for anything about angels, demons, or my past lives. I still had so much to learn.

I gestured at the huge buffet. "Please, eat anything you like. There's way too much for me."

He gave me a warm smile as he pushed off the wall and walked toward me. "Thanks."

With a plate of food in one hand, I headed into the library. My eyes immediately landed on the sword on the wall behind Lucifer's desk, and I swallowed back the memories of dead gargoyles it brought to the surface. Was I a fighter in one of my past lives? How many times had I wielded Lucifer's sword before?

I set the food down and found the area of the library with the books on history and mythology, and then spent the next few minutes pulling out everything that looked even remotely helpful. I spread them out on the floor and sat in the middle with my plate beside me, munching on food while perusing old tomes and newer books alike.

Hours passed, and I still felt like I knew nothing. I sighed and put the book on Hades and Persephone down in my lap. It was informative, but how was I to know how much was true and how much was legend? I'd been through a dozen books on angels and demons and the Greek gods, but I wasn't sure I'd really learned anything new. Now my neck was starting to crick from leaning forward over the pages, and my butt hurt from sitting on the hard marble for so long. I let out a long sigh and began massaging my neck, hoping it would loosen my tight muscles.

"Everything all right?" Gadreel asked, from where he sat in an armchair. He'd been alternating between eating and idly playing on his phone while I'd been in here. Not a fan of books, it seemed.

"Just a bit stiff." I stood and stretched some more, then crossed the room to sink into the armchair beside him. Sitting on the floor had been a terrible idea, but it was the only way to see all my books. "I've been trying to research angels and demons, but it's such a big topic. I'm not sure why I thought I'd be able to learn everything in a few hours."

Gad chuckled softly. "It's probably easier to just ask one of us. We'll tell you whatever you want to know."

"I appreciate that." I sat up straighter and tucked my feet under me. "How did you come to work for Lucifer?"

"I'm one of the younger Fallen, which means I'm only a few centuries old and was born in Hell as a Fallen, not an angel, unlike Azazel or Samael. I fought in Lucifer's army in the Great War back in the 19th century, and since then I've worked my way up through the ranks and proved my loyalty, until Samael made me his assistant."

It was something of a relief to hear he wasn't as ancient as the others, even though I would definitely not consider *a few centuries old* to be young. "The Great War—the war against Heaven, right?"

He nodded, with a sad smile. "I knew you then. In one of your previous lives. Do you remember?"

I shook my head, but the feeling that he spoke truth lodged in my chest. "Can you tell me about that life?"

"I'd be happy to. You were a beautiful Fallen angel

named Lenore with raven-black hair and wings, born around the same time as I was in the 18th century. We fought together, side by side, and you were a fearsome warrior."

"A warrior?" My eyes slid to the sword on the wall again. Was that when I'd gotten my fighting skills?

He leaned his head against the high back of the chair and grinned. "Oh yes. You cut down so many angels in Lucifer's name. But you were also kind and funny, and like now, you loved books. You would often go to Earth and hang out in London, talking to the gothic writers there like Lord Byron, Mary Shelley, and Edgar Allen Poe. You inspired a lot of their stories, actually."

"Really?" My eyes widened at that. It was a relief to hear I'd done something in that life other than kill angels, and I'd always loved all those old gothic books—to hear I'd actually met the authors and inspired some of their stories was really incredible.

He chuckled at that. "Yes, and Lucifer encouraged it. He liked that they were writing about the creatures of the night."

I let out a long sigh. "I wish I could remember it."

"It might come back to you in time." But then his smile dropped and he looked away. "Although maybe it's better you don't remember."

"What do you mean?"

"You died on the battlefield of Hell. An angel in gold armor cut you down right in front of my eyes. You took your last breath in Lucifer's arms, whispering his name, and many of the Fallen wept for days over your loss." His face was a mask of regret, as he sucked in a deep breath. "For what it's worth, I killed the angel who did it. I just wish I'd been a little faster and could have saved you instead."

I'd scooted to the end of the chair as he talked, held captive by this glimpse into my own life and death. I wasn't sure how to feel about this new information—sadness? Regret? Confusion? All I had was loss and emptiness. "I had no idea about any of this."

Gadreel looked stricken as he leaned forward as if to comfort me. "I'm sorry. Did Lucifer not tell you about this?"

I shook my head. "No, he's been very sparse with details about my past lives so far."

He rested a hand on my shoulder and offered me a weak smile. "I'm sure he would have told you this eventually. He's been very busy lately with the attacks and all that."

"What's going on here?" Lucifer's dark voice made me jump.

Gadreel jerked his hand back as if he'd been burned. I took in our shifted positions as I'd moved closer to listen to his story. Our knees nearly touched, and we both sat on the edges of our seats. *Too close.*

"Gadreel was just telling me about how he knew me in a previous life," I said, as I scooted back in my seat again.

Lucifer stood in the doorway, and he took my breath away with how handsome he was, even doing absolutely nothing except filling out a black three-piece suit. "Is that so?"

I gestured toward my pile of books on the floor. "I've

been reading up on angels and demons and mythology all day, but I still had so many questions. Gadreel was kind enough to share what he knew."

Lucifer crossed the room and bent down before me, sliding a hand behind my neck as he kissed me hard. Then his dark gaze shifted to Gadreel. "You're dismissed."

His kiss left me breathless, and he spoke in a low, threatening voice, but I couldn't figure out why. There was no reason for him to be jealous. I didn't have any feelings for Gadreel. That was even more obvious after such a hot kiss like that.

Gadreel brushed past us, back stiff, and strode from the room.

"That was rude," I said to Lucifer, crossing my arms. Days ago, I would never have spoken to him that way. Now? I'd lost all my fear of him. "Gadreel guarded me all day per your orders, and was just answering my questions."

Lucifer considered me with his fierce gaze, but then bowed his head slightly. "I suppose I overreacted. When I came in and saw you two like that..." His face darkened again, his hands clenching into fists at his side. "I always suspected Gadreel had feelings for you when you were Lenore, though you claimed you were only friends. But everyone loved Lenore. Entire poems were written about you."

"Why didn't you tell me about that life?"

He reached up to touch my face as he gazed at me with sadness in his eyes. "That was your most recent life before this one, and sometimes the pain of losing you is still strong. It's hard for me to speak of it, though I'd planned to tell you eventually. I'll tell you about all of your lives, if we have time. There's simply a lot of them to get through."

I nodded, leaning into his light touch. "I guess that makes sense. I'm just eager to learn."

"You always have been." He hit me with a devastating smile, then stepped back. "Come."

He led me across the room to one of the bookshelves, and his shadowy wings erupted from his back. With one powerful stroke, he lifted off his feet and hovered at a top shelf I hadn't reached yet. He grabbed a small black book and lowered to the ground, his wings disappearing behind him.

He offered me the book, bound in black. "This was yours."

I carefully took the tiny book, which was old but well preserved. *Collected Works of Edgar Allen Poe*. On the title page there was an inscription that read, "For my muse, my Lenore." Underneath it was Poe's signature.

I quickly looked up at Lucifer. "Is this real?"

"Oh yes. I've looked after that book for a long time for you."

"Holy shit. I'm *the* Lenore. In *The Raven*?" I turned the pages to find *The Raven* and read the poem to myself, then repeated one line out loud. "A rare and radiant maiden whom the angels name Lenore, quoth the Raven 'Nevermore.'"

Lucifer's lips quirked up. "He wrote another poem

about you too, simply titled *Lenore*. Poe was quite obsessed with you."

"Wow." I flipped the pages, which cracked with age as I turned them, and found the other poem.

"Hannah, please trust me on this. I plan to tell you about Lenore and all your other lives, but I know from past experience it's better to introduce these things gradually, or otherwise it becomes quite overwhelming for you. Coping with past lives and being fated mates with the devil is a lot to ask of any woman." He leaned forward and cupped my cheek. "Even one as extraordinary as you."

It *was* overwhelming, but I had this urgent need to know too. I shook my head and closed the book. "I want to remember so badly. I often have these vivid dreams, and I always thought it was because I read so many books and had such a strong imagination, but now I'm wondering if it could be glimpses of my past lives."

"It's possible. I'm surprised you haven't remembered more by now, or at least remembered me, but more should come in time." He rubbed his hands together. "Now, we have two more nights of sin, and tonight's is lust. Oh, you should see what I have planned."

I held up a hand, as an idea hit me. "Hang on. You've picked the activities every night so far, but now it's my turn."

He blinked at me, cocking his head. "Your turn?"

"For days I've done everything you wanted, and yes, it's been pretty incredible, but tonight we're going to do what I want for a change."

"You don't even know what I have planned." His fingers

trailed down my neck, brushing the top of my chest like a tease. "Trust me, you'll like it."

I sucked in a breath and tried to control my desire. "I'm sure I would, but I need a break from this lifestyle. A little sense of normality amid all the madness of the last few days. Please."

"Very well, I'll allow you to choose tonight's activities." He sounded skeptical, and I sensed it was because it was hard for him to give up control after many lifetimes of being king.

I lifted on my toes and gave him a quick kiss. "Don't worry. I'm sure we'll both be naked by the end of the night."

I was rewarded with a sensual grin. "Now that sounds more like it."

20

LUCIFER

"Here we are," Hannah said, as a bell jingled above our heads.

I guessed she'd pushed a door open, but I couldn't see because she'd instructed me to keep my eyes closed, in a voice that said she meant it.

"You can open your eyes now."

She nudged my arm, but... Fuck, did I have to? I was deliberately keeping my eyes shut against the fear they might fall out once I opened them and saw wherever she'd brought me. If the stench of stale beer and too much cheap cooking grease—not to mention the undertones of puke and piss—were anything to go by, I definitely wanted to keep my eyes closed. Very firmly closed. Perhaps with a padlock.

I tried to grin, but it came out more like a grimace. "Are you sure we're in the right place?"

"Yep, this is it."

I took a deep breath, even though the alcohol in the air was so strong just inhaling it burned my throat, and opened my eyes. I looked around in apprehension. We were in some sort of seedy dive bar, the sort of place I would never visit on my own. The interior had neon lights that flickered and blinked, although due to short circuit rather than design. Far too many pool tables took up valuable seating space and an entire side wall was devoted to old slot machines, many with dark, cracked screens. Ripped vinyl seating seemed to be the order of the day along with dated plastic tables where the top coating was lifting and scorched.

An enormous man in dirty jeans and a leather vest—and nothing else—stumbled past us, and I glanced down at my Armani suit, feeling rather overdressed for the locale.

This was where she'd brought me? And they said I was a torturer.

"Is this truly what you chose for lust?" I couldn't hold the question in any longer as I tried not to look as horrified as I felt. Of all the places in Las Vegas we could have gone to, she'd picked this dingy old bar?

Hannah laughed, and seeing her eyes sparkle with mischief was almost enough to make up for this wretched place. "Come on, let's go order some food and drinks."

She led me to the bar, and I admired her in those tight black jeans and that draping top, both of which came from her new wardrobe, though she didn't stand out in this place like I did. I wouldn't have chosen to spend any moment of my immortal life with these other human specimens, but if this made Hannah happy, so be it.

She hopped onto one of the red barstools, and I took the one beside her. I nearly rested my elbow on the bar and barely contained my yelp as I yanked away from the surface. More than one layer of dirt and grease graced the dark wood. Enough that my jacket sleeve might have never recovered from such close contact.

"What are we doing in here when you don't even drink?" I asked Hannah.

"I found this place on one of those lists of 'best food in Vegas off The Strip.'" She shrugged as she flipped open a laminated menu with peeling edges. "I thought it'd be fun to do something different. Take you out of your element for a change and see what happened."

A crusty old bartender ambled over, acknowledging people left and right as he approached us. He made a pretense of wiping the bar with a stained rag. "What'll it be?"

"Four chili dogs with everything on them. Fries and onion rings." She paused and I stared at her in horror as she described six different ways to cause a heart attack. Not that I could have one, of course, but I worried about her own mortality. "And a root beer."

"What'll you have to drink?" The bartender tapped his fingers on the bar while I considered which wine would taste best with fried foods.

"Malbec?"

He stared at me, his face blank.

"You don't have wine, do you?" Instead of horror, I only felt resignation. I glanced behind him at the various bottles and waved a hand. "Just bring me some of the house beer, whatever that is."

At Hannah's giggle, I swung my attention back to her while the bartender walked away to get our drinks. I straightened my suit and asked, "Does this amuse you?"

"Very much so. It's a nice reversal, seeing you so out of place." She raised her eyebrows and gave my suit a once-over with a grin, although the hand she skimmed down my thigh spoke much more of appreciation than amusement. "This is how I always feel around you, with your fancy penthouse and gourmet foods and private helicopters. Tonight I wanted to see what Lucifer was like without all the money, luxury, and power."

I leaned close and brushed my lips across her ear. "You can take away the money and luxury, but power? Oh, I still have plenty of that, darling."

Her eyes flared with desire as I sat back, just as the bartender set two drinks in front of us. I picked up my plastic cup and took a sip. It tasted thin and watered down but wasn't completely undrinkable.

"Besides, I have a hard time believing you'd ever eat here if it wasn't to torment me," I added, once he'd left again.

"Probably not." She glanced around and wrinkled her nose. "But it's closer to the kinds of places I'd normally eat at than anywhere you'd take us."

"Then I shall endeavor to enjoy slumming it with you, as the mortals say."

She burst out laughing at that, and the sound of it made

all of this worthwhile. I'd do anything she asked if it brought out that kind of reaction. Damn, how I'd missed being with her. She'd always loved to challenge me, and it was wonderful to see she felt comfortable enough already to do it now. Her fear of me had vanished, and though she may not remember me yet, she knew me on some deep, subconscious level.

Her laughter trailed off as the bartender plopped two grease-spattered plates of chili dogs and fries in front of us. Eating this meal without getting it all over ourselves was going to need a miracle.

Well, challenge accepted.

With my gaze meeting hers, I picked up the chili dog and took an enormous bite. Flavor and heat exploded in my mouth, but it was nothing I couldn't handle. Then I set the food down and grabbed a napkin from the smudged chrome holder and carefully wiped grease off my fingers. "Your turn."

She took a bite next, but her chili dog fell apart as she did, making a huge mess that tumbled down to her plate. She laughed as she tried to salvage it, and I handed her some fresh napkins. "Wow, that is good. Although I'm not sure it's worth the, um, ambiance."

"No food is worth this," I muttered, as two people in the corner started yelling at each other in high-pitched voices, then suddenly leaped up and started making out over the table.

We kept eating anyway, dipping fries in the chili as we watched a lady in a pink tutu who couldn't be a day less than ninety use one of the slot machines. At least we were never bored.

"What did you do today?" Hannah asked, as she grabbed an onion ring.

"I questioned the dragon we captured, but once again he proved resistant to my powers, which shouldn't be possible." I bit down hard on an onion ring, trying not to let my frustrations show. The fact that dragons were also turning against me and trying to kidnap—or worse—Hannah meant this truly was a larger conspiracy. One I'd need to deal with soon. Tomorrow, in fact, at the Devil's Night ball.

"I nearly pissed my pants when I saw that thing," Hannah said. "I can't believe dragons are real."

"They are, but there are very few of them left. It's unheard of for so many to attack at once."

She lifted her eyebrows. "What does that mean then?"

"That someone powerful is trying to undermine me." I shrugged casually, even though my blood heated at the very idea. When she looked uncertain, I reached over and rested my hand on her knee. "You don't need to worry. I'll deal with it."

She nodded slowly as she drank some of her root beer. "How many kinds of demons are there?"

"Six, or seven if you include the Fallen, although there's some debate over whether they count as demons or not."

Her eyes lit up. "One for each deadly sin?"

"Exactly, although the deadly sins were so named by angels. Still, they mostly fit. Pride for Fallen, naturally. Shifters are wrath, though their emotion is more like passion. Imps are envy, although they mainly thrive on attention."

"You said last night that dragons were demons of greed."

"Yes, it's where the whole dragon hoarding stereotype comes from."

She tilted her head as she considered. "Lilim are lust, obviously. What about gluttony and sloth?"

"Gargoyles, like the ones who attacked you the other night, are sloth. They can turn to stone and they feed on sleep." I finished my food and used my napkin to wipe my hands. "As for gluttony, that would be vampires. They require blood to survive, just like in lore, and they're very charming."

"Glad I haven't met any of those yet." She gave my shoulder a playful shove. "I can't possibly handle any more charm."

We finished up our meal and I was surprised to find that in this dive bar with her I'd been having a great time. Even with the greasy chili dogs and weak beer. All I needed was Hannah by my side to feel complete, no matter the locale.

As we stepped outside I said, "Now that you've had your fun, let me take you to do one of the things I'd originally planned for tonight."

Her brow furrowed. "No more private helicopters and thousand-dollar dresses, please."

I held up my hands. "I promise I won't spend a penny on this particular endeavor."

She twisted her lips, like she was contemplating saying no, but then she nodded. "Okay. I suppose we can see the

Mob Museum and the world's largest slot machine some other time."

"Wonderful." I held out my hand and my blood pumped harder when her fingers wrapped around mine. Then I cloaked us in shadow so any stray gazes wouldn't notice us before lifting Hannah in my arms and launching into the air. She tightened her grip around my neck, but not like she had with the dragons. She trusted me not to drop her.

My chest humming with pleasure, I took us higher and higher, holding Hannah so she could see the city beneath us. The hustle and bustle, the lights and the music, all of the chaos that was my home. We didn't talk, just held each other as we flew over the city, enjoying the feel of being close as the cool night air bent around us.

Eventually, I landed on the top of the Stratosphere Tower, the tallest structure in the city and the perfect spot to lord over it like a king and queen gazing across their domain.

"Welcome to The Strat. Best view of the whole city." I put my arm around Hannah's shoulders and she leaned against me.

"It's beautiful." She turned to look up at me with those bright eyes that missed nothing. "But why do you live here and not in Hell?"

My chest tightened with long-repressed pain. "After thousands of years of war against the angels, Hell became uninhabitable. Heaven too. Our numbers were dwindling, and it was clear both our races would die off if something didn't change. Archangel Michael and I met in private over many years, discussing how to negotiate peace between our kinds. In the end, we signed the Earth Accords and called a truce, then brought all the angels and demons to Earth, closing off Heaven and Hell permanently."

Her eyebrows darted up. "The angels and demons were okay with that?"

I let out a bitter laugh. "Hardly. Many were angry with us at the time. Hell, many are still angry. Archangel Michael even lost his life over it. But it was the only way to save our people, and I stand by the decision."

Her hand found mine and she squeezed it. "I'm sure you did what was best. But...why Vegas?"

"About forty years ago, when I realized we couldn't live in Hell anymore, I started building up Las Vegas to be a safe haven for demons, where they can feed on humans without harming them or exposing our kind to the world. Here, humans are allowed to indulge their sins, and demons can reap the benefits."

The wind whipped strands of her golden hair across her cheeks. "And the Fallen?"

"The Fallen act as the...keepers of the demons, you could say. I have strict rules about not harming humans, and one of the requirements of the Earth Accords is that we keep our presence hidden from the mortal world. My Fallen make sure the demons stay in line."

Her face softened as she gestured at the sparkling city below us. "You did all this, creating this entire empire, just to protect both humans and demons. To make sure we could live in peace."

"And angels," I said, deflecting her praise with a smile. "Can't forget them."

"And angels." She reached up and touched my face in wonder, and the look in her blue eyes captivated me like nothing else ever could. "Tell me again how you're the villain of this story?"

Before I could respond, she pressed her lips to mine and stole my breath. The kiss quickly grew heated, as my tongue explored her mouth and she tangled her fingers in my hair. I let my hands skim down her back to firmly cup her ass, so tight in those hot little jeans, and she let out a little sigh.

"Take me back to the penthouse," she whispered.

21

HANNAH

"Already?" Lucifer drew away with a small chuckle and a teasing glint in his eyes. "The night is yet young. We could still see the sights, grab a souvenir, eat a bite of dessert."

"I'm ready for the lust portion of our evening."

I gripped the front of his shirt, the small buttons pressing into my skin. I kissed him with renewed passion, trying to convince him of my need as he gathered me in his arms. The feel of his tongue gliding across mine distracted me from our surroundings so much that I didn't notice he'd taken off until we were already high in the air.

I pressed my lips to his neck as I watched the view over his shoulder as he flew toward The Celestial, his wings moving silently through the night. I wanted more of what he gave me the other night, and my body hummed with need as I pressed against him.

He landed on the balcony outside his room and the door pushed open ahead of us. It was hard to tell in the night, but it seemed as though a shadow had opened it. As soon as he entered the room, his wings disappeared and he set me down, but he didn't let me go.

"I need you." My voice came out husky and full of desire, and I began unbuttoning his shirt as he slid the jacket off his shoulders. I walked backward into the room as I slipped my finger under his belt, drawing him after me. His cock pressed against his pants, seeming to guide his way, and I smoothed my hand over the bulge, making him groan softly.

After one last stroke across the front of his pants, I returned my attention to his buttons before he grew impatient and yanked his shirt off and threw it to the floor.

"Mmm…" I pressed a series of open-mouthed kisses across his neck and collar bone as my hands explored the shifting muscles of his taut stomach. "Let me count the sins… Greed." I kissed his neck again. "Lust…" A deeper kiss to his mouth. "Gluttony." I stroked his tongue with mine before drawing it into my mouth. Then I pressed my hand to the bulge in his pants once more. "And pride."

He lifted an eyebrow as a corner of his mouth gave an amused quirk. "It is my sin, after all."

"Want to show me how proud you are, Lucifer?" I asked as I drew his zipper down. I caught my breath as his huge cock sprang free of his soft black slacks.

I sank to my knees, and his fingers immediately laced in my hair, his fingertips pressing to my scalp as all of my focus fell on the hard length in front of me. I closed my eyes as I traced my fingers lightly over the soft skin of his cock and a growl rumbled through him.

"Tease," he ground out, his voice rough as his fingers tightened in my hair.

"Not used to a little temptation, Lucifer?"

He rumbled another growl and I grasped him with a little more pressure as I stroked his full length. He inhaled sharply, and I took the sound as encouragement, pressing the flat of my tongue to his skin in a long lick. I swirled it around the head, listening as his breathing became ragged.

"Hannah." He murmured my name so quietly I didn't know if he was even aware he'd spoken.

In reply, I slipped the head of his cock between my lips. He groaned, driving his hips forward, and I opened my mouth wide as I accepted more of him. He was so big it was a challenge, but somehow I knew I could take it.

He pushed into me a couple of inches then pulled slowly back out, giving me a chance to even out my breathing. I chased him with my mouth to take more of him as I worked my hand at the base. I bobbed my head lower each time, and he moved his hips rhythmically with me, his breathing increasing in tempo with every thrust he made.

As I closed my eyes, all of my other senses took over. The texture, the taste, the smell, and the sound of Lucifer. It all rolled over me, and the moment took me home. I hummed my pleasure over his skin, while he thrust into my mouth.

"Hannah," he whispered hoarsely. "You always were the one to make me fall. Not pride. You."

With a groan, his fingers tightened around my head, forcing me to suck him deeper, just as his cock surged between my lips. Then his hot, salty seed shot into my mouth and down my throat. I took it all as I looked up at him, his face gazing down at me as he came.

He gripped my arms and yanked me to my feet, his eyes blazing with hunger. "Now it's my turn. Take off your clothes."

I stripped slowly, removing my shirt and jeans, then my bra and panties. He watched me the entire time, stroking that long cock, which was still hard, even after that. I should have expected that the devil could go for more than one round. My pussy pulsed with the knowledge of where he wanted to be, and where I craved him so badly.

He removed the rest of his clothes next, way too slowly for my liking, although I soaked up the sight of his sculpted, naked body. Both impatient and in the mood to tease him, I slipped my fingers between my thighs, gliding them over my wet slit. I groaned as I touched my clit, suddenly unsure who I was teasing more. "Envy."

"Don't let me get to wrath," he muttered as he reached for me, drawing me flush against him, his cock needy as it pressed into me. "That's my pussy, and I'm going to be the one to fill it."

I shivered at the darkness and sin in his low voice, but I glanced up at him with a smile. "Promise?"

He growled and walked me backward, faster than I

could keep up with. My back hit the floor-to-ceiling window looking out over Las Vegas, and he grabbed my ass and yanked me up, wrapping my legs around him. His cock entered me hard and fast, without warning, filling me completely. He swallowed my gasp with his mouth, his kiss rough and demanding, while he plunged his tongue and his cock into me.

I reached across his back to where I knew his wings were hidden by some kind of magic, then wrapped my arms around his neck. I slid my fingers along into his lush, dark hair, holding on tight as he pounded into me relentlessly.

With my naked ass pressed against the window, I was on display for anyone who might look over. Maybe someone in one of the other hotels, or one of the Fallen flying outside on patrol. The thought that someone could be watching us made the whole encounter even more sinful.

Against my back, the glass was cool, but my skin felt like it was on fire. Lucifer's strong arms moved me up and down on his cock while his hips rocked into me. His entire body fucked me so thoroughly I wasn't sure I'd be able to walk afterward.

I was getting close, so close, thanks to his intoxicating rhythm, but then he suddenly pulled out of me, setting my feet back on the floor. My need for him skyrocketed and I started to protest, but then he spun me around, so my naked body faced the windows. He held me against him, snaking his hand down to my clit, pinching it hard as we gazed out at the bright city lights with our reflections imposed over it.

While his cock nudged me from behind, he played with

me, teasing me, tormenting me. One hand on my clit, and the other on my breasts. My pussy throbbed, aching for him to fill me again, and I whimpered.

"Lucifer, please."

He buried his face in my hair, then nipped lightly at my ear as his fingers stroked my wet folds. "Tell me this pussy is mine."

"It's yours. Please. I need…"

He pinched my nipple hard. "Yes, what do you need?"

I gasped from the mix of pain and pleasure. "I need you inside me."

He pushed me forward, my hands splayed against the glass, then entered me roughly from behind. My nipples tightened painfully and I arched back against him, needing him to fill me completely. He felt so huge in this position, like he was tearing me apart, and I loved every second of it.

In the reflection of the mirror I watched him fuck me from behind, his hands on my hips, his eyes red and wild. His wings flared out behind him, his black feathers exuding darkness, and the sight of him in his true form made me want him more. Only I could make the devil lose control like this.

"This is what you want," he said, between hard thrusts. "You want me to fuck your tight little pussy so hard you feel me for days."

"Yes, yes, yes," I cried out, as he pounded into me, my breasts shaking from the impact.

He grasped my hair, yanking my head back. "Now you're going to come, and you're going to scream my name so loud everyone in The Celestial will know the devil's the one fucking you."

With that, he reached around with his other hand and stroked my clit, setting me off like a bomb. I convulsed around him, my knees growing weak, and only his hands holding me kept me upright. I screamed his name as a violent orgasm ripped through me, like nothing I'd ever felt before. My hips bucked back against him, wanting it to never end, while he kept rubbing my clit and filling me up. Only when I felt like I was bursting with pleasure to the point I'd surely die did he let himself go too. I felt it when he came, like a rush of power leaving his body, his wings flaring and his red eyes looking at me in the window's reflection. Like he was staring right into my soul.

Then he picked me up in his arms, our naked bodies cradled together, and he carried me to his bed. He set me down on it, while I tried to remember how to breathe, and he lowered himself beside me, his wings fading away into the darkness of the room.

I turned to his face and stroked his cheek, with a delirious grin on my face. "And now, sloth."

"I'm not done with lust just yet," Lucifer said, as he spread my thighs and ducked his head between them, wringing another orgasm out of me with his tongue and his fingers, making me scream his name again and again.

I had a feeling it was going to be a long night...and I was definitely not complaining.

22

HANNAH

My hair tumbled over my left shoulder in shiny blonde ringlets. Damn, it looked good. I sat in a robe, feeling sexy and sultry before the gorgeous gown even went over my head. The matching bra and panty set under the robe did their part as well, the lace detail against my skin reminding me I was wearing bedroom underwear—the kind I wanted Lucifer to see.

I met Zel's dark eyes in the mirror. "For a badass killer, you do a great job on hair."

"What, a girl can't be multi-talented?" Zel tapped me on the nose before going back at it with the wand of black goop. "Hush, or I'll mess up your mascara."

This was it. My last night here with Lucifer, appropriately known as Devil's Night—the night before Halloween. But then what? I was free, I supposed. The devil's bargain hadn't extended past seven days. It would be time to head back to Vista and check on my shop. But the thought of leaving made my stomach clench.

"There." Zel stood back and squinted at me, casting a critical eye over her workmanship. "You'll do."

I gazed at myself in the mirror, amazed at how Zel had turned me into some kind of ethereal beauty. But sudden anxiety suffused me. "Will everyone know who I am tonight?"

"Without a doubt." Zel paused in the act of putting lids back on the makeup we'd used. "Lucifer doesn't look at other women the way he looks at you."

The words sent a shiver of pleasure-laced apprehension down my spine as they confirmed what I already knew. What Lucifer had told me. Still, it was nice to hear it from someone else, someone who was a... I paused, considering. Was Zel a friend?

I studied her closely, noting the slightly red skin on her legs, barely visible under her tight leather skirt. She'd mostly healed from the attack, but the traces of it were still there. A reminder that she'd protected my life over and over. "Zel, were we friends in any of my past lives?"

Her movements stopped as she stared off into space. When she finally looked up at me, it was through the mirror, her mouth set in a grim line. "Sometimes, yes."

"And the other times?" I touched her arm lightly.

Her face became hard as stone. "It's hard being friends with someone you know is going to die."

With those words, she walked out of the bathroom, preventing me from asking more. I sighed and stared at myself in the mirror, at the hair and makeup Zel had so carefully done. She must have been close to me in a previous life when I was also human. Compared to demons, our lives are short, our bodies fragile. I could understand why she'd be hesitant to get close to a mortal, only to lose them a few years later.

Did Lucifer worry about that too?

How could I be in a relationship with an immortal, knowing I would grow old and die, while he stayed exactly the same?

I left the bathroom and found Zel sitting on my bed, to my surprise. She was staring at nothing, and I wondered if she was distant with me because she wanted to protect herself against the pain of losing her friend again to the ravages of a mortal life.

She stood as I approached and went to the closet. "Let's get you dressed."

I nodded as she helped me step into the gorgeous, shimmering black gown with the crystal stars and moons on it. The fabric fell about me, lying softly over my skin with the lightest of pressure, skimming my curves and making me feel beautiful. When I turned, the cloak flared behind me, like something from a dream.

Zel pulled a matching mask out from behind her back. It was also black and covered in crystals, like a starlit night. As she tied the ribbon and wove it into my long ringlet with her dexterous fingers, I asked one last question.

"Can humans be made into demons? Or Fallen?"

She snorted. "No. Impossible."

Damn.

She handed me a tiny purse that seemed to be made entirely of sparkling crystals, and turned me toward the door. "Go. Lucifer is waiting and the ball is starting soon."

I hesitated, overwhelmed at the idea of attending a demon ball. "Will you be there too?"

"Yes. I'll be guarding you the entire time from the shadows."

I reached out and rested my hand on her upper arm, giving her a warm smile. "Thank you."

She shook off my hand, scowling without meeting my eyes. "Just doing my job."

I stepped out of my room and entered the living room, then paused to take in the man in front of me. Tonight was October 30, known as Devil's Night, and if any man looked like he deserved an entire night named after them it was him. In his shiny black tuxedo every inch of him radiated power, charm, and dark, dangerous masculinity. He looked like a sexy supervillain that people on the Internet wrote fanfic about. No mask, though. I supposed when the masquerade ball was in your honor, you were the only one who didn't need a mask.

"You're gorgeous," he whispered. "Absolutely stunning."

"Thank you." I did a little twirl, the fabric swishing around me. "You look pretty incredible yourself."

He held out his arm. "Shall we?"

I walked with him out of the penthouse and into the elevator. Was I ready to face a ballroom full of ancient demons?

No, I really wasn't. But what choice did I have?

The elevator kept going down, down, down, as if we were descending all the way to Hell. I hadn't seen which button Lucifer had pressed, but we traveled past the underground parking garage, and when the doors finally opened, an enormous ballroom was revealed in front of us. The room was dark, with only roaming spotlights and bright stars on the ceiling illuminating the room, making it feel like we were outside under the night sky. I glimpsed many people in masks and gorgeous clothes moving about the room, and a large silver throne at the other end, but otherwise much of the room was a mystery to me. Unlike the demons here, I couldn't see in the dark.

"The Devil's Night ball is always designed to look like Hell," Lucifer explained, as he watched me gaze across the room with an expression that probably looked a bit baffled.

"I thought Hell was supposed to be all fire and brimstone."

He gave a bitter laugh. "Only because of angel propaganda. Hell is the realm of night and darkness. It only burned when the angels set fire to our world."

As we stepped into the room, people started noticing he'd arrived and began to bow. Within seconds, the entire ballroom full of masked demons sank to their knees or bent at the waist, honoring the King of Hell in respectful silence. I tried not to widen my eyes too much behind my mask as we walked toward the throne, but every gaze was on us. On *me*.

Hundreds of demons, all watching me. They must know

I was human, an imposter among them, only here because Lucifer demanded it. Every one of them could probably kill me with the slightest thought.

Lucifer gestured for everyone to rise, and then began pointing out people in the crowd, first nodding toward a woman in a slinky silver dress with shiny, jet black hair. "That's Belphegor, or Bella, the Archdemon of gargoyles," he told me in a low voice. "She lives in Paris and oversees much of the European demon affairs."

The mention of gargoyles made my skin tingle, and I studied her closely, but she kept her head bowed and never met my eyes. With her silver mask on, I couldn't see much of her face anyway.

Lucifer led me forward still, pointing out more people of note in the crowd. "The man in the red and gold mask is Mammon, Archdemon of the dragons. He lives in China and handles that part of the world for me."

Mammon was huge and built like a truck, with jet black hair and eyes that I swore were glowing orange. He glared at us as we passed by, and I really would not want to meet him alone in a dark alley. Or any of his other dragons, for that matter. I'd seen enough of those for one lifetime, thank you very much.

"The woman beside him wearing green is Nemesis, Archdemon of the imps," Lucifer continued.

My jaw dropped at that. Nemesis was a demon? Not some mythological goddess or abstract concept? She had bright red hair and sensual curves, but barely even glanced my way, too busy with a crowd of admirers flocking around her.

I couldn't help but feel a bit shell-shocked at seeing so many powerful people, and I didn't fail to notice that these were all the Archdemons who might be responsible for the attacks over the last few days. A whisper of fear trickled down my spine, but I had to trust in Lucifer. He wouldn't have brought me here if he thought I would be in any danger. Besides, Azazel would be protecting me from the shadows all night long. Only that knowledge made me feel a tiny bit better.

Closer to the throne, Lucifer stopped in front of a woman who was more beautiful and alluring than anyone I'd ever seen in my life, even with a red leather mask on her face. Her dark hair was in an elaborate coif that suited her bone structure, and she had green eyes that rivaled Lucifer's.

He gestured toward her. "Hannah, I'd like you to meet Lilith, Archdemon of the Lilim."

"It's good to see you again," Lilith said, and even her voice was sultry. "But you don't remember me, do you?"

"No, I don't. I'm sorry." Should I remember her? Was she another person who'd been close to me in one of my past lives?

"No matter." She leaned in close, as though sharing a confidence. "I'm incredibly grateful for your part in rescuing my son, Asmodeus. He should be around here too some-where, and I'm sure he'd like to thank you himself."

I couldn't help but raise my eyebrows. "You don't look old enough to have an adult son."

"My dear, you flatter me." She made a dismissive gesture, her fingers fluttering. "It's but one of the benefits of being an immortal."

"How are your daughters, Lilith?" Lucifer asked. I sensed he was closer to this Archdemon than any of the others.

Lilith's face showed genuine affection as she spoke of her children. "Olivia is settling in nicely as mediator between angels and demons. Thank you again, Lucifer, for helping her get that position." She looked around and then smiled toward a couple talking to a tall man with long black hair. "Ah, Olivia and Kassiel are over there with Baal now."

The woman named Olivia looked a lot like Lilith, with the same seductive beauty that was hard to take your eyes off, but the dark-haired man beside her, Kassiel, sparked an odd reaction in my body. My heart beat faster, almost painfully, tugging inside my chest in a physical reaction I couldn't explain. I lifted my hand and rested it over the bodice of my dress as I waited for the response to the man to die away. Then it vanished as quickly as it came upon me. How odd.

"And your other daughter?" Lucifer asked, as if he was genuinely interested.

Lilith inclined her head slightly. "Lena is still recovering from her time with that awful cult, but she improves every day."

I had no idea who they were talking about. What cult? But I didn't ask. Lucifer had been a good sport when I took him to that seedy dive bar, so I figured I owed him this. I could smile and nod along with these people, even if their conversation did make me feel like a child at an adult party.

"Excuse me." Lucifer pressed a kiss to my cheek. "I must speak with Fenrir. I'll return in a moment."

He headed over to speak with a large, bearded man with wild gray hair who stood in the corner. The long-haired man named Baal joined them a moment later.

"I have no idea who any of these people are," I muttered.

"Fenrir is the Archdemon of shifters, and Baal is the Archdemon of vampires." Lilith cocked her head. "You know, I think this might be the first time all the Archdemons have been in one building in decades. Lucifer demanded our presence here tonight. I wonder if he has something planned for us."

Had he summoned them here because of me? But why?

Lilith slipped her hand in the crook of my elbow as she led me to the buffet. "Don't worry about the others. They're all jealous. Who wouldn't want to be on the arm of the Demon King?"

Maybe she was right. Tonight's sin was supposed to be envy, after all. I watched Lucifer as he prowled across the room with barely restrained power in every one of his movements, and noticed the way everyone responded to him. Treating him like a king.

And me?

I was Persephone being claimed by Hades, and I had no choice but to enter his underworld and become his dark queen.

23

HANNAH

L ilith and I grabbed a few fancy appetizers to eat at the buffet, and I was grateful to her for sticking by my side even though she didn't know me at all—at least, not in this life. As an introvert, parties were hard enough. Add in the fact that I was the lone human at a ball full of demons and it was hard not to run back to the penthouse as fast as I could.

"Ah, there's my son now," Lilith said, raising her hand to wave him over.

The man who approached could only be described as sex on a stick. With dark hair, bronze skin, and muscles galore, he looked like some kind of international model on a billboard somewhere. He wore a plain black mask and a black suit, oozing sex appeal with every step, although he didn't make my heart flutter the way Lucifer did. He looked like the kind of guy you had one crazy, unbelievable night with, and then never saw again. In that Fuck, Marry, Kill game he'd be Fuck every time.

Unless you're Brandy, maybe.

"Hannah, this is Asmodeus," Lilith said.

He reached out to take my hand, then bowed a little and brushed his lips against my knuckles, sending tingles through me. I hoped Lucifer wasn't looking, or Asmodeus might be flying against the wall soon. "An honor," he said, his husky voice sliding along my skin like silk.

I nearly fanned myself. Shit, I needed a cold shower after five seconds in his presence. How had Brandy withstood a *week* of this? No wonder Lucifer had said there was no way she could have resisted leaving the bar with him.

"I've heard a lot about you," I said, after extricating my hand.

"All bad things, I hope?" he said with a wink.

I laughed, unable to resist his charm. "Things I had a hard time believing until now."

Lilith pressed her hand to Asmodeus's face. "Have you been feeding? You still look a bit weak from your ordeal. I'm sure any number of demons here tonight would be happy to help."

He pulled away. "I'm fine, mother."

"All right, dear." She ruffled his hair with obvious love, then excused herself to speak to someone else, leaving me alone with the incubus.

"You're Brandy's friend." He said it as a statement, his

voice becoming more serious. "I've heard a lot about you too, and it seems I owe you my thanks."

I shrugged, the action making my shimmering cloak flutter. "All I did was nudge Lucifer in the right direction."

"You're a good friend. Brandy is very fond of you." The way he said her name made me think he cared for Brandy too.

I remembered how she spoke of him at the spa. "I'm not the only one she's fond of..."

His shoulders stiffened and pain crossed his green eyes. "Brandy is special, but it's impossible for the two of us to be together. She knows that."

"Maybe, but I know Brandy better than anyone and she's never backed down from a challenge. She's also never spoken of any other guy the way she spoke about you."

He studied me. "May I tell you a secret?"

Err...me? I'd met the guy two minutes ago. But I nodded. "Of course."

He closed his eyes as if in pain and let out a shuddering breath. "I haven't slept with anyone since meeting Brandy. My parents want me to feed, and I know I need to, or I'll die. But I can't. I don't want anyone but her."

"But you can't have sex with her?"

"Only once, and then never again. Not without killing her."

"Is there no way around that?"

"No, there isn't. Unless..." He trailed off and looked across the room, his gaze landing on his mother. "There might be a way. But I'd have to give up everything. For a human I barely know."

I spread my hands. "I can't tell you what to do. All I know is that Brandy would love to see you again. Maybe all you'll have is one crazy, wild night together that you remember for the rest of your lives. Or maybe you both decide you want more and find a way to make it work. Either way, you should go to her."

"I think you're right," he said, his voice distant. Then he took my hands and bowed slightly. "Thank you, my queen. I always did appreciate your wise counsel. It's good you're back."

My mouth fell open. "You're welcome?"

He straightened the cuffs on his shirt. "I have a long drive ahead of me. I better get going."

"Give my love to Brandy."

With a nod, he vanished into the crowd, and I hoped I'd done the right thing. There was obviously something there between the two of them, and if nothing else they needed to get some sort of closure. Hopefully they'd be able to find a way to be together too.

And now I was alone again. I scanned the crowd for Lucifer, but didn't see him anywhere. Plastering a pleasant expression on my face, I worked my way to the edge of the room, nodding at people I didn't know and shaking more hands than I wanted to think about. The darkness along the walls was deeper, but there was also an area with tables. My feet throbbed in my heels, and I collapsed gratefully into the chair closest to the wall, then slipped off the expensive, sky-high heels.

Being a human among demons was intense to say the least, but it was far easier to handle from over here. The other guests barely paid any attention to the edges of the room, focusing all of their attention inward instead to observe each other, sometimes with suspicion gleaming in their eyes from behind those masks. It made for great people watching, though. *Demon* watching.

A small group sat at the table behind me, their faces shrouded in darkness. As I listened, relying on my mask to disguise exactly where I was looking, I learned that the demons were scandalized by some new woman who was half demon and half angel but was favored by Lucifer, and I was just leaning into the details of the story when a rough voice nearby caught my attention.

"It's true then. Lucifer's woman has returned."

"She's human though." The second person snickered. "We'll see how long she lasts."

My pulse kicked up a notch at their words. I glanced over, peering into the shadows and trying to make my movements so small that no one would notice my focus had shifted to the new conversation. I got a glimpse of a huge man with a red and gold mask. Mammon.

"Not long," he said. "Things are already in motion. Many of the Archdemons are involved. Soon Lucifer will be defeated, and it will be time to return to Hell."

His words were enough to strike fear in my heart. I had to tell Lucifer immediately. I bent to slip my shoes back on, then took a deep, fortifying breath and threw myself into the crowd. I darted between demons, trying to get to the center of the room so I could find Lucifer and warn him about Mammon.

When I was almost halfway there, one of the spotlights swung around and beamed down on Lucifer. I caught my breath at the sight of him, shadows playing across his face and his eyes burning with power. He stood in front of his throne and turned in a slow circle. A silver crown graced his head, throwing off fragments of the light as he moved, and it fit him as if he'd been born to wear it. The room quieted as everyone gave their attention to their king.

His commanding voice rang across the ballroom. "Someone in this very room has been plotting to overthrow me. Trying to take what is mine."

At first I assumed he meant his throne, but then his gaze found me in the crowd, like a caress only I could feel.

He meant me. I was the thing he considered *his*.

"All traitors will be punished." As he spoke, another spotlight illuminated the corner of the room, near where I'd been sitting, where Gadreel and Samael now led out four demons. I wasn't sure what kind they were, but I had a sneaking suspicion these were the demons involved in the attacks that had been captured.

The demons were pushed down so they knelt in front of Lucifer, facing the audience. Their faces were drawn with lines of tension and their hands were bound behind their backs, but otherwise they appeared uninjured. I could barely look into their eyes. Pure fear glimmered there as shadows began to snake round them. Like even the darkness was toying with them.

Lucifer began to pace slowly behind the traitors as he spoke. "These four—an imp, a dragon, a gargoyle, and a shifter—were all caught in plots against me. Tonight they will be punished."

I expected the audience to react in some way, but it seemed like everyone in the crowd was holding their breath, too terrified to move. Me included.

"I have been Demon King for thousands of years." Lucifer's voice boomed around the ballroom, echoing from the walls I couldn't see. "Though many have tried to over-throw me, all have failed. There's a reason I'm the King. Perhaps you all need a reminder?"

Then he bowed his head and took a deep, controlled breath. His shadowy black wings erupted behind his body, and I gaped at him along with everyone else in the ballroom. Tendrils of black, smoky energy crept around him coalescing and growing thicker, until they almost looked like inky black, swirling solids. I stepped forward, moving care-fully through the crowd again as the lines of black shadow wrapped around each of the demon's necks. Nobody moved but me.

"I do not tolerate insubordination." Lucifer snapped his fingers, and suddenly bright blue flame erupted from the darkness wrapped around the demons. The traitors screamed as the unnatural blue fire consumed them, lighting the room with eerie, flickering light. Everyone gasped, their faces paling, their mouths falling agape, but nobody stepped forward. I heard a few people whispering in shocked voices about hellfire, as the four demons turned to ash before our eyes.

Then the entire room bowed as one, lowering to knees of submission on the floor, until I was the only one besides Lucifer standing. I stared at him in horror as he surveyed the people kneeling before him, his wings spread wide with darkness trailing off them like mist.

He'd just...killed them. Right there, in front of everyone. And his people *bowed*. My breathing came in shallow, fast pants, and my dress felt like it was tightening around me, constricting my chest until I had no space for air.

Lucifer's gaze met mine with a dark smile, and he was triumphant. Proud. His eyes glowed red as he looked at me like he was encouraging my pleasure as well.

Because I was his queen.

And the worst thing was...a part of me wanted to smile back. To applaud him for what he'd done. They'd kidnapped Brandy. They'd threatened my lover. They'd tried to kill me. They deserved retribution.

As soon as everyone was upright again, I used their cover to take off running, sliding between bodies and moving as fast as I could while staying upright in my heels. My chest heaved as nausea roiled through me and my heart practically leaped out of my body. I made it to the elevator without anyone stopping me, but when I pressed the button, it wouldn't light up. Turning to see if anyone was trying to follow me, I noticed a door off to the right. With a fluorescent glow behind a small window, I realized what it was. A stairwell. Even demons needed an emergency exit.

I burst through the door and slipped my heels off, holding the skirt of the gorgeous gown as I sprinted up the stairs, my legs pumping and my lungs threatening to burst. We were a few flights down from the parking garage, and I shoved through the doors, then raced across the lot in my bare feet until I found another door leading to another stairwell outside. I had to get the fuck out of here.

As I stepped out into a side alley, I gulped in the fresh night air as panic threatened to overtake me. I'd known he was the devil. He'd said he was a villain. What had I expected? That he'd be someone different with me? Had I willfully ignored his dark side, or had I craved it? He'd never been anything but honest with me about what he was, but I'd been drawn to him anyway. He should have inspired fear in me rather than lust. But that was his job, after all. Temptation. *Sin.*

It didn't matter. The deal was over anyway. Tonight was the seventh night—Devil's Night—and I was done. Maybe I was Lucifer's reincarnated love, and maybe I wasn't, but either way, it was time to return to my real life. I didn't belong here. Not in this fancy hotel, not in these expensive clothes, and definitely not with the demons.

I put the shoes back on, not about to walk barefoot in a Las Vegas alley full of broken bottles and old piss. Then I pretended my feet weren't on fire as I shoved my panic to one side and summoned enough confidence to walk a straight line. No way I was going back in that hotel. I had a tiny little purse with a wad of cash and my phone in it, and that was enough to get me home.

A flash of light exploded nearby, the force and shock nearly knocking me over. A pair of gleaming copper wings were highlighted against the dark night sky, swooping down toward me, and in my already-panicked state I screamed. Strong hands grabbed me, lifting me up...and then everything went black.

24

LUCIFER

As I surveyed the room, taking in my followers and their show of loyalty, I wore a dark smile, my eyes glowing red. I hated doing shit like this, but it was necessary. A show of force to ensure they all knew I was their king. Demons needed a firm hand. Whatever this newfound conspiracy was, someone would come forward rather than risk my wrath. Then it would be settled. This shit had happened before and would happen again, and I'd deal with it every time.

Before I became king, the demonic tribes fought each other. When I left Heaven for Hell, I united the tribes under my banner, bringing order to the chaos. If it weren't for me, the vampires and shifters would still be at war, the dragons would still be slaves to the fae, and let's not forget the angels, who would have wiped out the lot of them if they'd had a chance. No matter how heavy my crown became, I never forgot that someone needed to rule the demonic horde, and it sure as shit had better be me.

Besides, I'd do whatever it took to save Hannah's life. If a show of force was needed to prevent more attacks and show she was completely off-limits, so be it.

As everyone rose and the music began playing again, I sank down on my throne, waiting for Hannah to join me. I should have made them bring a second throne out for her, but they'd planned this night before she'd come back into my life. If she was still alive for the next ball, I'd make sure she reigned at my side.

The demons and Fallen went back to their conversations and I gazed around the room, searching for a glimpse of Hannah. I'd seen her briefly, but then she'd been swallowed by the crowd. I noticed Gadreel flirting with Lilith, whose smile was tight and her eyes wandered, like she'd rather be anywhere else. He'd always had a thing for her, but who didn't at some point? And Gadreel had always been ambitious. It was one of the reasons I'd thought he was interested in Lenore too.

I rose to my feet and people hushed around me as I scanned the crowd. Where was Hannah? Earlier she'd been sitting at the side tables, but she wasn't there now. Nor was she with Gadreel and Lilith, or Samael in the corner, or at the buffet or the bar. I didn't see Azazel either, who was meant to stay on Hannah's tail all night.

My chest tightened in panic. Where could Hannah have gone? Had someone taken her? Was I about to lose her again?

Clenching my fists, I strode through the crowd. They parted in front of me, out of respect or fear, and a quick search confirmed Hannah wasn't in the ballroom anymore. I went to the elevator, wondering if she'd retreated to the penthouse, but it wasn't working for some reason. Someone was going to pay for that later.

My heart beat faster as I launched through the door to the stairwell and took the steps two at a time, up a few flights to the parking garage. I looked left and right as I reached the top, taking in the empty space, and spotted a tiny crystal on the ground in the distance. From Hannah's dress. She'd definitely come this way.

Maybe she hadn't been taken. Maybe she had run away.

Was she upset by what she'd seen in there? Killing enemies was par for the course among supernaturals, but she still thought like a human. Dammit. I'd forgotten she was mortal, and how sensitive humans were to death and violence. She remembered nothing of her previous lives, which meant all of this was new to her. I'd only known her for seven days, and that wasn't nearly enough for the truth about who she was to sink in. No wonder she'd panicked. She'd started the week meeting Lucas Ifer to beg for help in finding her lost friend, and she'd finished at a demon's ball where Lucifer himself had killed traitors in front of her.

Before I could tame my thoughts, Azazel ran around the corner, wearing a short leather dress with blades strapped to her thighs. "Hannah!" She stopped and sucked in a breath, her eyes wide. "She's been taken!"

"What happened?" I grabbed her shoulders and held

her firmly at arm's length as I searched her wild gaze. Azazel never panicked, but there was definitely something that had her spooked.

"I kept my eyes on Hannah all night, staying close to her from the shadows. When you executed those traitors, she freaked out and split. She ran for the elevator, but it didn't come."

"Then what?" I tried to keep my own panic from increasing. There weren't many places I couldn't rescue Hannah from. Except death.

"She ran up the stairs and took off walking through the alley. I followed in the shadows from a safe distance. She clearly needed to be alone, and I tried to respect that."

My grip tightened on her shoulders. "And then?"

"An angel swooped down and picked her up before I could get close enough to stop them. I tried to go after them, but I was hit with a blast of light, stronger than I expected." She ripped herself out of my arms, her eyes furious—and upset too. "It knocked me back, and I lost them."

"Tell me exactly what you saw." Perhaps I could work out which of my Heavenly brethren would be so bold. Why would they take Hannah? Were the angels making a play against me?

"Copper wings. Female. I couldn't see any other details." She shook her head, her face tormented. "I'm sorry, my lord. It was my duty to protect Hannah and I failed. I accept whatever punishment you deem fitting."

I stepped back, seething. Copper wings... I knew an

angel like that. What I didn't know was why she would want Hannah.

Azazel kept her head bowed, awaiting my command. She'd been ordered to guard Hannah and she'd failed, and now my mate had been kidnapped. She should be punished for her failure, and she knew it. But Hannah wouldn't want that. I felt that in my gut.

I turned away from her. "You are dismissed, Azazel."

"My lord?"

"I think I know who took Hannah." My eyes narrowed as red hot anger pulsed through my veins. "And I will handle this myself."

25

HANNAH

My head swam as I tried to pry my eyes open, but they were so heavy. Eventually, I managed to get them to crack open. The room was blessedly dark, curtains pulled tight, though a sliver of light filtered through. It was daytime, but where was I?

Something didn't feel right. This didn't smell like my lightly perfumed room in the penthouse, where even the expensive fabrics had a scent all their own. And it definitely wasn't Lucifer's room with his decadent black silk sheets.

I sat up in bed and rubbed my eyes. I was in another luxurious bedroom, tastefully done in shades of cream and dusky pink. The enormous room was sparsely furnished, but it had more of a deliberate minimalist vibe than feeling half-finished, and I was struck by the sheer size of the space. If I yelled out, it would echo. As I let my brain wake up and recover from the night before, I took in the smooth wood dresser and intricate sconces on the walls, both painted the same shade of pink. It was like waking up on the inside of a strawberry cream dessert.

This certainly didn't look like Lucifer's style. Not when I remembered all the black and silver that filled his spaces or the very safe neutrals that his guest room boasted. Where was I?

The bedroom door opened, and sunlight filled the room from the hall on the other side, putting whoever had opened the door in shadow. The person flicked the overhead light on, and the room illuminated. It took me a second to realize who had walked in while my eyes adjusted to the unexpected brightness.

When I saw the person holding a breakfast tray, my jaw dropped. "Jo? What are you doing here?"

My older sister gave me a droll look. "I live here."

I watched her walk around the bed, barely believing what I was seeing. Jo looked like her normal, beautiful self, with hair almost the same shade as mine that ended just above her shoulders. She'd always had a grace and sophistication I could never match, with her billowy frame and radiant skin. Even her nails were shiny and perfect. Pink, naturally.

"You're safe." She set the tray in front of me and poured us both some coffee. The situation felt strangely familiar, and eerily close to when I'd woken up in my apartment after the car wreck. My mind tried to piece together what had happened last night, but everything was fuzzy after

Lucifer's display. But as my brain cleared and the coffee worked, I remembered more.

Someone had grabbed me in the alley of The Celestial. Someone with wings. Someone who knocked me out.

Someone who looked a lot like Jo.

I scooted back in the bed, suddenly desperate to put distance between us, not caring that the tray wobbled as I moved. Was no one as they appeared anymore? And why the hell could everyone fly?

"How do you have wings?" My tone was accusing, but I couldn't help it. For fuck's sake, my own sister—the last family member I had left—had knocked me out and kidnapped me. I was allowed to be a little upset. "Are you a Fallen too?"

She drew back and huffed, visibly offended. "Of course not. I'm an angel."

"An angel?" That didn't make me feel any better somehow, and it made no sense. "How is my sister an angel when I'm human?"

She sighed and seemed to choose her words carefully. "We were sisters in one of your former lives, when you were an angel. I've tried to protect you ever since."

I stared at her, the weight of her revelation almost more than I could handle after all the other things I'd endured in the last week. Was *everything* about my life a lie? Was I nothing but a collection of past lives, with people and events I couldn't remember, while everyone else could? I wanted to bury my head in the pillow and scream.

Jo must have sensed my inner turmoil because she stood.

"Take your time and rest. Eat some breakfast. The shower is through that door, and the closet is beside it. I've put a few things in there you can wear." She moved to the door, lingering there as she twisted her hands together. "Come see me whenever you're ready."

She left me alone, which was a relief because I needed time to get my head on straight. I was still in my ball gown, and it was wrinkled to high heavens. Hopefully not ruined.

I was starving too, since all I'd eaten last night were a few fancy appetizers, and I devoured the omelet Jo had brought me. Then I took a quick shower and quickly dressed in a cream blouse and navy blue slacks that were obviously Jo's. Now that I was fully awake, I wanted answers from my so-called 'sister.'

I found Jo in the living room, a massive space all done in white and gold, with huge windows offering spectacular views of the bay, from the Golden Gate Bridge to Alcatraz Island. I automatically moved toward them, pressing my fingertips on the glass as I looked out. We were up on a hill, and a view like this, in a house this enormous, had to have cost a fortune.

I turned toward my sister. "Shit, Jo. I knew you had money, but..."

"I do all right for myself." She sat on a soft-looking sofa and watched me like I was an injured deer about to bolt away. "You've never been here, have you?"

I didn't reply. She knew fully well I'd never been here. If I had, maybe I wouldn't have been as overwhelmed by Lucifer's shows of wealth. I'd offered to come visit her numerous times in San Francisco, but she'd always made some kind of excuse, and had come to see me instead. Had she been hiding this from me, maybe even purposefully keeping me away to protect her secrets? Was anything about her true?

"Well, you're here now." She gave me an encouraging smile. "And I'm glad to have you as my guest."

Was I her guest? Or was I a captive again? I moved through the vast living room, taking in all the displays of wealth. Her aesthetic was the exact opposite of Lucifer's, with white trimmed in gold, and just like his place, it was seriously lacking in plants and flowers. A display case held dozens of tiny little angel figurines, some looking quite old, others made of crystal. I studied them as I asked, "Why did you bring me here?"

Jo clasped her hands in her lap as she looked up at me. "I had to get you away from Lucifer. You're in danger around him. As long as you stay here, I can keep you safe."

"Jo, you don't understand. Lucifer is my mate. I've had all these past lives with him. He isn't a threat to me." Or was he? After what I'd seen last night, I wasn't so sure.

"I understand more than you do. I've lived an awfully long time, and I've seen many of those past lives of yours. What you don't understand is that Lucifer is the villain. He's been lying to you this entire time. Manipulating you. Controlling you. As he's done with all humans for thousands of years." She tilted her head, her eyes full of pity. "Did he even tell you about Adam and Eve?"

I hated to admit there was something Lucifer hadn't told

me, but I had to know what she was talking about. "No, he didn't."

Her mouth took on a sad smile. "I thought not. Why am I not surprised somehow?"

Her superior tone grated at me. This particular tone was so familiar that it must've bugged me in one of my lives before, and my subconscious knew it. I tried not to glare at her. "What about Adam and Eve?"

"Your very first life was as Eve."

My heart skipped a beat, or maybe even stopped for a full minute. "*The* Eve?"

"Yes, the very one."

I blinked at her several times as I tried to process this new revelation. "How?"

"You were married to Adam and had three sons with him, but then Lucifer abducted you and claimed you as his mate. Adam wasn't happy about that, as you can imagine, and he sought revenge. He killed you."

I blew out a breath as I processed everything she'd said. Hearing about my past lives was always a combination of difficult and intriguing, but this one was especially hard for me to believe, if not for the sense of rightness in my gut when she spoke.

A week ago I'd been book-loving Hannah from the florist shop. Now I was Eve. Persephone. Lenore. All great women from literature and mythology. Talk about a heavy legacy to live up to.

I dropped onto the couch across from Jo. "That is pretty

shocking, but I don't see why that puts me in danger from Lucifer."

The pitying look in her eyes increased ten-fold. "There's more. I'm just not sure you're ready to hear it yet."

"Just tell me already," I snapped. Damn, I was so tired of everyone knowing the truth about myself except for me.

"After your death, all three of you were cursed for all eternity. Your fate is to be reborn and die violently, usually in Lucifer's arms, in an endless cycle of death and agony. Lucifer's curse is knowing this will happen and being unable to stop it. And Adam's curse is to be reborn every time you are...and to kill you again and again, before dying at Lucifer's hand."

"No, that...that can't be true." I recoiled in horror, my pulse spiking through the roof. It was suddenly hard to breathe, but I managed to suck in a ragged breath somehow.

Jo came to sit beside me and rested a warm hand on my back. "I'm so sorry, Hannah. I wish it wasn't true. But deep down you know it is, don't you?"

I nodded, but then my head dropped and my vision blurred. I found myself in Jo's arms, leaning against her as she held me close, like she had in those early days after the car accident. Like she was still my sister.

Why hadn't Lucifer told me any of this? He'd been slowly doling out information to try to stop me from getting overwhelmed, but this seemed important. Maybe he was right though—this was really fucking overwhelming.

Or maybe he worried I wouldn't live long enough for it to matter.

Was that what was happening here? Was it time for me to die now that I'd found Lucifer again?

And where was Adam in this life? Were all the attacks his doing?

"Who cursed us?" I asked, gripping Jo's shirt as I looked up at her with wide, desperate eyes. "Is there a way to end it?"

"I don't know," Jo said, as she drew me into a hug again. "I wish I did."

An endless cycle of death and agony. That was my fate. And there was no way to escape it.

26

HANNAH

Once again, I found myself in a vast library, although this one wasn't as impressive as Lucifer's. Jo had a large collection of books, but she lacked the ancient vases and dark artwork that made Lucifer's library so remarkable.

I'd retreated here after speaking with Jo, when everything she'd told me had just seemed too big and impossible. When life became too much, the best solution was to retreat into a good book, or turn to them in the hopes of finding answers.

With a book on demonology in my lap, I sat in a white suede chair near windows overlooking the bay. The sun had turned the sky the entire range of reds, golds, and yellows as it sank down to the horizon. Sunset on Halloween, and not at all where I'd expected to be.

I'd spent the last few hours reading up on angels, demons, and the devil. I'd perused everything from Dante's

Inferno to some ancient scrolls Jo had that required me to use gloves. Every single thing I read depicted the devil as evil incarnate. A beast. A monster. In every story of good and evil throughout all time he was the villain.

How could I have been so wrong about Lucifer? Had he been deceiving me, tricking me into caring for him? How could I reconcile the man I knew in private with the one I'd read about in these books, or the dark king I'd seen at the Devil's Night ball?

Was Lucifer the root of all evil, or the thoughtful, protective man who'd do anything for me? Was he the villain in this story, or the one keeping the demons in line and the humans safe from them?

Unfortunately, coming to the library had only saddled me with more questions this time.

The doorbell rang, and I decided that was a sign I should take a break anyway. I headed for the front door, just as Jo ran in with a sword in her hand and a fierce look in her eye.

"Don't open that!" she yelled. "It might be someone after you."

"I doubt they'd ring the doorbell if they were trying to kill me," I muttered.

Jo checked the security camera and lowered her sword, then grabbed a bowl shaped like a pumpkin sitting by the door. "Just some kids. I forgot it was Halloween."

With a chuckle, I opened the door to a trio of trick-or-treaters. One of them was dressed as a little red devil, to my great amusement, though Jo's tight smile told me she didn't feel the same. We dropped some candy in their bags and then they scampered off to the next house. I smiled after them, enjoying the brief moment of normalcy.

As I turned away and began to close the door, it suddenly slammed open, crashing against the wall. Something cold and dark passed through me, and when Jo and I whirled around, Lucifer stood behind us. His black wings were spread wide as darkness swirled around him and his eyes blazed red. Shadows played across his face and his hands were clenched in fists at his side. He looked pissed as hell, and my traitorous heart beat faster and filled me with longing.

His gaze raked over me, like he was checking I was unharmed, before they landed on Jo. The entire room got darker and colder, like his anger was sucking all light and warmth from the surroundings. Jo raised her sword, which now glowed white, while Lucifer conjured a shadowy blade of his own made of pure darkness. Then he surged forward toward her.

With my heart in my throat I dodged in front of him, blocking Jo with my body, certain that neither of them would hurt me. "Stop!" I yelled. "That's my sister!"

Lucifer drew back, his inky dark sword held high as he looked from me to Jo. "How is that possible?"

"It was in one of my past lives," I explained, though it hit me then that Lucifer should probably know that... Shouldn't he?

They stared at each other with hard expressions, until some sort of understanding passed between them, but that only made him angrier. His voice grew so loud it shook the walls. "Did you do what I think you did?"

"I had to," Jo said. "All I want is to protect her. From Adam. From you." She pointed her glowing sword at him. "It's always you!"

"I'm her mate!" he roared.

I watched them like I was a spectator at a tennis match, back and forth as they yelled and exchanged meaningful looks. There was clearly a lot more to this story than either of them had told me. I wanted to snatch away both their swords and give them each a time-out.

I held up my hands between them. "I wish someone would let me in on what the *fuck* you're both talking about! I'm sick of everyone hiding things from me. Can I have the whole truth, please? And put your damn weapons away already!"

Lucifer's darkness blade disappeared like vanishing smoke. He spread his hands and bowed his head, as if to say he'd play nice. I looked at Jo and narrowed my eyes a little. She sighed and put her sword on the entry table.

"May I have a moment alone with Hannah?" Lucifer asked. I was surprised by how polite his voice had become. "I promise I won't steal her away."

"Absolutely not," Jo declared. "Out of the question."

I turned to her. "I'll be fine. I spent a week with him and I'm unharmed, aren't I? And if I want answers, how else can I get them if I don't talk to him?"

"Fine." She huffed as she narrowed her eyes at Lucifer

over my shoulder. "You can use the library, but I'll be in the living room. And leave the door open!"

I rolled my eyes. What was I, a teenager with her first boyfriend?

I led Lucifer into the library, where he eyed all the books I'd pulled out. He picked up the copy of Dante's Inferno and snorted, shaking his head as he tossed it back in the pile.

"I see you've been doing some research," he said, his voice dripping with disdain.

"Is it true?" I asked in a low voice. "Am I Eve?"

"Yes, it's true." He arched an eyebrow. "What else did Jophiel tell you?"

"Jophiel?" To me she'd always been Jo. I'd just assumed it was short for Joanna all this time. Now I was beginning to realize I didn't know a single thing about her.

"Indeed. Your 'sister' is an Archangel. Did she mention that?"

I pinched the bridge of my nose, trying to contain my frustration. "No, she left that part out."

"Of course she did." He reached for me, but I quickly stepped back, and he paused. "Are you afraid of me?"

"No, I just..." I turned away and drew in a breath. "I have a lot of questions."

He sank down in the chair I was sitting in earlier and leaned back, then gestured lazily at me. "Ask away, darling."

"Is it true that I was married to Adam before you? That you abducted me and made me your mate?"

He let out a sharp laugh. "Abducted is a strong word. Trust me, you weren't happy being married to Adam. He was still in love with his first wife, Lilith, and he had a horrible temper. He's the kind of man who charms you with flowers, poems, and promises, and only once he has you in his grasp does he reveal his dark side."

"And you're not the same?"

"No, I'm completely up front about my villainous nature." He smirked at me as he leaned forward. "You ran away with me to escape Adam."

I swallowed hard. "But he followed us. And then...he killed me."

Lucifer's eyes darkened. "He did."

"And this curse? Is that real too?" I clenched my throat, suddenly finding it hard to breathe. "Is my fate to die over and over at Adam's hand?"

He rose to his feet and stepped toward me, with pain and sadness written across his face. "I wish I could tell you that wasn't true, but I never lie to you, Hannah." He reached up to touch my cheek, and this time I didn't flinch away. "I've watched you die hundreds of times, and each time my heart shatters into a million pieces. My only solace is that I know one day you'll return to me, but it's little comfort as you take your last breath in my arms." Darkness swirled around him like angry tentacles. "And then I usually rip that fucker's heart out."

An endless cycle of love and death, for all eternity. I blinked back the emotions threatening to drown me. "Why didn't you tell me?"

He brushed his thumb under my eye, catching a tear before it fell. "It wasn't the right time. You were just beginning to accept the supernatural world and your place in it as my mate. How could I add this burden on top of everything else? I planned to tell you about the curse eventually, but only when you were ready."

"I'm not sure it's possible to ever be ready for a revelation like this." I drew in a ragged breath. "Do you know where Adam is now? Do you think he's behind the attacks?"

"I don't know." Tension tightened the corners of Lucifer's mouth. "My people have been looking for him, but haven't found anything yet. All we know is that he must be human, since he's reborn in a pair with you. It seems unlikely he could be behind the attacks unless he's sided with some of the Archdemons somehow. Though he has gotten very crafty over the years..." His voice trailed off as he considered, but then he met my eyes again. "It's more likely the Archdemons are trying to overthrow me again. It happens now and then, but my display at the ball should make them reconsider."

I shuddered a little at the memory. The darkness holding the traitors in place, the blue hellfire that turned them to ash, the way everyone bowed... And the worst part of all, how it had secretly thrilled me, deep down, to see them punished.

"It bothered you, I see," he said, cocking his head. "When I couldn't find you at the ball, I feared the worst, but then I suspected you might have run away. I was almost relieved when I'd learned Jophiel had taken you."

"I *did* run away." I stepped back from him, my eyes wide. "I'm not sure what to make of you, Lucifer. History doesn't exactly paint you in the best light. And in every one of these—" I indicated my large pile of books. "They tell the same story, over and over—that the devil is the personification of evil."

"They also say I have horns and a pitchfork, and that's obviously not true." He cast a dismissive glance at my pile of books. "History was written by the angels, who have long sought control over Earth. They've hated me ever since I rebuffed their control and fought for humans to have free will. They paint me as the villain, making me their scapegoat, blaming all evil on me. As if any one person could have such power."

He sounded bitter, but there was something else in his voice too. Vulnerability. Pain. Despite all my hesitations and fears, my heart ached for him. If he was telling the truth and they'd made him out to be this horrible monster that he wasn't, that was incredibly sad. It would be a hard life to live, and lonely too. Especially in the long years while he waited for me to be reborn.

But was Lucifer telling the truth? Or was he deceiving me? I couldn't tell. I'd learned so much about myself and the world over the past eight days, but I wasn't sure of anything anymore.

"Lucifer I... I need some time to think."

He moved close and touched my face again, with the lightest of caresses. "I know this is a lot for you to take in, but it will all make sense in time. Come back with me to the penthouse. You know in your soul we're meant to be together, even if you're uncertain about everything else. Your place is by my side, ruling as my dark queen."

I pulled back, out of his grip, and shook my head. "I'm not ready for that. It's too much. Please just...give me some space for now."

"You want me to leave."

"Yes. Go. Please. Before this gets any harder."

He searched my eyes, like he didn't want to believe what I was saying, but then he bowed his head and stepped back. Without another word, thick darkness swirled around him, the shadows dancing and claiming him as their king.

When it cleared, he was gone.

27

LUCIFER

S pace. Hannah wanted *space*.

Fine. I could give her that. For now.

But that didn't mean my business here was finished.

Using my power to become darkness, I slipped through Jophiel's extravagant house until I found her office. White walls, white distressed desk, white chair... What a bore Jophiel was. If she hadn't been an Archangel and the CEO of Aether Industries, she'd hardly be worth my notice. Except now it seemed she was apparently Hannah's sister, though that was impossible. To my knowledge, Hannah had never been an angel in any of her past lives, and she certainly wasn't one now. Her wings would have long emerged by now if she had been—plus I would have sensed it.

I pushed back Jophiel's white chair and sat in it, then kicked my feet up on her desk, knowing the sight of me invading her space would drive her mad. It only took a few minutes of playing on my phone before she arrived.

She jumped when she saw me at her desk, and then her eyes narrowed with a look of pure, unadulterated hatred. "What do you want?"

The sight of her made my blood boil too, but I flashed her a devilish smile. "I want the truth. Isn't that your area of expertise?"

Her mouth twitched at that. As an Ofanim, Jophiel was an angel of truth...and was one of the best at concealing it. All Archangels had a special, unique power—and Jophiel's allowed her to erase or hide memories. "The truth will only hurt Hannah."

"I'll be the one to decide that." I rose from her desk slowly, the shadows gathering behind me like menacing wings. "You stole some of my memories, didn't you? Of a past life where Hannah was an angel. And your sister, apparently. Now you're going to put them back."

She raised her haughty little nose. "Why should I?"

I turned to shadow for a split second to glide through the desk, then I grabbed her by the throat while my eyes turned red with rage. "Because I demand it."

We stared each other down, her body glowing with light and power as she faced me. The high and mighty Jophiel and I had never gotten along. For years, she'd blamed me for killing her former lover, Archangel Michael, even though I never would've done such a thing. He and I had once been enemies, that much was true, but we'd worked too hard to end the war and establish peace between angels and demons. Why would I kill him after all that effort? His death nearly undid the treaties as it was. Now we knew Archangel Azrael was behind Michael's death, and he was in Penumbra Prison—a place where the angels, demons, and fae kept the worst supernaturals locked up. Yet she still hated me.

"I don't take orders from you," she finally gritted out.

I tightened my fingers around her throat, my darkness filling the room like ink. "Not even you can resist an order from the devil."

"Villain," she muttered. "All you do is lie and kill."

I arched an eyebrow. "Enlighten me on the truth then. You know I didn't kill Michael."

"But you did kill my father!"

I rolled my eyes. Not that old excuse for her continued behavior. "Phanuel attacked me, as you well know. It was self-defense and we were at war then. We aren't any longer."

That only made her glare harder at me. "Not at war? Tell that to the angels and demons who died at Seraphim Academy last year."

"We both know that was Azrael's doing." I cocked my head. "Wasn't he your former lover as well? I heard the other Archangels have been suspicious about your loyalties lately."

"My loyalties are to other angels and to my family," she snapped. "Including Hannah. It's your fault she's doomed to die, over and over. I won't let you hurt her again."

I sensed she was talking about something specific, something from this past life of Hannah's that I couldn't remember. My anger exploded and wrapped inky darkness around her. "Show me," I demanded, and even the Archangel Jophiel couldn't deny a command from the King of Hell.

She finally relented with a sharp nod, and I let go of her. She drew in a ragged breath and then reached up to touch my forehead. Light burst in front of my eyes and warmth flooded my skull, radiating out from Jophiel's touch as memories rushed through my mind. My anger washed away, replaced with a potent mix of happiness, pain, and grief, and I nearly stumbled under the weight of it. Within seconds I was hit with everything from the relief of finding my mate alive again, to the joy of being with her every moment I could, to the heartbreak of losing her.

I stepped back and bent over, gripping my head, as the memories consumed me. Our first meeting, our first kiss, our first time making love. Long talks into the night where she made me question my beliefs. Flying together, her wings silvery white against the moonlight. And then losing her in a way too painful to even focus on.

When all of it faded to a bearable level, I was left with the true knowledge of Hannah's angelic life, and what the two of us had shared together.

And everything we'd lost.

My anger returned with greater fervor than before, making it hard for me to even think. An entire life with Hannah had been erased from my memories by Jophiel, who had no right to do such a thing. I held myself tense as I spoke through gritted teeth, then lifted my red eyes to

Jophiel again. "How dare you? You've hidden this from me for years. Not to mention what you did to Hannah..."

"I only did it to protect her!" Jophiel said, as she stepped back from my rising darkness. There was nowhere for her to go. Her back hit the door and she glowed brighter, but she wasn't a fighter. Not really. We both knew she had no chance against me.

"I should make you pay for what you've done." My magic gathered around me as my wings unfurled, my darkness eager to do my bidding. I breathed through it, the desire to lash out and punish her for her actions almost overwhelming every other thought in my head. It would be so easy to let the darkness tear her apart limb by limb, a fitting punishment for her crimes, which I now knew went above and beyond erasing memories. But then I thought of Hannah in the other room, and the way she'd jumped in front of me to save this wretched angel. No matter what Jophiel had done, they were sisters, and I couldn't hurt her.

I reined in my dark desires with effort. When I folded my wings and snapped them away, the shadows receded. "I won't punish you." Then I smiled, and not in a nice way. "No, I'll let Hannah do that when she learns what you've done."

Jophiel shuddered a little, but then looked me in the eye. "We both know my actions have kept her alive this long. Leave Hannah here with me. I can protect her better than you can."

"Never," I growled. "Her place is by my side."

The second I said the words, doubt crept in. Perhaps the

angels could do a better job of keeping Hannah safe. I'd done a shit job at it for thousands of years, after all. This newly remembered life of hers only proved that even more. Every time she was reborn, I swore to myself I'd protect her and that this time it would be different, and then I failed. Over and over.

My memories weighed heavily on me as though they were as fresh as the day they were created, and though I detested Jophiel, I knew she would protect Hannah with her life. Yet I couldn't give up my mate completely either.

I moved to the window beside Jophiel's desk. "I'll leave Hannah with you...for now. But when she wishes to return to me, you must allow her to do so."

She sniffed, back to being haughty. "Shall we make a deal for her time, like you did with Demeter over Persephone?"

I should have known she'd get in one last jab by reminding me of that mistake. "I'm done making deals."

I pinned her with a dark look, before turning to shadows once again and heading outside, into the night. I hovered there, invisible to any mortal who might look up at the sky, as I watched Hannah through the library windows.

Children walked along the street below me in their costumes, many of them dressed as the creatures of the night I ruled over, while Hannah leafed through book after book. Reading about me, no doubt.

Halloween had always been my favorite of Earth's holidays—a night when everyone embraced their inner wickedness and allowed themselves to love the darkness. Tonight though, it was me who was haunted.

My chest ached as I watched Hannah, wishing I could go to her, but doing my best to respect her wishes. I reached out as though I could touch her, imagining her soft skin under my fingertips, then clenched my hand into a fist. Damn this curse. It had killed her hundreds of times, putting her through so much agony, more than any one mind could possibly bear. No wonder she could only see glimpses of her past in her dreams. Anything more would shatter her mind. And me? The curse had destroyed me emotionally over and over, hundreds of times throughout the years, and would continue to destroy me still.

Could I go through this again? Could she? How many more times must we suffer?

Perhaps it was time to end this curse...but I didn't know if I could bring myself to do the only thing that would stop it.

The price was far too high. A sacrifice, and one I'm not sure I could make.

28

HANNAH

S unlight wanted me to wake up, but I clamped my pillow over my head and ignored the bright, shining ball of fire in the sky. After Lucifer had left, I'd sat at the table in the library, reading about angels and demons until well into the night. When my eyelids had started drooping, I'd come to lie down in the bedroom Jo had let me use, hoping that staying up so late would help me sleep better.

I should have known that wouldn't work. It never did.

Violence had crowded my dreams, and what I now knew were events from my past lives had echoed through my head, leaving me sweaty, rumpled, and still tired. Gadreel had been in one of them, wielding a sword, presumably from my life as Lenore. I didn't remember any of the other dreams except in snippets that disappeared like fog when I tried to chase them.

No matter how hard I tried, I couldn't get back to sleep.

I rolled over and groaned. In all the time since the accident, only when I slept beside Lucifer had I slept well.

Lucifer... My heart ached at the thought of him. After only a few days of knowing him, I already missed his presence, even though I wasn't sure how I felt about him. Or what my place in the world was anymore.

When I walked into the huge, white, gleaming kitchen, Jo looked up in surprise. "I was just about to wake you. I made breakfast, if you're hungry. Eggs, bacon, and toast."

"Thanks," I mumbled, as I headed straight for the coffee pot. I still wasn't happy with my 'sister,' and I couldn't pretend otherwise. She'd hidden so much from me, and I suspected there were so many more things she hadn't told me yet. But she was an angel...one of the good guys? Right? Or was that a lie too?

"You made the right choice by staying here," Jo said with a self-righteous smile, as she made up a plate for me. "I can protect you from Lucifer."

I grabbed the plate from her hand, annoyed at her words, but also hungry. Did I need protection from Lucifer or from her? Jo—*Jophiel*—wasn't even my real sister, and she'd lied to me for years.

"Is anything about my life real?" I asked, as I sat at her round breakfast table.

Jo took a chair across from me. "Our relationship is real. That's never been fake."

"But you're an Archangel!" I sputtered, then glanced around the house, which was like something out of an HGTV show about mansions I could never afford. "I'm only realizing now how little I knew about your life. How separate you kept me from it. How you knew all this time I was Lucifer's mate and didn't tell me."

"Only to keep you safe." She spread her hands out on the table. "Hannah, I had to keep my life separate from yours to protect you. If you came to visit me, for example, you might attract the attention of others in the supernatural world, which I knew could lead Lucifer and Adam to you. But if you went about your life believing you were an ordinary human, you'd remain hidden."

I was getting tired of everyone knowing the truth except for me and using the excuse of trying to keep me safe like it absolved them of all their crimes. But at the same time, maybe I was alive now because of Jophiel's actions.

"What about the accident? My parents?"

Jophiel's face turned pained. "Your parents are dead. I didn't lie about that."

I sensed that was true, at least. I took a moment to eat some of my food, which was delicious. I wondered if Jophiel had really made it. I'd never seen her cook before.

"You can stay with me as long as you like," Jophiel continued, a smile lighting her face. "Now that you know about the supernatural world, I no longer have to hide things from you. I can tell you all about your life as an angel. Oh, you can even meet my sons!"

I nearly choked on my bacon. "Sons?"

She nodded, her eyes proud. "Yes, I have two of them. Callan and Ekariel. Callan is the son of Archangel Michael and Ekariel is the son of Archangel Azrael, though I hope you won't hold that against him..."

The more Jophiel talked, the more I felt like she was a stranger, and like my entire life was a lie. The only thing that felt real anymore was the time I'd spent with Lucifer. How did that make sense?

I pushed my plate away and buried my face in my hands. "All I want is to go back to my old life of a week ago, when I was just Hannah who worked at a flower shop and lived in Vista. Hannah, who didn't know about angels and demons and past lives, and had no one trying to kill her. But that's impossible now. There's no forgetting this."

Jophiel rested a light hand on my back, as if to comfort me. "Actually, it is possible. I can remove your memories and make you forget all of this ever happened. I could hide you from both Lucifer and Adam. You could go back to being an ordinary human again who knows nothing of the supernatural world."

I looked up at her. "How?"

"It's one of my angelic gifts."

The idea was tempting, but only for a second. I shook my head with a sigh. "No, I don't really want to forget. I don't think it's possible to run away or hide from this anymore. This is my life, my curse, and my fate. I have to accept it. Somehow." I drew in a ragged breath, but then sat up straighter. "And I will. Eventually."

"And then you'll die again and start all over," Jophiel said, her voice sorrowful. "I don't want to lose you, Hannah.

I realize you feel like you don't know who I am anymore, but to me, you're still my sister and I love you."

I started to say the words back to her too, but I couldn't get them out. I didn't know how I felt about anything at the moment. Especially her.

From across the house came the faint sound of my phone ringing, saving me from having to answer Jophiel. I set the coffee mug down and hurried to the guest room just in time to see Brandy's name flash across the screen.

"Hey Brandy." I glanced at the hallway, out where Jophiel was, and decided to step onto the balcony. "Are you okay?"

"I'm fine. Good, actually. How are *you* though? I've been texting you, but you haven't answered. I got worried and had to resort to actually using my phone to make a call, ick."

I laughed, and it was so nice to have a moment of levity after the events of the last few days. Damn, I missed Brandy and her cheerful, stubborn exuberance. No matter how much life shit on her, she always found a reason to smile.

"Things are...complicated," I admitted. "I've learned a lot of things over the last few days that have made me question my entire life."

"What sort of things?"

I leaned against the balcony railing and stared across the bay covered with wispy fog, while the cool air tickled my hair. "Things like I'm supposedly Lucifer's soulmate. And I've lived hundreds of lives before this one."

"What? Like some reincarnation thing?"

"Exactly like that. Lucifer finds me in each life, but our happiness never lasts."

Brandy let out a low whistle. "That's some deep shit right there."

"No kidding. I'm at my sister's house now. Which is also complicated." I blew out a breath, suddenly really tired of my problems. "Tell me what's been going on with you. Did you get home safely? How's Jack? And Donna?"

"They're both good, and yes, I got home fine. Lucifer made sure of that. He also paid all our bills for this month and the next, to cover the time off we both had to take from work. I could hardly believe it."

"I had no idea." I pressed a hand to my chest as the longing for Lucifer became so strong it actually hurt. It was just like him to do something like that, without even telling me.

"I thought I was done with demons," Brandy continued. "I told myself it was for the best, too. But I couldn't stop thinking about Mo, I mean, Asmodeus. Then he showed up at my front door in the middle of the night. He said the two of you talked, and then he got in his car immediately to come see me. So whatever you said to him, thank you."

"I just told him he should talk to you. The rest was all him."

"And we did talk, and so much more..." She giggled, like she was sharing a naughty secret. "Let's just say the Lilim's reputation as sex demons is well-deserved. Then he went trick-or-treating with me and Jack. Can you believe that?"

It was hard to imagine Asmodeus going trick-or-treating

with a little kid, but it definitely proved he cared a lot for her, and made me like him even more. "Asmodeus said there might be a way for you to be together?"

"He told me the same thing, but it sounds dangerous. He's gone back to Vegas to speak to his mother about it." She let out a dreamy sigh. "It's crazy but...I think he's the one. Maybe this soulmates stuff is actually real. I mean, I never in a million years would've guessed I'd fall for a demon, or that they even existed, but here we are."

I stared across the bay, though my heart was somewhere else entirely. "I know exactly how you feel."

"Do you?" Brandy asked. "Because if so, then what the fuck are you doing at your sister's house?"

I bit out a laugh at her bluntness. "Like I said, it's complicated." I closed my eyes as my voice lowered to almost a whisper. "He's the *devil*, Brandy. Red eyes. Black wings. Hellfire. The actual devil."

"Well, no man is perfect."

"I'm serious. I've... I've seen him kill people."

She was silent for a moment. "Did they deserve it?"

I chewed on my lip as I considered. "One was involved in your kidnapping. The others tried to kill me."

"Then you have your answer. He was protecting his family in the only way he knew how. Just like you did when you came to Vegas to find me."

"That's not really the same thing..."

Her voice softened. "Hannah, you have the best heart of anyone I know. Follow it, and I know it won't lead you astray."

My throat choked up a little at her kind words. Jophiel may call herself my sister, but Brandy was the one who'd always been there for me and never kept secrets. She was the true sister of my heart. If she thought I should give Lucifer another shot, even after knowing everything we did about demons, then maybe I wasn't crazy for wanting the same thing.

"I love you," I told her, my pulse racing faster as I made my decision. "And I'm going to follow my heart. Back to Vegas."

"I love you too, and you better call me and tell me everything that happens."

"I will, I promise. Say hi to Jack and Donna. I'm not sure when I'll be back."

"As long as Lucifer keeps paying your bills, it's not a problem," she said, with a joking tone. "But seriously. I won't ever forget what you did for me. I've got your back, no matter what happens."

"Thanks, Brandy."

We said our goodbyes and hung up, promising to keep each other updated. I wanted to hear what happened with Asmodeus too, and if they found a way to be together. But first I had to get back to Lucifer. I wasn't sure about much of anything anymore, except that I only felt like myself when I was by his side. Maybe he was a villain to the rest of the world, but to me, he'd always been a hero.

I went inside and put back on the sparkling black gown and uncomfortable heels from the ball, leaving Jo's clothes behind. Then I shoved my phone back in my tiny little purse and checked my cash. I had plenty to cover gas money and a pair of flip-flops, because no way was I driving for hours in these freaking heels.

I stepped out into the hallway and glanced around, but didn't see or hear Jophiel anywhere. I considered finding her and explaining that I had to go, but I honestly wasn't sure she'd let me leave. She'd try anything to make me stay. Anything to prevent me from returning to Vegas—to Lucifer.

But fuck that. This was my life, and I was taking control of it.

Yesterday Jophiel had given me a brief tour of her gigantic mansion, including her four-car garage, and that's where I was headed now. Once there, I found a panel by the door that had a row of key fobs, which no doubt unlocked one of the ridiculously expensive cars before me. I took a moment to eye up the cars—a burgundy Porsche SUV, a black classic Rolls Royce, a yellow Lamborghini, and a silver Audi—and then grabbed a pair of keys. I rushed over to the Lamborghini, because when you're stealing a car from your angelic 'sister', you might as well go big.

When I got on the street, I found the button to put the top down and cranked the radio. My hair blew out behind me, immediately getting tangled up, and I kicked off the heels and tossed them to the passenger seat.

Vegas, I was coming for you. Consequences be damned.

29

LUCIFER

After my encounter with Jophiel, I returned to Vegas, keeping my word to give Hannah some space even though it tore me apart to do so. Besides, my people still needed a king, and Samael said he wished to speak with me. I had some questions for him too.

The sun had barely risen by the time I arrived in his office. He was on his computer, completely absorbed in whatever he was looking at, but he glanced up sharply as I entered.

"Did you find Hannah?" he asked.

"Yes, she was taken by Jophiel." I slammed my hands down on his desk, making him jump. "The Archangel gave me back my memories. Turns out, my mate was once an angel, and we were together before the Earth Accords were signed, when our relationship was forbidden. No one knew about us, except Jophiel...and my most trusted advisor."

Samael's chair squeaked as he rolled back and looked at me in alarm. "Lucifer, I can explain—"

I clenched my teeth. "You kept this a secret for years. Why didn't you say anything?"

"I thought the pain would be too intense. I thought it might be better if you didn't know. Less agonizing. For both you and Hannah." The look on his face, the twist to his mouth, said he was tortured by the decision, but that only made me angrier.

"Keeping those secrets was not your decision to make." I kept the desk between us, or I would've been too tempted to grab his throat like I'd done with Jophiel. "Did you set up Brandy's kidnapping to bring Hannah back to me? Are you behind the attacks on my mate's life?"

He held his hands up in supplication. "Of course not. I wanted to keep Hannah away from you, not bring you together. I assumed Jophiel had her hidden somewhere, but that suited my ends. It kept you both safe and alive."

"Not safe enough. Someone found her and brought her here." I fixed him with a glare as I asked questions I'd never wanted to voice. "Have you ever thought about taking my place? Or becoming the leader of the Fallen?"

He drew his shoulders back. "I'm offended you would even ask me such a thing. I've been your closest friend for thousands of years and have always served you well. You're questioning my loyalty when I've never given you any reason to do so."

"You're the only other person who knew about Hannah's life as an angel. What was I supposed to think?"

"There is someone else who knew. Adam." Samael returned to his desk and took a seat. "That's why I asked you to meet me, actually. At the ball, Gadreel told me he'd tracked down a human who might be Adam."

"Where?"

"He didn't say."

I took the chair across from Samael and stroked the rough stubble on my chin as I considered this news, my gut telling me something wasn't right. I scoured my memories, including the ones Jophiel had just returned to me.

When Eve had been reborn as an angel, I'd believed only Samael knew about our relationship, but maybe I was wrong. Maybe someone else knew too. I'd never found Adam in that life—normally I tracked him down and killed him as retribution for what he'd done to my mate, but Jophiel intervened first and took my memories. I never even knew what he looked like. Could he still be alive?

In every life, Adam was reincarnated as a pair with Eve. If she was born human, so was he. Except when she was Lenore. The one who'd killed her was an angel, according to Gadreel. When I'd found them, there'd been a dead angel beside her, his sword covered in her blood, and I'd simply assumed that the curse didn't differentiate between an angel and a Fallen.

But what if it did?

Now someone had lured Hannah to Las Vegas, for the sake of bringing her back to me. Why? Just to take her away again, knowing it would hurt me more now that we'd found each other. But how?

My mind followed the trail of clues. Asmodeus said he'd received a text from Samael ordering him to seduce her, but Samael claimed he'd never sent it. It had to be someone close to us, someone who knew too much, who had access to everything.

Someone like Samael's assistant.

Someone who spent too much time chasing both Lenore and Lilith.

Gadreel.

Could it be? Could Gadreel be Adam? Had he somehow defied the curse and stayed alive when Eve was reincarnated again and again?

I leaned forward, anger simmering under my skin. "Where is Gadreel now?"

Samael's mouth tightened. "I haven't seen him since the ball."

Darkness swirled around me. My fury couldn't be contained, and with it came fear for Hannah's life. She was in more danger than I'd realized. "Find him, and bring him to me. Now."

30

HANNAH

The drive from San Francisco to Las Vegas took way longer than I expected, and even with only a few quick stops, it took me the entire day to get there. By the time I rushed up to Lucifer's penthouse, night had fallen and The Celestial was waking up. Vegas truly was a perfect city for demons, where most of the action happened after dark.

I found Lucifer in his library sitting behind his desk, a glass of whiskey beside him and an ancient-looking tome in his hands. He rose to his feet as soon as he saw me, and my heart skipped a beat as our eyes met and I was hit with the full force of his magnetic presence. Then he quickly crossed the room in a few long strides and swept me into his strong arms. Before I knew what was happening, his mouth came down on mine and he kissed me hard, as if he hadn't seen me in years, while his fingers tangled in my hair like he was never going to let me go. My hands gripped his soft white shirt while his tongue swept against mine and I wondered how I ever thought I could live without this man.

My *mate*.

"You came back to me." He pulled back just enough to study my face. "You had us all worried."

I was still dazed from his kiss and it took a second for his words to register. "Worried?"

"Jophiel texted me when you drove off with her car. Nice choice, by the way." His lips quirked up in amusement as his thumb idly stroked my cheek. "Both of our people have been looking for you ever since. You shouldn't have driven all that way without anyone protecting you."

I shook my head. "Lucifer, I can't live in fear all the time. I may be cursed to die, but I'm ready to accept my life by your side. For however long we have."

"Even though I'm a villain? A monster? The root of all evil?" His eyes gleamed red as he spoke, as if he were challenging me to run away again.

I reached up to stroke his eyebrows and the dark stubble on his jaw while I gazed at him, accepting him completely, red eyes and all. "I don't care how the world sees you. You're not evil. Not to me."

He gripped my arms tightly. "Only because of you. Your light keeps me from turning completely to darkness. I would be lost without you."

I trailed my fingers down his neck. "I'm here. I'm yours."

He closed his eyes and inhaled sharply. "Say it again."

Sliding a hand behind his neck, I drew his face down to

mine and brushed my lips across his. "I'm yours."

"Yes, you are." He yanked me against him and turned my soft kiss into something much more, something that made red hot desire race across my skin. "Across the vastness of time, you're the one thing that stays mine."

My heart beat faster with his words and his touch, my need for him becoming overwhelming. I quickly unbuttoned the top of his shirt, while his hands skimmed down my black, sparkling gown. The gown I'd worn to the ball as his guest. As his queen.

"You're still wearing this dress." He unclasped the attached sheer cloak, and it billowed to the floor. "I love seeing it on you."

I smoothed my hand down the front of it. "It's probably ruined now."

"It's perfect. Just like you."

He drew the gown above my head, and I raised my arms, delighting in the feel of the silky fabric drawing across my skin and leaving it exposed to the cooler air. When I lowered my arms, Lucifer's gaze raked down my body like a caress. Then he unclasped my bra, freeing my breasts, and I loved the way he looked at them with fire in his eyes. Like he'd never seen anything he wanted more.

He took a step toward me and the dark hunger in his gaze made me tremble. He took each of my breasts in his strong, masculine hands, feeling the weight of them, rubbing his thumbs along my taut nipples. Then he lowered his mouth to one of them, tasting me with a slow lick that made me moan. His mouth thoroughly explored my breasts, his rough stubble grazing my sensitive skin and leaving the slightest burn behind. I wanted that burn to continue all over me. I wanted Lucifer's fire to consume me.

After sliding his fingers across my midriff with agonizing slowness, he slid my panties down. His fingers tickled along my thigh, leaving a path of desire from my pussy to my toes. Ready to explode from the heat and desire coursing through me, I ground against him, desperate for a little relief from the ache inside. My fingers fumbled for his trousers, yanking them open, searching for his cock. It didn't disappoint as it sprung forward, and I wrapped a hand around it, savoring the feel of his size and length in my palm.

With one arm, Lucifer shoved everything off his desk, the ancient texts falling unheeded onto the floor, before he gripped my hips and set me on the edge of it. Then he dug his fingers into my thighs and pulled my legs far apart, exposing my wet folds to him.

He slowly kneeled in front of me. "It's been far too long since I tasted you."

"It's only been a few days," I said with a delirious laugh.

His tongue slid along my slit, one long, slow stroke before he looked back up at me. "Exactly. Far too long."

He lowered his head again and I moaned and grabbed his hair as he dipped his tongue inside my pussy, pushing until he filled my entrance with wet warmth. He fucked me like that with his tongue, driving me wild, and then suddenly moved to take my clit into his mouth. He hummed, the vibrations teasing while I writhed on the edge of his desk.

He kept a firm hand on my hips but adjusted so his arms wrapped completely around my thighs, holding me in place. He spread my pussy open and sucked my clit harder, causing me to cry out in earnest as I begged and moaned. My hips tried to thrust against his mouth as he took me higher and higher. With my hands planted on the desk behind me, all I could do was throw my head back and chase the pleasure as it built, my every nerve tingling in anticipation. But then he stopped.

"No." Lucifer pulled back and let go of my thighs. "Not yet."

"Lucifer," I begged. "Please."

He rose to his full height, then gripped his perfect cock and stroked it slowly, making my mouth water. When I was about to drop to my knees and start begging, he stepped forward and continued his torment by sliding his cock up and down my folds, getting the head slick with my desire. I whimpered a little, and a satisfied smile crossed his face at my desperation. When he looked at me like that, I knew exactly why they called him the devil.

When I couldn't stand a second longer of his teasing, his cock pushed inside me, and it was everything I needed. Thick, hard, and long, a perfect fit for me, like we'd been designed as a pair. He went slow this time, drawing out each thrust and retreat, and I felt every single inch as he moved inside me. He teased my breasts and stared into my eyes the entire time, watching my reaction when he stroked and pinched, when he plunged in deeper, when he claimed me again and again.

Then he pushed me back so I lay flat on the desk, and he grabbed my legs and lifted them up, hooking them over his shoulders. The position allowed him to sink even deeper into me, and put me completely in his control. All I could do was take what he was giving me.

His hips began to roll and lift in a slow, sensual rhythm, his cock hitting me in spots I never knew existed. With one hand he held me in place, and with the other he rubbed my clit, knowing the exact way to touch me to make me lose my mind. Of course he did. He'd been making love to me for centuries, whereas this was all new to me.

"Tell me you're mine and I'll let you come," he said, his voice rough with lust.

"I'm yours," I managed to gasp. "Always yours."

He moved harder and faster, hitting that spot over and over while he teased my clit, and the pressure built until I couldn't hold back any longer. Just as I began to tighten around him, he dropped my legs and reached down to slide one hand under my head to grip my hair. As the orgasm swept through me, he tugged my body up to press against his chest, then claimed my mouth with a rough kiss. He kept thrusting into me the entire time he came inside me, and all I could do was moan into his mouth against the delicious tug of his hand in my hair, while he drew out every last second of my orgasm.

He held me close against him, and I buried my face in his neck as our hearts raced together. Our breathing slowed to a normal rate, but he didn't let me go.

"Don't leave me again," he said, though it sounded more like a plea than a demand.

"I won't," I promised, as I took his face in my hands and stared into his shockingly green eyes. My favorite color, and only now did I realize why.

"You will," he said, with a sharp intake of breath. "You always do."

My chest tightened at the inevitability in his words. "And you always find me again."

"I'm not sure how much longer I can do that," he confessed. "Each time you die, I lose another part of my soul."

"We have no other choice." I stroked his face. "Not even death can keep us apart. Somehow we'll find a way to be together, no matter how much time or distance comes between us."

"Not even death," he muttered, his eyes turning distant.

"What is it?" I asked.

He finally pulled back from me and picked up the ancient books on the floor. "I need to do a little research. I'll join you in the bedroom shortly."

I stretched in a way that drew his eyes back to my naked body. "All right. I could really use a shower after my long drive."

He gave me a quick kiss, but I could tell his mind was elsewhere already. He sat behind his desk, cracking open one of the old books, and I watched him for a moment, wondering what research could be so important...and why his mood had shifted so suddenly.

31

LUCIFER

S he'd returned to me. I'd hoped for it, but I wasn't sure it would happen before the curse struck again and we began the cycle of love and death once more. A cycle I had grown weary of, but wasn't sure we could escape.

While my people had been searching for Hannah, I'd been going through Samael's old journals in Aramaic, the ones he'd written to document the ancient days. In those thin, cracked pages he described the curse as it happened, and once again I scoured the tome hoping for answers, but found nothing I didn't already know. There was only one way to break the curse, but it would destroy us both. And possibly the entire world with us.

Could I make the ultimate sacrifice?

For her, I would do just about anything... Except this, perhaps.

I quickly sent off a few texts anyway, calling in a few favors. Now I had to wait.

While I drummed my fingers on the cover of one of Samael's journals, Hannah returned to the library, her hair wet from her shower. Now she wore one of the slinky nightgowns I'd bought her, which just begged to be pushed up to her thighs or even ripped off completely.

She covered a yawn with her hand. "Quit reading those old books and come to bed already."

"Yes, dear," I said, as I rose to my feet. I'd worry about breaking the curse tomorrow. And find Gadreel, while I was at it. Where was that bastard now? I took Hannah's hand, realizing she didn't know about him yet. "There's something I need to tell you."

"I suspect there's still a lot you need to tell me." Then her eyes widened. "Actually, there's something I need to tell you too. Something I heard at the ball. I completely forgot about it until now, but—"

Her words were interrupted by a loud crash outside the library. I immediately shoved Hannah behind me, while shouting broke out from the entrance of the penthouse. Was it Gadreel?

I turned to Hannah and took her face in my hands. "Stay in the library. You'll be safer here."

She nodded, her eyes wide with fear, and I kissed her deeply, fearing it might be the last time. She hugged me tight and then I headed out of the library, closing the door behind me. Without any windows, the library was the safest place in the penthouse for Hannah at the moment, and I had to deal with whoever was invading my lair.

I rushed through the living room, and from the corner of my eye I spotted dark shapes outside my windows flying back and forth in ominous patterns. I had no time to worry about that though, because at the entrance of my penthouse stood a tall, hulking man with hands turned into reptilian claws, now dripping with blood.

The blood of my guards.

"Mammon," I growled, as I surveyed what he'd done. All of my hand-picked, loyal guards lay dead at his feet. "So you're the one behind all this."

The ancient Archdemon of the dragons let out a haughty laugh. "Hardly. I'm but the first of many who want your downfall."

I drew my darkness around me, preparing to fight. "Then you'll have the honor of being the first to die."

He let out a massive roar, making the floors and window shake, and dragonfire burst out of his mouth. I smothered it quickly with my darkness, almost offended. He should know better than to think that would work.

"Why?" I asked. "Has your greed overcome you? You think you can steal my throne and be the next Demon King?"

"It's time for someone else to lead the demons." He swiped at me with his claws, and I easily dodged and avoided them, my movements flowing like smoke around him. "You never should have forced us to abandon Hell. It was our *home*."

"A home that could no longer sustain us," I reminded him.

He ignored me as he kept attacking, knocking over all my furniture in the process. "And a truce? With *angels*? Come now Lucifer, surely you didn't think that would work."

"You'd rather we kept fighting forever, while our numbers dwindled to nothing?" I cringed as he threw a chair into my bar, destroying dozens of bottles of my finest alcohol. "I did everything to save our people. The future of our race was at stake."

"*Our* race? You're not even a real demon!" He blasted me with another mouthful of dragonfire, which I blocked with a wall of darkness. His face began to redden, his frustration becoming obvious. "Angels never belonged in Hell. Once we rid ourselves of all the Fallen, we'll reopen Hell and begin to rebuild it."

We'd neared the huge windows overlooking Vegas now, and I had a clear view of the battle going on outside. My dark-winged Fallen angels fought in the skies against both dragon and gargoyle attackers, with blasts of fire and shields of darkness fighting for dominance of the air. I spotted both Azazel and Samael out there, but no sign of Gadreel anywhere.

"You plan on destroying all the Fallen?" I asked, cocking my head. "But what of Gadreel? Isn't he working with you?"

Mammon snorted. "Gadreel is nothing but a tool the Archdemons have used to weaken you. He gave us the information we needed, but he's a pawn. An inside man, if you will. He serves us, like all your Fallen will soon. They'll be on their knees before the Archdemons, where they belong... or they'll be dead. Along with you."

His threats against my people made rage boil up inside me. "I am the true Demon King, and you will kneel!"

With a wave of darkness, I pushed Mammon through the windows into the night sky and launched after him, my dark wings spreading as I dove. Blood red scales slithered across his skin as his own wings erupted, his body shifting into his massive dragon form faster than I expected.

We wove and dodged through the sky amid the other fighters, though they gave us a wide berth. Mammon scraped at me with his enormous claws, but I pulled back, trying to avoid the pointed tips. He was too fast though, and one of the massive claws caught me, gouging a jagged split from my collar bone to my abdomen.

I went into a spin as I fell toward the city streets below. Pain washed through me, but the darkness forced my body to heal, and I fought for control over my flight. My wings beat strongly, lifting me back up, chasing the man who dared lead a revolt against me, who dared endanger Hannah.

He banked and whirled, flying high over the city lights, above the fighting around us. Pushing out my wings, I soared upward as fast as I could, and moved just in time as a blast of orange dragonfire erupted from Mammon's mouth, the heat intense even over the distance.

He'd left himself vulnerable by spewing the fire. It took him precious seconds to coordinate his massive body for movement, and while he swung his head to try to locate my position, I made my way around him. I dropped onto his back, almost grateful for the opportunity to rest a moment while my body burned with the effort of healing. His leathery wings beat against the night air as he fought against the sudden addition of my weight.

Dragon hides were nearly impossible to penetrate due to their scales, but I pushed my darkness into his ears, his eyes, his nostrils, choking him. I wished for a moment I had my sword, Morningstar, but it was in the library with Hannah. Probably for the best. Instead I unleashed my hellfire, bright blue and charged with the magic of both Heaven and Hell, fueled by both light and darkness. A gift I rarely used because it was so destructive, and one that only I possessed. Well, along with Belial, but I hadn't seen him in years.

In a desperate move, Mammon dropped from the sky, unseating me as his weight plummeted from underneath me. He spun frantically, trying to put out the hellfire, the only kind of fire that could harm him. It went out, but I'd managed to injure him at least.

I followed him down, but he banked again and maneuvered around me. Staying on his tail, I chased him high into the air, before I got close enough to sling out my darkness like a whip and wrap it around the base of his wings. I yanked hard, and the popping of his wing joints reverberated through the sky like thunder and skittered along the threads of my dark magic.

He plunged from the sky as he tried to escape, but I made sure my threads of darkness held his wings just enough so that he couldn't move. Pointing myself downward, I flung my feet onto his chest and held my darkness like a rope, pulling on his wings while letting another tendril of magic wrap around his throat. We kept falling, but I controlled it with my wings as Mammon struggled underneath me.

"You can't kill me," I said, glaring into Mammon's eyes. "Concede defeat and I'll let you live."

"Never," he growled, baring his fangs. "Even if you stop me, there will be others. This is just the beginning, Lucifer. You have no idea what's coming. For you and your little bitch."

Fury consumed me at his words. He could insult and threaten me all he wanted, but now he'd insulted Hannah, and I was done playing around.

Narrowing my eyes, I unleashed my hellfire again, the destructive magic rippling over his scales like lightning and tearing him apart. He let out a mighty roar as it consumed him, dragonfire spewing from his mouth in every direction, and I snapped my wings, sending me backwards and away from him. He lit up the night like a display of fireworks, until all that was left were his ashes as they blew away in the wind.

At his death, the other dragons below us let out a wailing roar, and then they loped away, giving up the fight. The remaining gargoyles hurried after them on their bat-like wings, the battle over. It surprised me to see it hadn't been just my Fallen fighting the gargoyles and dragons, but a few angels had joined the battle—the ones I'd texted earlier. I hadn't expected them to respond so soon, and I began flying toward them.

A scream and a crash from inside the penthouse struck me with sudden terror. Dread filled my chest as I rushed toward more battle sounds and noises of struggle echoing from the library—where I'd left Hannah.

32

HANNAH

L ucifer had been gone for only a few seconds before I grabbed the sword off the wall—the same one I'd used against the gargoyles, the one I seemed able to use without even thinking about it. Lucifer's sword, from back when he'd been an angel. Hopefully nobody would come into the library, but I had to defend myself if they did. Assuming I remembered how to fight again.

Long minutes passed by, and the noises outside the library filled me with fear and anxiety, including guttural roars that made the floor shake. Then I heard a huge crash as if the windows were shattering, like they'd done during the gargoyle attack, and I couldn't wait any longer. I had to know if Lucifer was okay.

I threw open the door and ran out, swallowing hard at the sight of the penthouse torn apart again and some of the walls scorched with fire. Outside, Fallen angels clashed against gargoyles and dragons, while fire lashed across the night sky. I wondered if any humans in the hotel or down on the ground could see this, and if they thought it was another Vegas attraction. The magic of Sin City. If only they knew what *really* happened in Vegas.

Then Lucifer flew into view, and my heart pounded harder as he fought a red dragon a good three times his size. Was that Mammon? Dammit, I should have warned him earlier about what I'd heard at the ball, but it had slipped my mind after Jophiel kidnapped me. I gasped as Lucifer streaked upward, far out of my sight, chasing the dragon. I ran for the balcony, my slippers crunching on broken glass, hoping to see where they went.

My only warning of approaching danger was a faint whisper behind me. My instincts took over, and I whirled in time to yank up Lucifer's blade and slice through tendrils of shadow magic that had been about to grab me.

The sword glowed bright white as Gadreel stepped forward out of the darkness. His grim smile sent tremors of terror through my heart, especially when he squared off, pointing a sword at me that looked similar to mine, except it blazed with darkness instead of light.

As Gadreel and I shifted positions, like we were about to dance, I prayed my muscle memory would hold and that I was a good enough swordswoman to match Gadreel.

"Why are you doing this?" I asked. "I thought we were friends! Or at least we were, back when I was Lenore."

He slashed forward, on the offensive, and I blocked him with my glowing sword. We weren't fully fighting, not yet.

He wanted to feel me out. Probably checking to see if I had enough fight in me in this body. Asshole, I had plenty.

"You know why," he said, his voice cold. All traces of fun-loving Gadreel were gone, leaving a stranger in his place. "Deep down, you've always known my true identity. Haven't you?"

I nearly dropped the sword as clarity swept through me. My hands trembled and I stepped back, but I managed to whisper his name. "Adam."

A cruel smile spread across his handsome face. "I've come for you, my wife. As I always do."

I leveled the glowing sword at him. "Stay away from me!"

His face darkened, and he attacked again. I had to dance and move quickly to block him. As we fought, we dodged upended furniture and broken glass, unintentionally moving back toward the library. The battle was balanced, and somehow I knew in my bones that this was a fight we'd fought a hundred times before. An exhausting thought that lent a feeling of inevitability to all of it. Was it even possible for me to win against him? Or would he strike me down just as Lucifer returned?

"Jophiel thought she could hide you, but I always find you," Gadreel snapped. "You belong to *me*, Eve, not Lucifer."

He found me... My jaw dropped, though I kept my sword raised. "Did you have Brandy kidnapped?"

He inclined his head slightly, with pride shining in his eyes. "I knew it would bring you to me."

"Why not just kill me in Vista? That seems a lot easier."

"Where's the fun in that?" He gave me a maniacal grin as he advanced, making me step back. "No, it's much more satisfying to bring you to Lucifer and give you some time to fall in love again, so it hurts him even more when I take you away. Like he stole you from me."

"Lucifer is my mate, not you," I shot back at him, as I stepped into the library. "I don't even know you!"

He looked oddly hurt at that. "How do you not remember me? *Me?* After everything I've done to you?"

The way he said it made me want to vomit, but I had an idea. "What if I left Lucifer for you? Would that make you stop?"

He let out a horrible, menacing laugh as he came toward me. "Oh, Eve, you're the same in every life. You think you haven't tried that before?"

Damn. I was out of moves. Except as he drew closer, I grabbed the vase of Hades and Persephone, silently saying an apology to the long-dead artist, and threw it at Gadreel's head. It hit him perfectly, using precise aim I didn't know I possessed, shattering into a hundred pieces. Giving me just enough time to stab him in the shoulder with the light blade. He screamed and stumbled back, like he was on fire. I already knew from the gargoyle attack that the blade seemed to do extra damage to demons—and Fallen too, apparently.

His dark blade glanced downward as he cradled the wound, and I used the second of vulnerability to my advantage. Darting forward, I sank my blade into Gadreel's chest, driving it into his heart as his eyes widened with shock. The sword's white light increased, shining between us.

I gave him a triumphant smile. "Never expected me to kill you for once, did you?"

I yanked out the sword with a twist and stepped back. He rocked forward, clutching at his heart as he sank to his knees. He hit the floor hard, and I pressed a hand to my chest, sucking in a deep breath and trying to calm my racing heart.

Holy shit. I'd killed Gadreel.

Adam was dead. Was the curse broken?

Then a horrible laugh came from his body, even as his blood spread across the floor. Like some kind of zombie, he forced himself up off the floor with a groan. Ripping his shirt apart, Gadreel proudly displayed his chest, and I watched in confusion as the torn flesh and skin knitted back together.

I stumbled back, shaking my head, fear gripping my throat. "How?"

"Oh, Eve, don't you remember? Thanks to the curse, I can't be killed as long as you're alive. We're a pair in life and death." He stepped forward again, shadowy blade in hand. His eyes had changed. They were wild before, but now they were six steps past that. He'd gone totally dark. Pure evil.

"Together forever," he whispered, and terror rushed through me.

I tried to move, but I wasn't quick enough. I lifted my blade, but the dark swinging sword came at me so fast, with so much fury, all I could do was surrender to the inevitable. At least I would be reborn again.

The library door blasted open, breaking off its hinges, and a shield of darkness flew up around me, blocking Gadreel's attack. Lucifer strode through, his eyes blazing red, his shadowy wings fully extended. He crossed the room to me in a blur of darkness and threw me behind him, protecting me from any further attacks with his own body.

Gadreel took one look at Lucifer and paled, the color draining from his face. He turned and sprinted toward the broken library door, sweeping Lucifer's old book from the desk as he darted by—the one Lucifer had been reading when I'd found him earlier.

In the living room, glass shattered and fell toward The Strip below as Gadreel launched through the last remaining windows with a burst of energy and force I hadn't expected. His pale gray wings carried him into the night, and I almost expected Lucifer to go after him, but he turned to me instead.

His red eyes faded back to green as he held my shoulders and scanned me from head to toe. Probably searching for signs of blood or other injuries. "Are you hurt?"

"No, I'm fine." I threw myself into Lucifer's strong arms. "I'm so glad you're okay. When I saw you out there fighting a dragon, I feared the worst."

He held me close against him, running his hand up and down my back. "It was Mammon. He and some of the other Archdemons have been plotting against me, and they're working with Gadreel. He's Adam, you know."

"Yeah, I figured that part out," I said with a slight shudder.

"I was about to tell you when we were attacked." He looked in the direction of the library and his frown deepened. "And now he has Samael's journals. This is bad. Very bad."

With a ripple of magic, Lucifer's darkness snaked out and flipped over one of the leather couches. It had large gashes in it, like it had been shredded with huge claws, but he sat on it anyway. Then he sighed before rubbing his hands over his face—the most defeated I'd seen him.

I sank down beside him. "Why is that bad? What was in that book?"

"It's an account of what happened long ago, written by Samael. I was going through it to see if there was a way to break the curse. But there's more in that book. A lot more." Lucifer turned his gaze toward the window, looking in the direction Gadreel had flown off in. "And now Adam has it."

"I killed him." The fight played over in my head, and fear gripped my throat again. "But he didn't die. He said he can't die while I'm alive. Why didn't you tell me that part of the curse?"

Lucifer took my hand, turning it over as he looked at my skin, as if committing me to memory. "I assumed Jophiel told you about it."

"She must have left that part out." I had a feeling she'd left a lot of things out.

He wrapped an arm around me and held me close, and I leaned against him until the shock of the attack slowly receded. But when it did, I was left with a horrible dread for the next time it would happen. And the next, and the next...

"We have to end the curse," I said quietly. "I can't keep doing this. Living and dying, over and over. Finding you and losing you again and again. Living in fear of the day Adam would end my life once more." I turned toward him, but he was staring off into space, his brow furrowed. "Did you find a way to break the curse in Samael's notes?"

"Yes, there is a way." His dark gaze lifted and his eyes met mine, but now they were hard. Cold. A little terrifying. "But there's a price. There's always a price."

"Whatever it is, I'll pay it," I said, though a flicker of doubt lodged in my chest.

"Will you?" He let out a haunting laugh, as darkness began to gather around him. "Or am I the one who will suffer for all eternity for the crime?"

I stood up and backed away, my skin suddenly cold. "I don't know what you're talking about. How do we break the curse?"

He stood and stalked toward me like a predator, backing me against the wall. "Do you trust me, Hannah?"

Words failed me for a moment, as the darkness seemed to close in around us like a cage. Was he trying to scare me? If so, it was working. But I knew in my heart he would never hurt me. He was my mate, the other half of my soul, and he loved me.

"Yes, I trust you." I reached up and stroked his face softly as I looked into his eyes. "I love you."

Pain crossed his face just before the darkness turned the room pitch black around me. All I could see were his red eyes, glowing like brimstone, and then the shadows wrapped around my body like shackles, holding me tight.

"Lucifer... What are you doing?" I struggled against the bonds he'd twined around me, but there was no resisting the devil.

He wrapped his strong, masculine hands around my throat. "I'm sorry, Hannah. It's the only way."

I couldn't talk, couldn't protest, couldn't breathe. I could only watch Lucifer's red eyes burn like an inferno as his hands tightened, cutting off my air. I tried to fight, tried to scream, tried to beg, but I couldn't move at all.

Pain exploded in my neck and lungs. Tears fell from my eyes. It grew harder and harder to see his burning eyes clearly as the darkness creeped into my vision and I struggled for air.

Lucifer was *killing* me.

How could he do this? Had I been wrong about him this entire time? As my vision blurred and my body grew weaker, Jophiel's words came back to me. *Lucifer is the villain. He's been lying to you this entire time. Manipulating you. Controlling you. As he's done with all humans for thousands of years.*

You're in danger around him.

His voice came to me in the darkness. "I love you, Hannah."

How could that be true when he was ripping the life from my body? Was this how he ended the curse—by doing Adam's job for him?

I'd made the ultimate mistake, trusting the devil with my heart. And the price was my life.

The darkness closed in, enveloping me completely as my lungs burned for the last time. Everything turned black as death finally claimed me, as it had done so many times before.

Except this death would be my last.

33

HANNAH

With a bright flash of light, life surged back into me... and with it came power.

And memories. So many memories.

My mind flooded with events from my past lives. Every single one of them. Eve. Persephone. Lenore. Countless other humans who lived short, brutal existences.

All of their lives came rushing back to me, filling my head with their pain, joy, love, and death, stretching back thousands of years. Too many memories for one mind to hold, even an immortal one. I screamed and thrashed, clutching at my head, trying to make the torrent stop.

Then the flood died off and the memories faded away like smoke. Only a few impressions remained, fragments from some of my lives, though I knew others were within my grasp if I needed them. Only one life remained just out of reach, clouded by another's magic. My true self had been stolen from me, my powers stripped from my body, now returned in death. But I still couldn't access those memories.

I sucked in a breath that felt like my very first one. Power swirled inside me like adrenaline. My skin tingled with magic. How was this possible?

Lucifer had killed me, but somehow I was alive.

No, better than alive. I was *whole* again.

But that didn't mean I forgave him for what he'd done.

I opened my eyes and slowly sat up, glancing at the small crowd of people gathered around me, before my eyes landed on Lucifer. My mate. My killer. My savior.

"Hannah?" he whispered.

Hannah? Hannah was dead. But like a phoenix, I was reborn. I didn't remember my name, but I knew one thing.

It was time to raise some hell.

ABOUT THE AUTHOR

Elizabeth Briggs is the *New York Times* bestselling author of paranormal and fantasy romance with bold heroines and fearless heroes. She graduated from UCLA with a degree in Sociology and has worked for an international law firm, mentored teens in writing, and volunteered with dog rescue groups. Now she's a full-time geek who lives in Los Angeles with her husband, their daughter, and a pack of fluffy dogs.

Visit Elizabeth's website: www.elizabethbriggs.net